Ber Carroll was born in Blarney, County Cork, and moved to Australia in 1995. Her first novel, *Executive Affair*, was inspired by her initial impressions of Sydney, and her exciting, dynamic work environment at the time. Ber now lives in Sydney's northern beaches with her husband and two children, whose constant interruptions and cries of 'Mum . . . *Mum!*' are no help at all to the writing process. Still, though, she loves them very much and has dedicated this novel, her fifth, to them both.

Ber's novels have been published in five countries, including Ireland. If you would like to know more about Ber and her novels, you can visit her website at www.bercarroll.com.

less than perfect

Ber Carroll

MACMILLAN
Pan Macmillan Australia

First published 2011 in Macmillan by Pan Macmillan Australia Pty Limited
1 Market Street, Sydney

National Library of Australia
Cataloguing-in-Publication data:

Carroll, Ber, 1971–

Less Than Perfect / Ber Carroll.

9781405039796 (pbk.)

A823.4

Typeset in 12.5/15.5 pt Granjon by Post Pre-press Group, Brisbane, Queensland
Printed in Australia by McPherson's Printing Group

Papers used by Pan Macmillan Australia Pty Limited are natural, recyclable products
made from wood grown in sustainable forests. The manufacturing processes
conform to the environmental regulations of the country of origin.

For Conor and Ashling

Part One

Chapter 1

The day I met Josh McKinstry is etched in my mind, its light, texture and sound, each and every fragment and feeling. At any random moment I can close my eyes and instantaneously, magically I'm transported back: 26 July 1997, my eighteenth birthday. My ears fill with the swell of music and voices in the sectioned-off corner of Maggie Maloney's where I had my party. The summery atmosphere washes over me, an atmosphere that is both consistent and convincing even though it's the end of a grey, overcast day in a string of such days that masquerades as the Irish summer.

Josh was not an invited guest at the party – well, at least not invited by me. He came with Liam, my brother, and some other friends. Their arrival was loud and disruptive, their voices amplified by the pints they'd had in the pub across the road. One of them made a beeline to the bar to get a round of drinks and the others hung their thumbs from their jeans pockets and exuded an air of superiority, making it clear that they'd come for Liam's sake, not mine. They were drunk, but not excessively so, the usual fare for twenty-one-year-old males on a Saturday night out. Nevertheless, my father stared daggers in their direction and his blatant disapproval added an underlying chill to the summery feeling. Liam returned Dad's stare with defiance and a touch of hatred.

My father was, and still is, a professor. He lectures students in ethics – you know, what's right, what's wrong. He's not a tweed-jacket, cigar-smoking kind of professor. He wears jeans and polo shirts. He's suave, youthful and, I suppose, attractive in a serious, straitlaced kind of way. Back then most of his female students were half in love with him. But they didn't know what he was really like. They didn't have to live with him, like Liam and I did, and Maeve, our younger sister.

The tension between Liam and Dad was so conspicuous that it had the potential to sour the whole night. Though they were standing a good distance apart, I felt I had no choice but to intervene, so I sailed across the room to arrive at Liam's shoulder. (I was the short one of the family.)

'You graced us with your presence.' I grinned.

'Aye.'

'I'm eternally grateful.'

Liam wrenched his gaze away from Dad. His pale blue eyes were the same shade as mine, and we both had red-gold hair. This colouring came from our mother, Paula.

'You're lookin' well, Caitlin.'

I was pleased. As with most brothers, Liam's compliments

were rare, insults more the norm. I wore a strappy top and capri pants, both in black. My skin was lightly tanned from a brand of fake tan that I'd discovered after much trial and error. My hair, vibrant next to my black clothes, fell thickly past my shoulders. I knew that I looked good, but it was nice to hear it confirmed. I had spent the whole day getting ready for this, my passage into adulthood. I was primed, not just physically but psychologically too. I was now the legal age to vote, to buy cigarettes and alcohol, to apply for a passport or a mortgage or both. I could marry without my parents' consent, and though I had no intention of doing so – I didn't even have a boyfriend – the sheer thought of it was enough to make me giggle. I'd been waiting for this freedom for what had seemed like my whole life.

Liam was temporarily distracted by the return of the friend who had gone to the bar. Lifting his pint of Guinness from the tray, he took a long drink, effortlessly emptying a third of the glass, fortifying himself for this obligatory family event. I sipped my own drink and glanced at Liam's friends. Some of the faces were familiar, some not. Every now and then I encountered Liam with a group of his friends in town, but he never brought them back to the house. He must have felt that he spent enough time at home, that meeting his friends was one of the few valid reasons he had to get out. I also suspect that he got a kick out of there being a part of his life we knew little about, maintaining an air of mystery about where he went and who with. In his own way, he too strove for freedom, and at twenty-one all the legal boxes had been ticked. He was missing just one thing, one core ingredient in what would surely have been a perfect recipe for independence: a job. Liam was unemployed.

Liam's friends were a motley group: different heights, physiques and looks, age the only thing they had in common. Now that they each had a prop, a drink, they'd taken their hands out of their pockets and there was a bit of friendly pushing going on as they took the mick out of each other. But one of them was quieter than the others, more reserved, and maybe for this reason my eyes were drawn to him. He was tall and there was something rather elegant about the way he held his head. His hair was dark and his eyes seemed like they would be too, though I couldn't see their exact colour from where I stood. He caught me looking at him and smiled at me, making my cheeks burn. Disconcerted, I looked away and sipped some of my drink.

'Maeve's sneaking back the hard stuff, I see,' Liam commented wryly, his eyes finding our sister.

Maeve was in a far corner, screened from my parents by her friends and swigging from a bottle of cider. At sixteen she was two years younger than me and impatient to be at my stage – on the cusp of leaving home and starting university.

I rolled my eyes. 'Dad better not see her!'

My father had rules for everything: no going into town alone until fifteen, no boyfriends or girlfriends until seventeen, no alcohol until eighteen or preferably never. Such rigidity had been frustrating for Liam and me, and we were both sympathetic to Maeve's predicament.

Furtively, I redirected my gaze from my sister to Liam's friend. By now he stood a little apart, evidently not participating in any of the conversations around him. He wore a grey T-shirt and dark-blue jeans that sat nicely on his narrow hips. His body was slim but there was strength across his shoulders and in the curve of his upper arms. How did Liam know him? From school? From the tech?

'Liam . . .' I began, my mouth suddenly dry. I'd never had this sort of conversation with my brother before now. He was far too private about his friends for me to even get the chance. 'Liam, who is –' I stopped mid-sentence as I noticed the subject of my query coming towards us.

Liam looked at me quizzically. 'What?'

'Never mind,' I said hastily.

In a matter of moments he was next to me, so close that one arm, both slender and muscular, was almost touching mine, his dark eyes looking expectantly at Liam as he waited to be introduced.

Liam was slow to take the hint. I urged him on with a stare of my own. 'Caitlin, this is Josh McKinstry,' he said eventually.

In those first few moments I was struck by two things. The first was that Josh was Protestant. I could tell this from his name alone. I noted his religion like a reflex but I wasn't put off by it: Clonmegan was one of the few towns in Northern Ireland where Catholics and Protestants got on well together.

The second thing I registered was the intense manner in which his eyes focused on my face. I sensed his concentration, his antici- pation of whatever words would come out of my mouth. His intentness was so extreme that I became tongue-tied and didn't say anything at all. He filled the awkward moment with a smile, a beautiful, unfaltering smile, which made the hesitation in his speech all the more evident.

'Hello, Caitlin.'

His voice was so indistinct that I hardly understood what he'd said. I immediately thought he must be drunk, *really* drunk, the kind of drunk when one can't even manage to speak coherently, and I felt totally deflated.

'Hi, Josh,' I returned in an unimpressed tone.

I became aware that Liam was looking at me, his eyes strangely watchful. I knew that look. Liam would use it as he waited for me to get the punchline to one of his jokes, or to realise that he had the winning hand of cards. Now he was waiting for me to realise something about Josh McKinstry.

'Josh is deaf,' he supplied when it became evident I wasn't going to work it out of my own accord.

I didn't know what to say in response. None of us knew what to say. I gulped the last of my drink and noticed Liam doing the same with his. As the silence stretched out, I found myself wondering what it would be like to be enclosed in such never-ending quiet, what it would be like to have nothing at all to listen to, nothing but your own thoughts.

'How do you know each other?' I eventually asked Liam in a polite voice that was nothing like the cocky tones I would ordinarily use with him. Too late, I berated myself for not speaking more slowly, for not turning my head so Josh could have a clear view of my lips.

'From football.'

That made sense. The soccer team had every religious denomination: Catholic, Protestant, Methodist, Presbyterian, all united as they chased after a leather ball and endeavoured to embed it in the other team's net. Liam was sports mad. He played Gaelic football and hurling as well as soccer and rugby – anything with a ball, anything to fill the long days.

Josh smiled again, pointed to my empty drink, and asked with a motion of his hand if I would like another.

'No, thanks,' I replied, and shook my head as an afterthought. 'I'm okay for now.'

I looked at Liam, trying to avert another silence before it happened, but he was gone, back to the fold of his other friends, and Josh and I were alone. After a few long moments I realised that what I thought was silence wasn't that at all. There were voices all around me, and music belting from the speakers: Oasis, 'Wonderwall'.

'Have you always been deaf?' I mouthed the words slowly, and touched my ear when I said 'deaf'. Immediately I felt embarrassed, both by my crude signing and what might be perceived as a tactless question.

'Born that way,' he replied, again his voice thick and almost unintelligible.

It was hard for me to comprehend that he'd never heard this song, or any other song for that matter. Did Josh mind that he couldn't hear the music? Or that he couldn't hear my voice? Or the rise and fall of conversation and laughter around us, combining with the music to form a rich and varied background tapestry. I tried to shut out the noise, to imagine real, pure silence, but I couldn't. The noise was like a heartbeat, it kept the atmosphere alive, and even if it were gone the memory of it would continue to beat in my head. Maybe I would have more success at imagining real silence later on at home, when I was in bed thinking back to this moment.

His gaze was all encompassing, as though he could tell exactly what I was grappling with in my head. My eyes shied away, dropping down to his sensual mouth, and then down again to his slender fingers. Of course, he would rely on his other senses all the more: I knew instinctively that his mouth would kiss tenderly and skilfully, and that his touch would be similarly refined and assured. By the time my eyes were drawn back to his, I had already fallen a little bit in love with my brother's friend.

I can remember the details of that night as though it was yesterday, but it was more than twelve years ago now. I remember being glad that the forecast rain had stayed away, that my 'waterproof' fake tan would not be put to the test. I remember my mum looking mildly stressed, fussing that the guests had enough to eat and somewhere to sit, if they wished. I remember my father, his disapproval of Liam broken by spells when he tried too hard to look like he was relaxed and enjoying himself; Maeve bright-eyed and unsteady and keeping well out of Dad's line of sight; Mandy, Carly and Sinead, my closest friends, dancing and having the time of their lives, as yet unaware that I had met Josh McKinstry and seen my future in his eyes.

At the end of the night, 'Happy Birthday' was played over the sound system and a circle formed around me. I swung from person to person, and was kissed, hugged and congratulated before being twirled to whomever was next. All the while I was aware of exactly where Josh was standing in the circle, and I counted down until, dizzy and exhilarated, I got to him. He hugged me and kissed me, his lips melting on mine and every bit as tender as I'd imagined them to be. I didn't move on to the next person in the circle. I stayed with Josh for the rest of the night and, indeed, for much of the following year.

Chapter 2

September in Belfast was rainy, grey and disappointing. The city scared me, with its graffiti, armoured cars and simmering tension; it felt as though I was walking in on the end of an argument that could flare up again at any moment.

Despite this, or maybe because of it, I was thrilled to start university, to further my education and pave the way for my future. I wanted to get the best qualifications possible because I had already decided that I was emigrating, leaving Belfast and Ireland. I didn't plan on sticking around and being unemployed like Liam.

I had the choice of commuting with my father to the city each day or staying in student accommodation. I chose to stay at Elms Village, only a fifteen-minute walk from the university – a relaxing start and end to the day, much nicer than sitting in a confined space with my father for over an hour each way. The

Elms consisted of several beautiful red-brick buildings set amid grassy grounds. I had a wee second-floor room furnished simply with a single bed, desk and chest of drawers. It was south facing, and daylight streamed in the window even when the weather outside was dull, which was most of the time.

As I began my Bachelor of Arts in English and sociology and life as a student, Josh and I were already established as a couple. We had become very close in the space of a few months, his deafness accelerating our closeness as we bypassed the coyness and game-playing of normal early-stage relationships, developing a rapport that was intimate and mature beyond our years. I settled into the compact room at the Elms with a sense of anticipation, keenly aware that a few nights of the week Josh would visit, that we finally had somewhere to be together without watching out for my parents or his. As a couple we couldn't whisper sweet nothings – in fact any verbal communication was trying – and so our physical communication was enhanced. The slightest touch of his hand would cause me to shiver. His gaze was sometimes so profound that it was like a caress, a form of foreplay. At that stage in our relationship we weren't having sex, but we were on the verge. In the narrow single bed in my room we took our physical relationship a step further, and a step further again.

'I love you,' he'd murmur, the words thick and garbled.

'I love you too,' I would reply. And I did love him. Wholly, without reservation.

Always we stopped at the very brink, breathless and a little delirious, and it would take a while for my heart to slow down enough to fall asleep, my half-naked body entangled with his.

Josh liked to leave the lamp on while he slept, to read my lips if I spoke during the night, and to enable him to see around the room and reassure himself that nothing strange or untoward was happening, because of course he wouldn't be able to hear if anything moved or creaked. Initially, I found the light disconcerting and had difficulty sleeping, but I got used to it. Other things kept me awake then, mainly excitement drumming inside me. I felt like I was on the precipice of my life. In three years' time I would graduate with first class honours – nothing less would do – and then I would leave. I didn't know where I was going just yet, only that I was going. And though it was early days with Josh, I knew that he would go with me. I couldn't imagine a future without him.

My father, at his lectern preaching to his students, spoke about different kinds of ethics. There are descriptive ethics, prescriptive ethics and virtue ethics, but I won't bore you with the details. Suffice it to say that ethics can be summed up quite conveniently with the following golden, over-arching rule: do unto others what you would have them do unto you. Unfortunately, that rule was far too simplistic for the social and political environment that we lived in. If there was ever a city to fuel debate on what was right or wrong, moral or immoral, justifiable or downright unjust, Belfast would have to be it. Neighbourhoods with separating walls, thick and high, topped with barbed wire. Buildings with graffiti and murals, hatred portrayed through art. Streets with kerbstones painted in blue-white-red or green-white-orange, Royal Ulster Constabulary officers with guns held across their bodies, and regular outbreaks of violence that were shown on the nightly news.

Dad was the king of the castle, presiding over the intolerance and hatred and violence, writing academic papers on it all and having excerpts published in the *Belfast Telegraph*, the *Independent* and, once, the *Times*. Occasionally he was on TV, usually after some atrocity or other when journalists sought him out for a comment. They filmed him with the university in the background and he always looked solemn, thoughtful and mortifyingly righteous.

At home Dad never missed an opportunity to instil his values in his children, even when we were small. Over and over again he'd test us.

'What are our core values, Caitlin?'

'Caring, honesty, accountability, respect for others, promise-keeping, fairness, and . . .' the last one always eluded me, 'and . . .'

'Pursuit of excellence,' he'd supply, looking deeply disappointed that I had forgotten.

I was only five or six when he made me learn the list. I didn't know what 'pursuit of excellence' meant, so it wasn't surprising that I couldn't commit it to memory.

It wasn't just the list, though. Dad would look for lessons in everything I did, everywhere I went, every single day.

'Was that very caring, Caitlin? Shouldn't you have helped your sister? Showed some compassion?'

'Caitlin, you're distorting the truth and being deceitful.'

'You did the wrong thing, Caitlin, and now you have to accept the consequences.'

'You weren't thinking, Caitlin. *Think before you act.*'

Needless to say, I chose my university subjects carefully so that I wouldn't have to attend my father's lectures. Those I received at home were more than enough!

Dad said I was the wild one, the one that needed watching, reining in. The truth was that I wasn't all that wild. I pushed boundaries no more or less than most kids; I answered back, flouted a few curfews and was sometimes lured into trouble when I forgot his set of rules and values and lived for the moment instead.

One incident stands out in my memory. I was eleven, and cycling with my friend Mandy. The sky was pale blue, the sun hidden behind one of many pillowy clouds, and the Sperrin Mountains spilled into the valleys alongside the curved, sloping road. We freewheeled side by side back towards town, our hair flowing behind us, the wind biting our faces.

'How much longer are you allowed?' asked Mandy when the road levelled out.

I didn't need to glance at my watch to know. 'Another twenty minutes.'

'What if I went in with you and asked?'

I pursed my lips. 'They'd still say no.'

Mandy, with her open face and unruly hair, had tried to understand the many restrictions that bound me: mealtimes, study time, leisure time, all measured precisely, like spoonfuls of medicine. Mandy had five siblings, one of whom was a very recent addition, and her parents were too busy to worry about rules and formalities. Their disorderly house was generally a relaxed and happy place to be. If Mandy wanted to go to a friend's house, all she had to do was ask; there was no need for a week's notice – unlike me.

'We'd better get going, so. God forbid you should be a minute late!' Mandy was quite adept at sarcasm: she had learned it from her parents who, despite all their children and the thousands of things they had to do each day, had not lost their sense of humour. 'Come on, I'll race you.'

Mandy darted ahead, laughing already at the unfair advantage she was taking. I lowered my head, tightened the muscles in my thighs, and drove my legs down on the pedals. It was only a matter of seconds before I sailed past her. 'Gotcha,' I called triumphantly over my shoulder.

At that moment, I was doing a number of things that were 'wrong'. I shouldn't have been racing. I shouldn't have taken my eyes off the road. I shouldn't have been so competitive or gleeful. Pride comes before a fall, my father would say.

My front wheel hit a pothole and the bike veered wildly. I tightened my grip on the handlebars, jerking them from side to side to keep my balance. I'd almost righted myself when Mandy, who hadn't noticed the sudden drop in speed, or the uneven terrain, careered into me. Our bikes tangled and we fell in a whirl of wheels and metal and limbs and cries of shock and pain. For a few seconds, neither of us could move or speak. Then we both tried to sit up.

'Are ya all right?' asked Mandy.

'Yes. Are you?'

'Aye.'

'Sorry,' I said, blinking back tears. 'I should have been looking . . .'

'I'm sorry too,' she said quickly. We exchanged wry, teary smiles.

A car stopped, mud splattered on its sides, a low trailer behind. The driver got out, a farmer with a cracked face and wiry hair. 'What about youse girls? Were youse doing the Grand Prix or what?'

The farmer put the bikes in the trailer and helped us into the car. It smelled of cow manure and there was loose dirt on the floor. Mandy sat in the front and gave directions.

'This will do,' I said when he pulled into my street.

'Which house?'

'We'll just get out here,' I told him.

'Afraid of getting in trouble with your ma and da?'

'Aye,' Mandy replied on my behalf.

We got out of the car and the farmer lifted down our bikes, with their bowed wheels and broken chains. 'Go easy on the driving, girls – soon it'll be cars and they're a lot more deadly than bikes!'

'We will. Thank you,' replied Mandy.

I added my thanks and watched the farmer drive away, the car's exhaust leaving a cloud of diesel fumes that caught in the back of my throat. 'My dad's going to kill me.'

'It was an accident,' Mandy protested.

'He'll say it was avoidable. He'll say I was being reckless.'

'Do you want me to come in?'

'Nah. That'll only make it worse.'

Mandy put her hand gingerly against her side. 'Ach, I'm sorer than what I thought at first. I'll be black and blue tomorrow.'

'Me too.'

'You've torn your pants.'

'Great – that'll get me into even more trouble.' I grimaced. 'I'd better go – I'll see you at school tomorrow.'

'Bye. Good luck.'

Mandy limped away, wheeling her bike on its only function-ing wheel. Manoeuvring my written-off bike in the opposite direction, I stopped outside our house and stood on the footpath with my torn knees and guilty face. I didn't want to go inside.

Mandy was a dot in the distance. I wished I could run after her, go back to her crowded house where the incident would be discussed openly and non-judgmentally and eventually laughed about. I wished, with a ferocity that brought a rush of blood to my face, that my family was more like hers.

Dad's daily contact with students and exposure to their lifestyle meant that he was quite in touch with the world: he listened to whatever music was popular at the time, took notice of fashions and trends, and used relevant, modern examples in his lectures. He kept up to date in his own rather deliberate way, and his stu-dents appreciated and respected him for it. Dad was also savvy enough to guess that Josh and I were making the most of our pri-vacy at the Elms. He would have been able to tell from our body language that we were physically intimate, and from our faces when we looked at each other that we were in love. 'Be careful, Caitlin,' he muttered once or twice, glancing in Josh's direction to make his meaning clear. This was his way of telling me to use contraception.

He always wore a slight frown when he greeted Josh; in

fairness, though, I don't think he was aware of this. His problem wasn't with me having an adult relationship as such – he knew it was par for the course at my age – it was that he didn't quite know what to make of Josh. Undoubtedly, there were a number of factors in Josh's favour. He worked as a plasterer and earned a decent living, unlike Liam. He came from a respectable family, albeit Protestant. He dressed well, he was obliging (he always helped clear the table whenever he ate at our house) and he was polite, always letting Mum walk through the doorway before him and things like that.

But the fact that Josh couldn't hear – that missing sense, that blatant imperfection – must have grated on my father, diminishing Josh in his mind. Perfection meant everything to him. He aspired to it in every aspect of his life, and he expected it from everyone around him, not least his children.

The fact that Liam, his eldest child, was unemployed was an acute embarrassment to Dad. Never mind that there were thousands of other young men and women unemployed at the time. Never mind that the Celtic Tiger, the boom occurring in the South of Ireland, seemed to have totally bypassed the North. Never mind that Liam's diploma in sport was useless in the face of the continuing political friction and violence that stunted investment in the sports and leisure industry, and all other industries for that matter. Liam was young, male and Catholic, and unemployment in that particular demographic was as high as thirty per cent. Never mind all that: more should be expected, and was expected, of Professor Jonathan O'Reilly's son.

'Can you just *stop*, Liam,' he would snap when he was no longer able to contain his irritation.

'Stop what?'

'Stop kicking the chair. Stop moping around the house. For God's sake, for *all* our sakes, find something to *do*.'

'And what exactly do you suggest I *do*, Dad?' Liam would snarl back.

'Go down to the sports complex and volunteer your services, for instance.'

'You mean work for free?'

'Yes, if that's what it takes!'

'They won't let me work without being on the payroll – insurance reasons. Any other ideas, *Dad*?'

'Can't you put on a suit and go into town? You never know what opportunities might happen if you get out there and meet some people face to face.'

'You mean gatecrash their offices? They don't want to see me, Dad. They have *no jobs*. It's a waste of my time and theirs.'

'Good Lord, Liam, you've some gall to call it a waste of your time! You've too much time on your hands, that's the problem. Can't you see that you won't get a job stuck inside the four walls of this house? It's laziness, sheer and utter laziness . . .'

'Being unemployed does *not* mean I'm lazy! *I'm not fucking lazy, okay?*'

The arguments exploded into raised voices, swearing and slammed doors at least once a week. In some ways I preferred the arguments to the strained, contemptuous atmosphere before and afterwards. At least the fights were honest.

As if the situation with Liam wasn't enough to contend with, now my father had Josh to deal with too. Josh, who couldn't hear, whose speech was unclear at the best of times, who had to grapple with all sorts of everyday challenges and who was not the kind of boyfriend he had envisaged for his eldest daughter.

'Don't get too serious too quickly,' Dad advised me more than once. 'You're only young.'

And: 'Are you sure that this is what you want, Caitlin? That Josh is what you want? Or, more appropriately, what you *need*?'

My father's wants and needs were different to mine. He wanted and needed me to be with someone strong, steady, mainstream, someone who had no obvious problems, because in his opinion I had enough problems of my own. Liam might have been the first of us to fail publicly at being perfect, but I had failed on an intrinsically private level many years before.

Josh and I *were* serious – nothing my father could say would change that – and his hearing impairment, though testing at times, was at the very base of my attraction to him. I connected with Josh at the deepest level – I understood his frustrations and fears better than anyone else could because I too had a handicap, a defect, something fundamentally wrong with me.

Like Josh, I was less than perfect.

Chapter 3

My fear of Belfast should have dissipated as I came to know the city better, but it didn't. The university quarter was located on the south side of the city, an attractive and apparently safe part of town. Within walking distance were the Botanic Gardens, the Ulster Museum, the Grand Opera House and numerous shops, cafés and restaurants. The campus was situated within three designated conservation areas with lots of grass and plants and trees. The buildings, some of which were more than a hundred and fifty years old, were imposing and steadfast and promised to students like me both a serious education and a sense of security.

The campus wasn't free of politics, though; quite the opposite. The students had political views and no hesitation in airing them. There was always someone ranting and raving and having their say, but it was honest and open and for that same reason it wasn't threatening. Politics aside, the students at Queen's studied hard and socialised even harder, just like students at other universities around the world. I often wondered if I was the only one who felt anxious and afraid.

I worried about accidentally walking into the wrong area, about being in the wrong place at the wrong time, about being attacked or getting blown up. Sometimes it was a relief to go back to Clonmegan on the weekends and holidays, to be in a small town that didn't need high walls or armoured cars, a town that was unified rather than segregated. Even the townscape in Clonmegan went some way to demonstrating a sense of unity, the skyline distinguished by the gothic spires of the churches, Roman Catholic, Church of Ireland, Methodist and Presbyterian harmoniously overlooking the town. And as you stood at Friars Bridge and observed where the Balowen and Glenrush rivers merged to form one, you could easily liken this confluence to that of the townspeople, separate outside the town but joined as one community inside it.

Belfast felt more benign when I was with Josh, when my hand was in his. We took walks down Royal Avenue, along the River Lagan and through the Botanic Gardens. Sometimes we went as far as the docks where the two decommissioned ship-building cranes, Samson and Goliath, presided over the slate-coloured water, the long corrugated-iron warehouses and the lines of multicoloured containers waiting to be transported somewhere else, rather like us all. On these walks I came to appreciate that our gritty surroundings were interesting and beautiful in their own unique way, and that any attractive monuments and architecture were only accentuated by the tough, unapologetic backdrop. I realised that Belfast was like a child who had been abused and neglected and misunderstood, but who wore its heart on its sleeve and had developed a resilient and lovable character. Still, though, Josh and I always stayed close to the city centre and I was thankful to have him by my side, his eyes on the lookout. He noticed things that I didn't, and I only ever felt any way safe when I was with him.

'Relax,' Josh would tell me, trying to massage the tension from my hand.

I tried to relax and came close sometimes, but never fully got there.

It took some willpower on my part not to see Josh every day. To prevent my studies from suffering I restricted the times he came around; as much as I loved him, I never lost sight of my degree, the reason I was in Belfast in the first place. I daydreamed about my graduation day. In my head I had a snapshot of myself in a black gown and mortarboard, holding a scroll – my degree, my ticket out of Ireland. Josh represented a complication to my dream, one I hadn't counted on. Because of his hearing impairment, he would find it harder than me to get a visa. And even if he did get a visa, he would then have to find a job wherever it was we decided to emigrate, a job as good as the one he had now.

We talked about our plans for the future like any other couple. I had more than two years to go on my degree and we reassured ourselves that we had time to work things out, to plan our escape to a more prosperous country, a country comfortable in its own skin, a country that did not know or need to understand the kind of conflict that split the North of Ireland in two. A place where one's name was simply what one was called, rather than a declaration of sides. Where religion and politics had their place but were not all-powerful.

'I want to go somewhere I can relax,' I'd say vehemently. 'Where the streets are safe no matter what neighbourhood I'm in.'

Josh wanted the same. 'Somewhere warm,' he'd add, his eyes faraway. 'Not just the climate, but how people treat each other.'

I would have enjoyed my first few months of university much more had I known that Belfast didn't pose any danger – well, at least not personally to me. I would have taken walks at times when Josh wasn't with me, when my eyes were tired or my head aching from stuffy classrooms and I needed some fresh, cold air and new scenery. I would have immersed myself wholeheartedly in student life, gone to pubs and house parties outside of what I perceived to be my 'safety zone'.

Little did I know that the danger I feared was, in fact, where I least expected it, where I felt safest and most secure.

My room at the Elms had a small telly, an old portable set that had belonged to my parents. When I was on my own, I rationed it between periods of study, a treat at the end of two hours' non-stop reading or a completed essay or assignment. When I turned it on, the telly felt like a flatmate, a voice in the room easing the silence and loneliness until Josh came around. Due to the misshapen aerial at the back the reception was patchy, but for all its obvious imperfections, I loved that box of colour and sound.

Josh loved it too. Most of the time. Television frustrated him almost as much as it fascinated him, teasing him with dialogue he couldn't properly follow and lifestyles he could never hope to emulate. He would flick through the channels, leaning towards the telly with the remote control in his hand – the signal didn't work unless you held it close and pressed hard on the buttons. He liked to watch anything to do with cars: design, road testing, racing, anything that involved a motor and four wheels. He would have loved a car of his own, to feel the curve of the steering wheel under his hands, to command the vehicle with the gearstick and clutch, accelerator and brake. He knew how to drive – his father had taught him – but he wasn't deemed fit for a licence because he couldn't hear sirens or car horns in the event of an emergency.

'It's not fair,' he'd protest, anguished by his exclusion from this aspect of everyday life more than anything else. 'All those lazy, incompetent drivers on the road, and yet they're allowed to sit behind the wheel and I'm not.'

I tried to console him. 'Maybe they'll change the rules when hearing-aid technology improves.'

'Yeah, maybe, but I could be an old man by then!'

When Josh had finished surfing the channels on the telly, we'd snuggle together under the covers and watch a film, usually a foreign one with subtitles, a quirky storyline and more nudity than the plot required. Those were happy times – the warmth of the duvet and his body next to mine, the small portable telly with its wonky aerial, its blurry screen a window to an exotic other world.

Initially I didn't take much notice of the peace talks that were reported on the telly.

'Talks between the political parties and the Irish and British governments have been going on for more than thirty hours now, through the day and night, and now into another day, in a monumental effort to reach agreement . . .'

It took a while for the television coverage to penetrate my cynicism. As far as I was concerned, there was always some politician talking to another, shaking hands and flashing phoney smiles at the cameras, but nothing ever came of those talks. Nothing happened other than the handshake, so firm and resolute, promising so much and delivering nothing at all. I imagined that both parties left with the best of intentions, and then at some stage reality intruded: thirty years of conflict; arms, hatred and history more powerful and dividing than any image of the future.

'Tony Blair and Bertie Ahern have not slept, leading to reports that it's not a matter of *if* agreement will be reached, but *when* . . .'

The chairman of the talks, a US senator, had been up all night too. Though the deadline for an agreement had passed, the news commentator sounded excited and hopeful. Maybe it was a similar sense of hope that made me break one of my rules and leave the telly on past the allotted time. I muted the sound and resumed my work on the sociology essay I needed to submit before the end of the week. A few laborious pages later, I glanced up to see that Tony Blair was speaking at a news conference; the talks had apparently ended. I turned the sound back on.

'Today I hope that the burden of history can at long last start to be lifted from our shoulders.'

The agreement had been signed by the British and Irish governments and by most of the political parties. It was called the Good Friday Peace Agreement.

When Josh came over later that night, we watched more

coverage on the agreement. Great Britain and the Republic of Ireland were to amend their laws and constitutions regarding Northern Ireland, which would now have its own assembly with devolved legislative powers. From this point, any change to the constitutional status of Northern Ireland could only follow a majority vote of its citizens. All paramilitary weapons were to be decommissioned and prisoners released within two years. Referendums in Northern Ireland and the Republic of Ireland would hopefully secure public endorsement of the agreement.

The phone rang and I picked it up, knowing who it was even before he spoke.

'Are you watching the telly?'

'Yes, Dad.'

'This is an important day, Caitlin, a day to remember.' He sounded a little giddy. He'd always said that peace wasn't possible without both Britain and the Republic of Ireland giving up some of their claim on the North. This agreement validated his views. I could see him in my mind, a smile of genuine satisfaction brightening his face, a celebratory glass of red wine in his hand.

'Aye, Dad. I know.'

'Goodnight, so.'

''Night, Dad.'

Josh and I celebrated in our own way. That night, in the narrow single bed, he moved inside me for the first time. The bedside lamp was on and I saw wonder and ecstasy on his face, and knew that he could see the same expression on mine. It was as though the last barrier separating us had lifted away, and the fact that we had waited and not rushed this side of our relationship made it all the more significant and precious.

'I love you,' he said afterwards.

Of all the times he told me he loved me, I remember this one the most vividly.

'I love you too.'

We fell asleep, bodies entwined, the lamp casting us in a gentle glow.

The following month we voted in the referendum, holding hands as we arrived at the voting hall, walking past flyers thrust in our path and ignoring last-minute pitches from party representatives. Technically we represented opposite sides – I was Catholic and Josh Protestant – but we wanted and voted for the same thing that day: peace, an end to violence, a better future.

Do you support the agreement reached at the multi-party talks on Northern Ireland and set out in Command Paper 3883?

Yes, we do.

Chapter 4

Loving Josh wasn't easy. It was wonderful and full of surprises, frustrating and hard work. He wore a hearing aid behind each ear, which enabled him to hear the odd word. He filled in the rest by reading lips. If we were out somewhere that had background noise – a pub or a busy street – the hearing aids didn't function properly and then all Josh had to rely on was lip-reading, which wasn't always possible. Things became particularly difficult when we were out socially with friends. He hated not being able to hear the banter, the one-liners, people talking over each other. Even though he was usually philosophical about his limitations, sometimes he became so frustrated he would walk off. I'd follow, steering him to a quiet corner where he could vent.

'I feel like the village idiot, only understanding half of what's being said,' he'd cry.

'I'll remind them to slow down and to look at you as they speak . . .'

'Don't! Don't say anything.'

'What do you want then?'

'I want to be able to fucking well hear properly!'

Obviously, there was nothing he or I could do to make this happen. All I could offer was silence: an acknowledgment of how unfair it was.

'Do you want to go home?' I'd ask out of courtesy. I knew that he didn't. In his heart of hearts Josh was a social being; he liked to be part of a crowd, despite occasionally feeling peripheral and left out.

'No, of course I don't. Oh, for fuck's sake, let's go back.'

Hand in hand, we would return to the group, everyone guessing why he'd stormed off and, for a short time, making a greater effort to include him.

When we were in Belfast, we socialised with my friends, students from my English or sociology classes, or with Mandy, who was training to be a hairdresser in a salon on Ormeau Avenue, and her boyfriend, Brendan, a mechanic. Josh liked Mandy and Brendan more than he did my university friends. He found it amusing that Mandy, with her somewhat haphazard appearance, wanted to be a hairdresser, and he liked that Brendan was quiet and introspective and sometimes drew diagrams of car engines for his benefit. It made me happy, Josh getting on so well with Mandy and Brendan.

While the boys were absorbed with talk of steering or suspension or torque, Mandy would lean close and shamelessly enquire, in a conspiratorial whisper, about my relationship with Josh.

'So, youse two are getting on well, then?'

'Aye, we are.'

'And he's good in the sack?'

'That's none of your business, Mandy!'

'Ach, come on, don't be so secretive. I tell you everything!'

Without my asking, Mandy had shared with me intimate details about her love life with Brendan, so much so that sometimes I could hardly look at him without blushing. Mandy fondly called me her uptight, prim-and-proper friend, while I laughingly referred to her as my slapdash, blabbermouth friend. I *was* a little uptight – who wouldn't be after living their first eighteen years under my father's roof? – but I was a good friend, I was loyal and Mandy had been my friend forever. My mother often stated that there were two kinds of friends: friends for a reason and friends for a season. Mandy fell into the former category. My own more conservative nature fed off her openness and irreverence towards rules of any kind, and she always made me laugh. If that wasn't enough reason to love her, she was as natural and open with Josh as she was with me. Mandy didn't know how to be anything but herself.

When we were home in Clonmegan we gravitated towards Josh's friends rather than mine and as a consequence I often found myself socialising with Liam. The boys frequently played pool in a dark, poky room at the back of one of the pubs in town. Initially, Liam was uncomfortable with my presence among his circle of friends.

'You must be joking,' he exclaimed the first time I turned up with Josh.

'Shut up, O'Reilly,' Josh responded with a friendly push.

Liam was equally unimpressed when I participated in the pool tournament they were running among themselves. 'Jesus, you're shocking, Caitlin. Don't you know how to hold a cue? Look, watch me. Steady does it . . .'

My pool skills improved dramatically under Liam's tutelage, which was driven more by embarrassment on my behalf than by brotherly love or concern. But gradually he got used to me being there, and quite often the only female present, and we became closer, more like friends rather than brother and sister. In that dark pool room I came to know him as a person. He would tell me things he'd never say at home.

'God, I *hate* it. Mum fussing over me like I'm still a child, Dad watching every move I make, always ready with a fucking opinion. Jesus, Caitlin, I need to get a job and a place of my own before I lose my temper some day and throw a punch at him!'

With his friends, away from the tension at home, I saw that Liam was good company, talkative, funny in an understated way. I saw that he was kind, considerate, and generous with the little money that he had. He was more sensible than some of the others, often the one to moderate their behaviour if they were getting out of hand, stopping them from launching their bodies across the pool table or using the cues to playfully, and quite painfully, whack each other on the head.

Sometimes, when he'd had too much to drink, Liam would hook his arm around my neck, half choking me. 'This is my sister,' he'd announce to his friends. 'Isn't she just great?'

I would smile sheepishly, waiting for them to unequivocally agree so that Liam would let go of me.

I realised that not only did I love my brother, I liked him too.

And I especially liked that Liam looked out for Josh, that he always did his best to include him in whatever conversation or social event was happening. I felt deeply grateful for this.

Josh's speech challenged me and I often struggled to understand him. His voice was nasal and his consonants were clearer than his vowels, particularly the consonants you say with your lips, like 'm' and 'b'. Invariably, he would lose the last sound in a word, as it was harder for him to hear that far. Though he practised and practised saying my name, it never sounded right.

I discovered that he wasn't deaf to music, as I had originally assumed. He could hear patterns, a beat, but not the pitch. I played CDs for him and he followed the lyrics by reading my lips, oblivious that my singing voice was just as off-key as his. He liked rap, Jay-Z and some Backstreet Boys, anything that had a strong rhythm. We had impromptu discos in my room, shimmying against each other before we ended up kissing on the bed.

Sometimes, I watched his soccer games on the weekends, standing on the sidelines, often in soft rain that wasn't heavy enough for the match to be called off. Josh was beautiful to watch, fluid as he ran after the ball, elegant when he extended his leg to kick it down the line or cross it towards the goal. I yelled encouragements that he couldn't hear. He was one of the better players on the team, the only problem being that he couldn't hear the whistle and often continued for a few seconds after play had stopped, smiling sheepishly when Liam or one of the others waved him down. When this happened, it brought a lump to my throat. I could see supporters of the other team, people who didn't know him, conferring, shooting curious glances at the young man with the dark hair and eyes, wondering what was wrong with him.

'He's deaf,' I wanted to explain. 'He can't hear. That's all. In every other way he's perfect.'

Josh worked as a plasterer for a small building company. His boss, Phil, picked him up in the morning and dropped him home in the late afternoon, either to his parents' house in Clonmegan or to my room in Belfast. Rather conveniently, most of their work was in the Belfast area. Once onsite, Phil took all the instructions and did all the talking to the client. He then communicated to Josh what needed to be done. He knew how to sign; his brother was profoundly deaf. Phil often commented to me how good Josh was at his job, how he could make the ugliest wall smooth, how his corners and finish were beautiful to behold. Though this praise for my boyfriend made me proud, it didn't surprise me. Josh was good with his hands in every way. He instinctively knew how to fix things, taking them apart and fitting them back together again. He was artistic and could sketch quite proficiently. And – something I wouldn't admit to Phil in a million years – Josh's hands knew how to caress and sweep the length of my body, how to bring me to a point where I hardly knew what I was saying or thinking, where he began or I ended.

Seeing Phil, a burly man with huge hands and bulbous fingers, signing so adeptly with Josh gave me the impetus to improve my own signing skills. As my relationship with Josh became deeper and more involved, so did our need to communicate on a more complex level. I asked him to teach me sign language and practised my skills by watching the RTE *News for the Deaf*, which was on after the main six o'clock bulletin. In a relatively short space of time I became quite good at sign language, with the added benefit, thanks to the news, of being very up to date on current affairs.

Occasionally Josh and I had arguments. Not shouting matches, like other couples; our conflict was expressed with angry gestures, furious glares and slammed doors. More often than not, the arguments spiralled from frustration: a failure in comprehension, having to repeat what we were trying to convey again and again, until one of us would throw up our hands and stomp off. Jealousy also reared its head, Josh fearing that I would fall for someone in my class, someone who could hear and drive and speak articulately, me telling him that he was being stupid and immature and that he didn't know me *at all* if he thought I would betray him like that.

We had other arguments too, normal ones that had nothing to do with his hearing. Arguments that were silly, unprovoked, with absolutely no substance. It never took us long to make up, though. One of us would seek the other out and apologise.

'Caitlin, can you let me in? I'm sorry, okay?'

I'd unlatch the door. 'I'm sorry too.'

'Fighting with you makes me feel sick inside.'

I'd nod, my own stomach churning. 'Let's not fight. Ever again. Especially not about something so stupid.'

Then we would hug, long, tight hugs where I felt like I was part of him and he was part of me, and I would think how very much I loved him, how lucky I was to have met him, and how perfect we were together.

My exams signified both the end of the academic year and the end of the routine I had going with Josh. I gave the exams my all, revising late at night so that my knowledge was fresh the following day. At the end of the two weeks I was completely and utterly spent but happy and secure in the knowledge that I had done well in the exams and in the first year of my degree.

I packed up my belongings at the Elms, amazed that I had enough to fill two big suitcases when I had initially arrived with just the one. In addition to the suitcases, I had several boxes filled with textbooks and writing pads, and garbage bags stuffed with clothes and towels and sheets, some of which belonged to Josh.

My father knocked on the door before coming in. 'Good Lord.' He surveyed the baggage. 'I'm not sure we'll be able to get it all in.'

It took a few trips up and down to the car, and between the boot and the back seat it all just about fitted. 'I'll do one final check to make sure I've left nothing behind,' I said as Dad settled in behind the wheel.

Back in the room, I took one last look around. The space looked small and bare and insignificant, as though Josh and I had never been there, as though we had already been relegated to the past, a memory. Next year the room would take on some other first-year student's personality. The bed, stripped down to its chequered mattress, would be slept in by someone else – one person, I assumed, not two. Josh and I would sleep in another bed in another room and make another year of memories together. Though I felt a little sad to be leaving this room and this year behind, I already couldn't wait for what was ahead.

In no time at all we were driving out of Belfast towards Clonmegan. As the concrete and uncompromising lines of the city gave way to the gentle roll of countryside, I dwelled on the year gone past. I felt grown up and more worldly than this time last year. I had lived away from home, fended for myself, and I now knew what it was like to love someone and to be loved in return. The fact that Belfast wasn't an easy city to live in, that it was unpredictable and sometimes rough, made me feel strong and more resilient.

And the fact that loving Josh could be hard too, that we had greater challenges and frustrations and limitations than other couples did, made me love him all the more intensely and completely.

Chapter 5

Josh and I strolled into town, hands entwined, the sky overhead more white than grey. I caressed the calluses on his fingers as they curled around mine. Town was busy – kids shopping with their mothers for school uniforms, teenagers scouting for jeans and CDs – and a sense of anticipation prevailed due to the carnival that would move through the streets later in the day. Some of the shops had tables outside displaying fresh produce, house wares, shoes, tempting passers-by with a faux-market feel. People meandered across the road and in and out of shops, relaxed but with a broad sense of purpose, unlike Josh and me, who didn't have any reason to be there.

When we reached Chapel Street, I touched Josh's arm and drew his gaze to my mouth. 'What do you want to do?' I asked.

He grinned in reply and used his free hand to rub his stomach.

I shook my head in mock disbelief; we'd had a sandwich at home only an hour or so earlier. 'I'm not hungry yet.'

'Have a look around the shops until you are?' he suggested.

'It's depressing looking at stuff I can't afford to buy,' I signed back.

We stood on the footpath communicating with a mishmash of sign, speech and facial expressions, oblivious to everything but our conversation until a dark-green car pulled in so close that it startled us both and Josh pulled me away from the kerb. Two men got out of the car and it seemed natural to exchange apologies, us for standing too close, them for not tooting to make us aware that they were pulling in. But the men were already walking away, their eyes fixed on the ground in front of them.

'Rude,' I mouthed to Josh.

He didn't reply, but he put his arm around my shoulders and drew me closer, his eyes on the men until they melded into the crowd.

We continued onto Main Street where we traipsed in and out of a few shops. I saw a pair of ballet flats that would be both stylish and practical for university when I went back after the holidays, and tried them on, knowing full well that I couldn't buy them. Unemployed like Liam, I was living off Mum and Dad. I had tried to get a summer job in town, dropping copies of my CV into the shops and sports complex, calling into the pubs and restaurants and imploring for a few hours' work a week, but the harsh reality was that Clonmegan had more students home on holiday than it had summer jobs. Mum would have bought me the shoes if I'd asked, but asking wasn't easy, not at my age, and certainly not with my father within earshot. My lack of gainful employment was a blot on his reputation, his ethic of hard work and just reward, and it provided me with an insight into how awful it was for Liam. To be honest, I felt quite guilty about my brother. In the past, witnessing his arguments with my father, I'd privately thought Liam wasn't trying hard enough to get a job, that he should make do with bar work or something in retail until his dream job eventuated, but I was now realising, first-hand, that any kind of work was hard to come by in our town. The next time we went for a drink together I would hook my arm around Liam's neck, half choking him the way he always did to me, and say sorry for not fully understanding and sympathising with him, and for not always taking his side in those clashes with my father.

As a result of my current and thankfully temporary brush with unemployment, I had already resolved to stay in Belfast next summer. I was still afraid of the city, of the violence that simmered beneath the surface, of the armoured cars and the RUC in their rifle-green uniforms who still had a presence despite the peace agreement, but I figured I had a much better chance of getting summer work there than in Clonmegan. I could have considered London or somewhere else in Europe but I wasn't prepared to leave Josh behind, not even for a few months. When I went abroad, he would be with me. It would be something we did together, as a couple.

With no choice but to leave the ballet flats behind, I wished that we had stayed at home, cuddled together on the couch, rather than embarking on this pointless trip to town. Window shopping every now and then was perfectly fine, but not for the whole summer. Then I remembered my father, his foul humour that had propelled us off the couch and into town in the first place, and decided this had been the better alternative after all.

Josh, now starving, steered me towards one of his favourite cafés, where we ordered drinks and food and smiled at each other in the subdued lighting. We'd been together just over a year now, my nineteenth birthday in July coinciding with our first anniversary. I couldn't remember my life without him. I couldn't remember what it was like to take a stroll without my hand being held in his or what it was like to wake up without seeing him or, at the very least, thinking of him. I knew what made him laugh, what he found frustrating or annoying; I could read his mood in a second. I knew the tender look he'd get on his face before he kissed me. I knew his touch, the differing pressure of his fingers when he was conveying comfort, or simple affection, or a prelude to sex. Being at home over the holidays meant we couldn't sleep together and I missed the closeness of waking up next to him, the luxury of feeling his naked body along the length of mine, the heat that radiated from his skin, the heaviness of his arm resting on my waist.

'I miss you so much.' I sighed. 'I must be the only student in the country who can't wait for the summer to be over.'

He nodded. 'It's been hard. When I wake in the morning, it feels wrong that you're not there. All day at work it's like something's missing – I don't feel right until I see you again.'

My fingers interlaced with his across the table. 'Next year will be different,' I promised. Next summer, in Belfast, I would have a job *and* a flat, and Josh and I would continue our physical relationship uncurtailed.

'For a start, let's try to get a double bed.' He grinned, and suddenly we were both fondly recalling our cramped legs and sore backs from the single bed at the Elms.

Josh's order came, burger and chips, and he ate with relish. It amazed me how he could eat so much and still be so lean. He burned off the calories so effortlessly. I had to watch my diet more carefully. My meal was a salad, chicken, bacon and croutons scattered among leaves of cos lettuce. Josh offered me one of his chips; I savoured it in my mouth, hot and salty, but refused when he offered me a second.

We were almost finished eating when it happened, a ruckus at the doorway, a police officer booming above the hum of conversation and background music, 'Evacuate the premises. Everybody out, please!'

'Why?' asked a woman who had only just received her meal.

'There's been a bomb warning. Everybody out! Now!'

I signed to Josh what had been said and we stood up from our table. He had his burger in his hand as we left the café and joined the stream of people making their way down the street. We didn't hurry; like everyone else, we didn't perceive the warning as a real threat. Josh chewed the last of his burger as we ducked under the tape cordoning off the street. People milled around, mildly annoyed at the interruption to whatever they'd been doing, waiting for the all clear so they could go back. Josh and I had no reason to wait; we'd had no reason to be in town in the first place.

'Home?' I arched my brows with the question.

He nodded absently, his eyes skimming the crowd, his expression becoming slightly perturbed. Though he took my hand and walked with me, he kept twisting his head, looking back. Something was making him more and more agitated.

'What is it, Josh?' I asked.

He stopped. 'Stay,' he said thickly, resting his hands briefly on my shoulders before walking back towards the crowd, his steps becoming quicker, more urgent, until he was jogging. I watched, confused and concerned. I saw him take strangers by the arm and pull them aside. I saw the puzzlement on their faces at being man-handled, and at his obvious lack of verbal skills. He succeeded in moving a few of them and then, through the gap, I saw it: the dark-green car, the one that had parked so close to us earlier. Something about it, about the drivers, had bothered him then, and now it was bothering him again. Josh relied heavily on his instincts. He saw things that others didn't, sensed things. Why was he moving people away from the car? Jesus, he didn't think that –

The blast was ear-splitting, so ferocious that it pushed me back and I fell to the ground. For a few moments I was dazed, oblivious even to the pain in my elbows, which had taken the brunt of my fall onto the unyielding concrete. I gingerly lifted one elbow, wincing as I did so, then the other, and stumbled to my feet. In front of me, where only moments before there had been a relatively ordinary scene from a relatively ordinary Saturday afternoon, a plume of black smoke soared into the sky, contaminating its whiteness, its purity.

And then the realisation hit me.

'Josh!' I screamed, rushing forward, arms outstretched as though I could save him.

Roof slates, fragments of wooden beams and shards of glass hailed down from the black cloud.

'Stay back.' Someone seized my arm. 'It's dangerous.'

I shook myself free and kept going. Closer, the road was littered with bodies and debris, water from a burst water pipe gushing over everything as though trying to cleanse the awful, awful mess. My screams mingled with all the other screams, all the other names being called.

I reached the spot where he had been standing, and there was nothing, nothing but a pile of rubble. I knelt and began to dig through the rubble with my fingers, my hands caked with soot, ash still raining from the sky and onto the sleeves of my denim jacket.

I sobbed, digging faster, more desperately.

I continued to call his name, knowing that he couldn't hear me, not even if he'd been alive. I remember pausing for a moment and listening to the guttural, almost inhuman screams of shock and horror and grief around me, and I felt grateful, overwhelmingly so, that he was deaf to those sounds. Some things are best never heard.

Chapter 6

A police officer took me by the arm and forced me away from my pile of rubble. 'It's deadly, love. The buildings are unstable and you could get injured yourself.'

I heard afterwards that the local hospitals were a hub of confusion, relatives running in and out of wards, shouting names of missing wives, husbands, sons and daughters, praying that they were lying injured on a hospital bed rather than in the makeshift morgue at the army base. Someone offered me a lift but there was no point: Josh wasn't at the hospital. I didn't have the consolation of hope that he might have gone into a shop on a whim, or dawdled too long talking to a friend. I knew exactly where he'd been standing when the bomb went off, and now he was gone.

An ambulance officer told me that the sports complex had been appointed a meeting place and I went there instead. When I got there, I used the public phone to call Josh's parents but they weren't at home. I tried my own parents, only to find the same. Mobile phones had not yet hit the mainstream, and chaos reigned as survivors were unable to quickly reassure worried relatives that they were safe and those with bad news, like me, were unable to pass it on.

I don't know how long I was at the sports complex. I sank to the ground, the wall hard against my back, and hugged my knees. I tuned out the howls of grief and anger and disbelief. My own screams had died inside me and I was left with a sense of being outside my body, looking on at myself with a sense of detachment.

Once, when I looked up, I saw Mandy, her face blotched from crying. She told me that her older sister, Fiona, was missing. I hugged her and tried to find words of comfort but at the same time I couldn't fathom that her sister could be missing, possibly dead, that Mandy's large irreverent family could be damaged in such a way. Fiona was even bubblier than her siblings, her hair highlighted an unnatural blonde, her fingernails polished in dazzling colours, her voice perky as she chatted to customers at the supermarket checkout where she worked. Fiona couldn't be missing. She was too loud and too vibrant to be overlooked.

Carly was at the sports complex, too, waiting to hear news of her aunt and cousin. She was pale – even her mouth looked white – and her mother and father and uncle, who stood to the side, were like ghosts hovering in the shadows.

Both Mandy and Carly asked why I was there, who was missing, but I couldn't answer, couldn't say the words. In scared voices they suggested names until I nodded. 'Oh, Caitlin. Oh, Caitlin.'

Finally Mum and Dad arrived, scanning the room frantically

before finding me alone on the ground. Mandy's family had been called into a private room and we all knew by now that you were only called into that room when the news was bad. Carly had drifted back to her family, each paler than the other but still hoping against all odds that a thirty-five-year-old woman and her ten-year-old son had not been among the fatalities.

Mum and Dad rushed to where I was slumped, their eyes widening at the soot caked on my skin and clothes, then looking into my face and finding an answer they couldn't bear to hear.

'No.' Mum shook her head.

'How can you be sure?' My father, always checking the facts.

'He . . . he was . . . standing right there,' I managed, but couldn't continue.

Dad got down on the floor beside me, on his knees. He crushed me to him, his torso shaking against my face. He was crying.

Shocked at this, I began to cry too, tears gushing and streaking soot onto his white cotton shirt. I was vaguely aware that we were making a spectacle and at any moment I expected him to pull away, to suggest we both compose ourselves until we were somewhere more private. But he didn't. He stayed with me, cried with me, until my eyes were empty and dry. When I finally pulled back from his embrace and got to my feet, he put one arm around my waist and one around Mum's, and we left the sports complex united in our grief.

Aesthetically, the funerals looked the same. Black jackets, white faces, grey skies, the sombre tones of priests and reverends, the sobbing bowed heads of the bereaved. So many funerals to go to: Fiona, Mandy's sister; the man who lived in the estate next to ours; a girl I knew vaguely from school; and a joint service for Carly's aunt and cousin. They blurred together, the funerals, and the most appalling thing was that by the end I could hardly distinguish Josh's from the rest. Black, white, grey. Black, white, grey. Mum went to the ones she could muster enough strength to endure, but Dad was there for all of them, by my side, his arm holding me up, and I was thankful because at that time I wasn't sure I could ever hold myself upright again.

Two months later, there was a meeting in town for the families of the victims; I went with Mum and Dad and Maeve. It was chaotic, people talking over each other, angry, grief-stricken, each one wanting their voice to be heard.

'Who did this? What are their names? Why haven't the police arrested them?'

They were all good questions but at that point nobody in the room had any answers. We knew only what had been reported on TV: the bomb had been planted by a group who was opposed to the Good Friday Peace Agreement. Apparently, there had been warnings, phone calls to the police and media, but the warnings hadn't been clear enough: the wrong area had been evacuated and instead of shepherding people to safety, the police had unwittingly directed them into the vicinity of the bomb, multiplying the deaths and casualties. Fifty-three people had died: Catholics, Protestants, women, men, schoolchildren and babies. Hundreds more were injured, with shrapnel wounds, missing limbs, horrific burns.

'These men have committed outright murder. They must be brought to justice . . .'

I thought of the two men I had seen get out of the car. I couldn't remember their faces but I remembered the colour of their hair and that they'd been wearing jeans and jackets. They looked normal, not the kind of men you'd expect to be driving a car loaded with four hundred pounds of explosives. Had they made the bomb themselves or was that someone else's department? How did one learn to make a bomb? Who had taught these men the rudiments of wiring and timing and all the other things they needed to know? I visualised a classroom scenario, an industrious atmosphere as the students worked with bent heads and dextrous fingers, the teacher, hands clasped behind his back, peering over their shoulders and commending their progress: today's subject, bomb making.

'They cannot get away with it just because the powers that be are afraid that the peace agreement will be compromised!'

Sounds of consensus reverberated around the room. There was a strong feeling that the police were proceeding too cautiously, afraid to rock the boat, to compromise the clearly overestimated peace agreement.

I sat in the meeting, listening to the anguished and uncontrolled outbursts. Men, women, teenagers, children, speaking without turns, airing their grief and confusion and their need to know that at the end of it all there would be justice.

Justice, it seemed, was the only thing that would ease their pain.

Eventually a man stood up and called for order. He said that we wouldn't get any answers unless we all pulled together, joined to form one voice. He was a soft-spoken, unassuming man but people listened nevertheless.

Before I knew it, my father was standing too, giving his unqualified agreement. 'I'll do all I can to help the families here tonight, to bring their concerns to the police and the political parties, and to ensure that the people responsible for this atrocity will be brought to justice.'

He sounded noble, inspiring even, and I could see from the faces around me that people were listening and responding to him in the same way they had to the man who'd spoken before him. They wanted to be led, to be taken charge of, and to have their voices channelled into one. But most of all they wanted justice, and that was my father's specialty. He knew all about justice and what was right and wrong. He'd been teaching it for years.

As I sat there listening, my hand in Mum's, we were both completely unaware that this was the beginning of a crusade that would in the end mean even more heartbreak for our family. By the time we filed out of the room, a committee had been formed and Dad was already in the thick of it. We left him behind, talking animatedly to the other committee members, and went home to a dark, empty house.

Over the following weeks and months, I analysed things more thoroughly. All those rules and values my father had preached about and stuffed down our throats replayed in my head, baseless all of them, a stupid waste of time and effort. *You'll be safe if you keep to the rules . . . A good life is one lived according to one's values . . .* I was a loyal daughter as much as I was a loyal friend. Despite my occasionally rebellious behaviour, I had essentially believed and trusted in those rules. The truth – that life was randomly and senselessly cruel and had no regard for rules or values of any kind, that safety was nothing more than an illusion – shattered my whole belief system.

I went over the events of that fateful day, picked them apart with the precision and objectivity of a forensic scientist, and came to realise my father's part in it all. And I saw this new committee, this crusade, for exactly what it was: a means of assuaging his own guilt.

I didn't cry in front of Dad again, instead retaining my tears for the privacy of my room or the shower. I pushed him away whenever he tried to hug me, comfort me or ask me how I was. We would not have been in town that day if it hadn't been for him. I could not get past that fact. And I could never forgive him for it.

Chapter 7

The keyhole was hazy, indistinct. I frowned at it until it came into focus. Lining up my key, I was on the verge of inserting it when the door was whipped open.

'What kind of hour do you call this?'

I blinked. My father had waited up for me. He was wearing his dressing gown, not a fluffy cheap thing but maroon-coloured velour, very suave. His stare reminded me that he'd asked a question. I glanced at my watch. The face was blurred, like everything else.

'Small hand on four. Big hand on two. Ten past four.' I looked up to add defiantly, 'That's am, of course, not pm.' I passed him in the hall and climbed the first few steps.

'You're drunk!'

I didn't grace this very obvious statement with a reply.

'I'm talking to you. Face me and show some respect,' he shouted.

I stopped, turned and viewed him from my elevated position. Even though I was drunk and full of resentment, I was struck by how handsome he was. His expression was stern, his brow lined with a frown, but the effect of his aqua eyes and high cheekbones prevailed over his mood. My father, the pin-up professor.

'Yes, Daddy,' I replied in a sarcastically sweet voice. 'I'm drunk. That's what teenagers do. Among other things, like taking drugs and screwing around.'

'Don't you dare speak to me like that!'

I saw the phone in his hand and realised that he hadn't been waiting up for me at all, that he'd been on one of his oh-so-important phone calls, at four o'clock in the morning!

'Who the hell are you to tell me what to do?' I spat. We glared at each other.

My mother appeared on the landing, with bleary eyes and tousled hair. 'What's going on?' she asked, looking from Dad to me and back again.

It was high time for her to ask that question. She'd allowed him to ignore her, to ignore us. She'd allowed him to comfort people he didn't know, to talk late into the night to strangers, while we were left to our own devices, neglected, cast aside for a higher cause.

'Why don't you ask *him*?' I said darkly.

'Caitlin, I don't like your tone,' Mum said.

'Can't you see what a hypocrite he is?'

'Caitlin!'

'He's there for everybody, everybody but his own family.'

The irony was that Dad was an expert on hypocrisy. *Hypocrisy is acting contrary to what one believes. Hypocrisy is deceitfulness, deception, duplicity, falseness, insincerity, phoneyness and two-facedness.* Professor Jonathan O'Reilly of Queen's University not only lectured on the subject of hypocrisy, he embodied it in his own everyday actions and behaviour.

'I'm going to bed now,' I declared.

Like all the bedrooms upstairs, the room I shared with Maeve was built into the roof. The ceiling sloped at the sides and I banged my head against it as I lurched towards my bed. I swore and rubbed my head before lying flat on my back, fully dressed, the room swirling around me. In her single bed on the other side of the room, Maeve was part of the merry-go-round. Maeve, Mum, Dad, Liam, me, round and round our faces went. How would it end, I wondered? What would it take to make it stop? To enforce some form of normality? Almost eight months had dragged by, each feeling longer than the one before. Were the men who parked the car that day back to normal? Had they been out tonight, drinking at their local, having a laugh with their friends? Did they ever stop to think of the fifty-three people they'd murdered? Of all the people in this town left with broken hearts and shattered lives? Did those men live normal lives now or did they still make bombs?

I'd gone back to university at the start of the new academic year and house-shared in an area of Belfast called The Holy-lands, which was rough and overcrowded. I desperately missed what I'd had last year. I missed the feeling of security at the Elms and I missed Josh so much that it physically hurt, stabs of pain that would start as soon as I woke up and continue through-out the day. I struggled through classes without a shred of the drive or focus that I'd had in my first year. I walked to and from university, robotic until a car would slide into the kerb to park, at which point I would be seized by panic and start to run. Loud or sudden noises made me jump in fright. Though the end of the academic year was only a few months away now and the finish line in sight, my nerves were stretched to breaking point and I felt I would hardly make the distance, that I couldn't endure another moment in this place.

This weekend was Easter and tomorrow morning we would go to mass as a family, followed by an early dinner of roast meat, potatoes and vegetables. Everyone in the family, including me, would go through the motions. I would sit in the church pew and at the dinner table pretending to be present, when in my head I had retreated to last year, when Josh and I had consummated our relationship and had our whole future in front of us, a future that seemed even better and brighter after the signing of the Good Friday Peace Agreement. A future that would still be intact if only we hadn't gone into town that day. If only that dark-green car had parked somewhere else. If only people had not congregated around it. If only Josh had not turned back to warn them. If only . . .

The bedroom continued to swirl around me and I imagined myself disappearing into a vortex that sent me hurtling back to last year. As if to mock such a fanciful idea, the room's turning slowed and everything became stagnant. I was lying on the bed, my face wet, sobs caught in my throat. There was no going back. I was stuck right here.

I heard a car pull up outside, our front gate being opened, footsteps coming towards the house. My first thought was that it was Patrick, the boy I'd kissed earlier on that evening and who had subsequently dropped me home. Even though I'd given Patrick my phone number, I didn't plan on seeing him again. He fell so far short of Josh that I'd had tears in my eyes as I kissed him. I'd been trying to numb the pain, to do something other than grieve, but now I was left feeling more lonely and bereft than ever.

No, of course it wasn't Patrick following me inside, he didn't even know me. It was much more likely that the footsteps belonged to someone from my father's group, one of the people who had access to him twenty-four seven, unlike his family.

I heard the sound of clanging glass, the footsteps retreating, a door slamming, an engine revving and moving away, but stopping again further down the street, the sequence repeated as before. It was the milkman. I fell asleep, relieved to have figured something out at least.

'You're making a big mistake.'

'That's what you think.'

'Qualifications mean everything.'

'No, they don't.'

'I can't believe you're doing this!'

'Well, I am.'

'Why? Why now? You've only got one year to go.'

'Because I can't stand it for another moment, let alone a year!'

My replies were quick. Sometimes I hit the mark and I hurt him. We were like fencers, our words swords.

'Please, Caitlin. You're a clever girl but clever often isn't good enough. You need your degree, that piece of paper. Sometimes it's all an employer has to go on.'

He could be quite persuasive, my father. He knew how to phrase things, how to strike that chord. He knew that beneath my pain and sorrow and the need to flee, there was ambition, battered and bruised but ambition nonetheless. He knew that I ultimately wanted to get a good job and to do well in the world.

'I've made up my mind, Dad. There's no point in talking about it anymore.'

'What are you going to do if you're not going to study?' He was at a loss. It was unimaginable to him that people could have lives and careers without an academic qualification.

'I'm going overseas.'

'Where to?'

'Australia.'

I'd chosen Australia for distance more than anything else. My parents wouldn't be able to 'drop over' to see me and neither would I be expected to 'drop home' for a visit.

I got to my feet. There was no point in staying a minute longer.

He looked up, his face weary and strangely vulnerable. 'Is it because of me?'

'Partly,' I replied harshly. Though our paths rarely crossed these days, I knew he was there in the background, somewhere on campus, be it his office, a lecture theatre or the canteen. And I couldn't stand it.

But of course it wasn't just him. There were many, many reasons. I would never feel safe again, not in Clonmegan or Belfast or anywhere in this country. I was sick and tired of religion and politics and their sheer divisiveness across every aspect of daily life. I'd had enough of the flags and threats that lurked around every corner. The low, grey skies left me claustrophobic and barely able to breathe. If I didn't get away I feared that I'd completely crack up.

I closed my father's office door behind me and for a moment it was just me and his secretary. She was stacking papers on her desk and I waited for her to look up. 'Can you remind him of Mum's birthday next month?' I hated to think of Paula sad and lonely on her birthday, without even a token gift from her husband.

The secretary blinked her cornflower-blue eyes. She was quite pretty; it was a rather odd time for me to notice this fact. 'I always remind him of birthdays. He's generally too preoccupied to remember . . .'

I nodded and left.

Outside the sky was lower and greyer than ever. Drops of rain started to fall before I left the campus. I quickened my pace and didn't once look back at Queen's University. As far as I was concerned, that era of my life was well and truly over.

Part Two

Chapter 8

Melbourne, February 2009

I slide the cue back and forth between my thumb and forefinger until it's steady. Then, with a fluidity that originates from a completely different time and place, I strike the white at its centre. It smashes into the other balls and scatters them around the table. One rolls into the bottom left pocket. I'm on stripes.

Derek's a silhouette at the far end of the table. He holds his beer bottle by its belly and his tie has long since been abandoned. There's no outward sign that he's in charge of the fastest-growing division in Telelink, a telecommunications giant in Australia.

I pot a second ball, the purple, and I can feel rather than see his patronising smile.

'Luck of the Irish, eh?'

I shrug. 'What do you think I should go for next?'

'Try the blue.'

This isn't good advice. There's no shot to be made with the blue and Derek knows this. I get him back by freezing the white against the wall.

I swig from my glass as Derek surveys the table. I should go home; I've had more than enough to drink. But I need to play Derek along a little bit further before calling it a night. He's one of my more difficult clients, his ego oversized and unpredictable. He regards his multimillion-dollar budget as a statement of power, and he spends it with a great deal of self-importance and flamboyance. I'm a good match for him, though, and I'm confident that I can channel his ego and budget into the single biggest order ever placed with Learning Space, the company I work for.

Derek balances the cue and leans forward. He has a nice arse, I think offhandedly, but he's not my type. He's too full of himself, too arrogant. I'm not his type either, with my fiery hair, pale skin and eyes, and faded freckles smattering the curves of my cheeks. I look Celtic through and through and Derek's taste in women, if his current girlfriend is anything to go by, runs more towards exotic.

He strikes the red in the wrong place and it stops short of the pocket. 'Close,' he says with a wry grin.

It's not close at all.

I gulp down more of my drink before taking the cue from his outstretched hand. I draw a mental line between the white ball and the one I'm aiming for, the green. It goes in, rolling along the underneath of the table with a satisfying rumble.

'Well done,' he says condescendingly.

I'm perfectly lined up for my next shot and it goes in just as nicely.

Derek, embarrassed that I'm better than him, looks around to see who's watching. 'Where did you learn how to play pool?'

'From my brother and his friends.'

'With pints of Guinness lined up on the sides of the table and Irish ballads playing in the background?' he sneers.

'Something like that.'

I scan the table. I could set up the last three balls, but that would piss Derek off even more. It's a fine line with him: he has to admire me, respect me; a little hate is good too, so that I can push him, like I'm doing now. But there is a line.

I clip the yellow and leave it deliberately shy of the middle pocket.

He puts down his drink. He has a purpose now: to regain dignity. He struts around the table. Squats. Measures. Bends over and gives a group of girls standing close by a tantalising view of his nice arse. He makes the shot and gets it in but he isn't lined up for the next one. This doesn't stop him from being inordinately pleased with himself.

'Hold on while I go to the bar.' He's gone before I have the chance to stop him. I'm tired by now, my body aching for rest. I've been playing to his ego all evening. Over dinner. Over drinks. This game of pool. Now more drinks. Still, though, if this is what it takes . . .

Derek re-emerges through the haze, tall and confident. People move out of his way. He hands me a bourbon and Coke.

'Did I ask for this?'

'Just drink it.'

Sometimes he's domineering and possessive with me, as though I'm his girlfriend, which I'm not and never will be. This do-it-or-else attitude is his way of flirting. He knows that I have his measure, that I will only allow him to act like this to a certain degree.

I don't like bourbon but drink it anyway. It tastes of my determination.

'Blue or orange?' I ask.

'Blue,' he replies.

The blue is in a slightly better place but it's still a challenging shot. I get the bridge and sit on the side of the table.

'One leg's meant to touch the ground,' he states with ill-disguised competitiveness.

'That rule's for people who are more than five feet tall,' I retort and cut the blue on the side. It spins into the pocket. The white draws back perfectly and I'm able to send the orange into the same pocket. I slide down off the table, not missing the look of annoyance on his face.

'So, Derek,' I begin as I size up the yellow that I left hanging by the middle pocket. 'Do you have firm dates for the training rollout?'

'It's scheduled for May,' he replies, mollified by my question: I'm seeking his business; he has the veto, the power.

'Do you have a better idea of numbers?'

'Approximately three thousand employees.'

'Do you still think the program will fit into two days?'

'At a push.'

'How about two long days?'

'How long can you make a day?'

'As long as you need it to be, Derek,' I say matter-of-factly. 'In fact, we can train your people through the night if that's what's needed!'

He hardly notices when I sink the black. He looks as though he's seriously considering it: training through the night.

The game is over and I nod to the group of men whose gold two-dollar coin rests on the edge of the table. 'It's all yours.' I smile at them, and then turn to Derek. 'Why don't we say 8 am till 7 pm, five rooms running concurrently?'

'How long would it take in total?'

'Three thousand people would go through in about eight weeks.'

He nods, suddenly looking impatient to go. He slings his suit jacket over his shoulder and I put my bag on mine. Outside it's warm but the sun has long gone.

'I expect a big discount,' he states.

'Of course.' I hide a grin.

'I mean it!'

'Don't worry. I'll take care of you.'

'When can you send me a quote?'

'Next week. I'll show the discount clearly.'

The quote will spark more haggling, maybe even another dinner and drinks. But it's close now, very close.

Derek spots a taxi and raises his hand. 'I'll talk to you soon,' he says as he gets into the cab.

He leaves me on the pavement to find a taxi of my own. Next week, or the one after, he'll be handing me a five-million-dollar order; apparently this exempts him from everyday manners.

I turn and begin to walk down the street. I'm not ready for a taxi just yet anyway. I want to stroll, clear my head, savour the moment, the city. The pubs have spilled onto the streets, there's a party under the stars, rock music swirling with conversation, laughter and a sense of excitement: Melbourne on a Friday night, the working week over, a long sunny weekend ahead. God, I love the atmosphere of this city, the distinct lines drawn between work and leisure, what's serious and what's fun. Everything so clear-cut and in its place, with no undercurrents of religion or politics. No history or past injustices to undermine the happiness of the present moment.

My first few years in Australia were tumultuous, a succession of different jobs, friends and places to live. I arrived in Sydney not knowing a soul and for a while I revelled in my anonymity. Living in a hostel and working casually, I gradually met some people, mainly backpackers in transit to somewhere else, and formed the kind of friendships that last until one or the other of you moves on, the kind that have no history and are based in the present only, and where you make a conscious decision what, if anything, you reveal about yourself.

After the hostel, I lived in an apartment in an old-style building in Bondi Junction. The apartment came with three bedrooms and two wild flatmates who clubbed and partied from one week to the next. I got my first permanent job, selling credit cards over the phone. It was hard work, cold-calling strangers, trying to persuade them they needed more credit, and nine times out of ten people hung up on me. It was useful grounding, though. It taught me how to make a good first impression, how to close a sale, and it was the first step in establishing my career.

A year later I moved to Brisbane where I started over with a new job, friends and flat. Another year saw my return to Sydney, this time to the north side of the city, and nine months later I moved to Melbourne. Melbourne instantly felt like a better fit. It had the right mix of foreignness and familiarity, of excitement and safety, and it was where I finally settled, or at least stopped running so hard and swinging so wildly from one thing to the next. I found a job that had good prospects for future promotion. I found an apartment that I could see myself staying in for longer than a few months. I found friends who were more than just drinking buddies.

Those first few years have morphed into a decade, ten whole years since that final scene in my father's office and everything that had gone before. The pain and loss and grief have reduced exponentially with each passing year, and now Clonmegan's just an ache deep inside me, so far embedded that I've learned to live with it and carry it around as I go about my life. Time is like a winter morning's mist, shrouding my memories of the dormered house where I spent the first eighteen years of my life; the bedroom I shared with Maeve, with its sloping roof and lavender-coloured walls, their exact shade becoming murky with the passing of time; the specific dimensions of the other rooms in the house, the ornaments on the mantelpiece, the pictures hanging on the walls and other small details, hazy and distorted; the smell of rain in the air, the sagging skies, the bright green grass in the garden. But some things I choose not to even try to remember, because I fear that my memories won't be blurred at all, but all too vivid to cope with.

Strangers often smile and ask where my accent's from.

'Ireland,' I respond with a reciprocating smile yet a touch of brevity in my voice.

Sometimes they persevere. 'What part of Ireland?'

'The North.'

At this, the subject is quickly dropped. Australians are too polite to talk about religion or politics, and the North of Ireland involves both.

I walk on, past more pubs and people, and though I'm tired and feeling the effects of all the alcohol, I'm buoyed by a sense of happiness and belonging. There's nowhere I'd rather be than in this city. I love its diversity, its beat. I love the ever-present and eclectic smells of food, the labyrinth of hidden laneways and alleys, the blend of old and new, east and west. It's easy to become lost in Melbourne, to be sucked so far into its way of life that you forget who you are and where you come from. And that's what I like the best.

Chapter 9

I yawn deeply as I wait for the tram. It's early on Monday morning, only 7 am, but there's a sizeable crowd waiting at the stop. Most of them are dressed like me in business suits and sunglasses, and hold fresh coffees in their hands. It's a beautiful morning in St Kilda, neither hot nor cold. The sun is coming up behind the skyline and when its full force is unleashed the temperature will rise to the high twenties.

The tram appears in the distance, covered in advertising pictures and slogans. Coffees are slugged back, empty paper cups tossed into a nearby rubbish bin. Handbags are unzipped and tickets located. The tram rocks in and the crowd, primed and impatient, surges forward to greet it.

I find standing space, smile at a man and woman who are so close it would be rude not to acknowledge them, and the tram takes off, gliding, clunking and squeaking. This never feels like a journey to work. Sometimes I feel like a kid on one of those trackless trains at the zoo, or a tourist, gazing single-mindedly at the passing scenery as though I've never seen it before. There's something very basic and unpretentious about riding on the tram: hanging on to keep your balance, the jerky cornering after smooth stretches, the claustrophobic lack of space. But there's something cosmopolitan and urbane about it too: whirring through the streets to the heart of the city, standing close to strangers and see-ing the colour of their eyes and the pores of their skin, and feeling as though you are part of the city rather than merely an onlooker.

I get off at Collins Street and walk towards my office, fall-ing in step with other striding commuters. The women wear tailored clothes, pencil skirts, fitted dresses and straight-leg trousers, mostly in black. Black is the unofficial uniform, the common denominator, the style not just of the commuters but of the city itself. Today I'm wearing a swishing skirt, a scooped short-sleeved top and stilettos, all black. The only colour in my outfit is my necklace, silver knotted around blue stones, and, of course, my hair.

'Hey, Caitlin.' Jo, the receptionist, smiles. 'Have a good weekend?'

'Yeah. How about you?'

'Busy. Too much on. Came to work to recover!'

Jo is joking. There's no time for 'recovering' at the Learning Space reception desk: the phones are relentless. Jo already has a queue of calls, most of them from lost, panicked trainees who aren't used to finding their way around the city.

She answers the next call in the queue. 'Yes, we're on Collins. Near the corner of Elizabeth. Keep walking . . .'

I continue on to my desk, smiling at people on the way. Learning Space is a friendly company, small enough for everyone to know each other and big enough to be dynamic, exciting and sometimes unpredictable. And there's something nice about the notion of training, of enhancing someone's education and skills and sending a better, more knowledgeable person back out into the workforce. Training suggests optimism, an openness to change, the possibility of a different future. It resounds with me, and for that reason I'm very good at selling it.

'Caitlin!'

Jarrod, my boss, has seen me pass his office and summons me inside. I change direction, stifling a sigh. I always prefer to have a settling-in period before facing Jarrod: he's hard to stomach first thing in the morning.

'Morning, Jarrod,' I say brightly.

Jarrod's face is angular and exact, just like his personality, and his eyes seem to stare rather than see. Even his hair has attitude, short at the sides, spiky at the front. He's excellent at reading clients and for him, like me, nothing is out of bounds when it comes to keeping the customer happy. Sometimes, though, all that's required is a smile and it's a pity he doesn't seem to realise this.

'What happened with Derek on Friday?'

Jarrod should really save this question for the sales meeting that's scheduled in an hour's time, but patience isn't one of his strengths.

'He's talking about discounts,' I reply. 'It's getting closer.'

'There's a board meeting next week. Will I know by then?'

I've never been to a board meeting and the thought of Jarrod going in there, making my deal look like his own, is enough to make jealousy ricochet throughout my body. The reality is that I'm a mere sales consultant and he's the manager. He is the face of sales while I'm background, invisible. I imagine that the board members love him. He takes himself and the business very seriously. He's articulate, well informed and respectful. The fact that he lacks a sense of humour would be barely apparent to them.

'That's cutting it tight,' I say in a voice which, to my credit, doesn't betray my feelings. 'I'm doing the pricing today. I expect some argy-bargy with Derek before he agrees to an order.'

'Will I call him?'

'No. If we push too hard, the whole thing could fall through. You know how perverse he can be.'

Jarrod nods: he understands. He won't make me push. He asked only because sometimes his impatience gets the better of his judgment, but once he realises this he always backs off.

'Was it a late one Friday night?' he asks.

His question is not as casual as it sounds. Jarrod has a rather unimaginative approach to entertaining clients, sticking rigidly to expensive meals and wines consumed within the limitations of a self-imposed curfew of 11 pm. He doesn't approve of my more flexible approach, and is better off not knowing about the beer, bourbon and pool playing that rounded off the night.

'Not very,' I reply evasively.

'Right. Well, show me the pricing when it's done, okay?'

'Sure.' I turn towards the door. 'Do you want this open or shut?'

'Shut.'

I leave, closing the door softly behind me. My workstation is in a quiet corner of the fifth floor, next to the window. I smile hello to Zoe in the neighbouring cubicle; she's already busy on the phone. Switching on my laptop, I swivel my seat to face the window while I wait for it to start up. The view is dominated by the building across the road, a high-rise exhibit of modern architecture with alternating layers of glass and thick concrete. The green area in front of the building is a nice focus for those moments when I need to stare at something other than my screen. This morning there are some bike couriers lounging on the grass, waiting to be radioed to their next job, and the usual smattering of office workers sitting on benches with coffees and newspapers. I turn back to my laptop but the phone rings before I have a chance to type in my password.

It's Jo. 'They're looking for you down on level four.'

'What's wrong?'

'The usual – food.'

It never ceases to amaze me that with all the different factors involved in the training business, the number one complaint is always food.

'I'm coming.'

Level four has its own separate reception area, the red feature wall behind the desk distinguishing it from the similarly kitted-out training floors on levels two and three. Nicola, the floor manager, stands against the red backdrop waiting for me.

'What's wrong?' I ask.

She rolls her eyes. 'The Roads and Transport Board have eaten Chambers Bank's breakfast, that's what's wrong! I've ordered some bacon-and-egg McMuffins to compensate, but Tanya insisted that you be told.'

Nicola, like me, is in her late twenties. She's originally from London but her parents are Greek and she has the dark hair, skin and eyes of her heritage. She's a very competent floor manager, adept at dealing with most crises. Tanya McManus, the complainant, is in the breakout area, her feet planted apart, watching us. Her hands are not on her hips but they might as well be. Tanya is a large woman. Her face is soft and round and she has big soulful eyes, but her cuddly appearance is deceiving.

'I'll talk to her.' I give Nicola a conspiratorial smile and walk over to where Tanya is standing. 'Nicola just told me what happened,' I begin in a sombre tone. 'I'm terribly sorry, Tanya.'

Tanya looks down at me over folded arms. 'Sorry is *not* good enough. This is meant to be a professional organisation... things like this *simply* shouldn't happen... the food should be closely *supervised* by your staff...'

Tanya is the learning and development manager for Chambers Bank, one of my most important clients. The bank's training needs are ongoing and they're one of the few clients who have permanently dedicated rooms. This is why Nicola called me down: Tanya's complaints, no matter how trivial, must be seen to be taken seriously.

'My people need to be *fed* and *watered* to keep their *energy* levels up...'

Tanya likes to over-enunciate certain words, which makes her speech pattern very uneven. I nod and make all the right placatory noises, though I suspect her gripe is driven more by her own sustenance needs than those of her trainees.

'The training program is gruelling, and they need to be *physically* and *mentally* alert...'

With some effort I keep a straight face until the McMuffins arrive and Tanya goes to load her plate with three of them.

'Caitlin, I'm really sorry.' The training coordinator for the Roads and Transport Board comes to take Tanya's place by my side. 'My guys should have looked at the name card. They thought all their Christmases had come at once!'

Being a government department, the Roads and Transport Board's food budget is basic: sandwiches and fruit at lunch, no morning or afternoon teas, and certainly no bacon-and-egg breakfasts!

'Don't worry.' At last I can genuinely smile. 'It was an honest mistake. I hope they enjoyed it.'

Back upstairs, I read and respond to emails until it's time to leave my desk again for the biweekly sales meeting. The only good thing about the sales meeting is that it isn't on every week. My male colleagues, Gary, Chris and Nathan, have adapted their styles to suit Jarrod's, discarding any sense of humour in the process, and are extraordinarily dull to listen to. Zoe is a relatively recent and much more interesting addition to the team. It's rather nice having another female around, and even nicer that she can be relied on to view things from a completely different angle to everyone else. She's the only bright spark in the entire two-hour-long meeting.

Finally I escape and return to the sanctuary of my desk, free at last to work on the Telelink proposal. The spreadsheet already has preliminary figures and key assumptions, some of which I now update. I detail the timelines, room availability and technology, working across a number of linked worksheets. When everything is complete, I run a sensitivity analysis to see how much negotiating space I have with the discount. I love this part of my job, playing with the numbers, coming up with a proposal that can't be knocked back by either Jarrod or Derek, the grudging admiration that comes over their faces as they see the extent of my work and the depth of my knowledge.

I continue until a feeling of light-headedness reminds me that it's lunchtime. Somewhat reluctantly, I save the file and close it down. Grabbing my bag, I pass by the ladies room on my way out. My hand has a slight tremor as I apply some lip gloss. I smooth down my hair, prick my skin in its usual spot and leave the light-bulb brightness of the toilets for the sunshine outside.

'Chicken on brown with Diet Coke?' The girl at the deli knows my order but not my name.

'Yes, thanks.'

While I wait for the food, I'm still thinking about the discount and where I should initially pitch it. I'll finish the proposal this afternoon, mull on it overnight and then get Jarrod's seal of approval before sending it to Derek tomorrow. Derek will respond in a few days' time with some nitpicks. I'll take him out for dinner and drinks and he'll hold out until the end of the night before stating what he really wants: a larger discount. With a great show of reluctance, I'll meet him halfway, we'll shake on it, and then I'll finally get the order. Five million dollars! My sales target will be blown through the roof. But it isn't just about the target, or even the commission cheque that will follow. There's more to it than that. Much, much more.

It's taken me a relatively long time and a lot of hard work to become established in my career. My ascension up the corporate ladder has not occurred in leaps and bounds; it's been a slow and sometimes difficult progression. I'm good in interviews – friendly and outgoing and charismatic, the right personality for a career in sales – but employers want letters after the names of their employees, particularly for roles that have a measure of responsibility or autonomy, and so my abandoned degree has come back to haunt me over and over again. Whenever I'm ready to change jobs, I resolve to look into how I can complete at the University of Melbourne what I started at Queen's University, Belfast. In moments of honesty and clarity, however, I doubt I have it in me to study again. Do I have the focus, the concentration required? Could I tolerate the solitude, the silence, the gush of memories? The career crisis always passes and I eventually make whatever move I sought to make and at the same time return the idea of finishing my degree to the too-hard basket.

Still, I've come into my own with this job at Learning Space. My four-year tenure makes up for my lack of qualifications, gives me a certain credibility, influence and status in the company. If Jarrod were ever to leave, I feel I could legitimately put my hand up for his job and be taken seriously as a worthy candidate. And I will be in a stronger position again when Telelink signs on the dotted line.

I pay for my sandwich and Diet Coke and walk purposefully back towards the office. The girl who ran away from Belfast is about to close a multimillion-dollar deal. Just the thought is enough to make me feel exhilarated, deeply fulfilled and, in many ways, redeemed.

Chapter 10

My week does not go to plan. It begins well: Jarrod pores over the completed spreadsheet, determinedly searching every figure, formula and underlying assumption for errors that aren't there to be found. The proposal is faultless. I'm my father's daughter in that respect, a perfectionist. Finally, he grudgingly signs his name, I courier the proposal to Derek, and this is where things go off track. Derek does not get back to me. The days pass and it becomes obvious that he intends to leave me hanging over the weekend. Not because he needs to think about anything further, I'm sure, but because he never misses an opportunity to demonstrate the extent of his power. By Friday evening, I'm anxious, frustrated and in an extremely bad mood.

I jump from the tram and cross the road and the manicured gardens to the beach. Yearning for the smell of the sea, I inhale and my nostrils are obligingly filled with salty air and my head immediately feels lighter. The beach is busy with high school kids, still in their uniforms, and office workers stopping for a swim on their way home. There's no better way to start the weekend, to restore equilibrium: the sea air, the bay and ocean beyond, the lapping water that leaves a line of froth on the pale, silky sand.

The beachfront is more urbane and sophisticated than the beaches outside Belfast, and the water of Port Phillip Bay more refined and polite than the Irish Sea. The waves lap in and gently recede, the motion predictable and soothing and suggesting a pattern if one concentrates for long enough. Normally I would be in the pub at this time on a Friday evening, not searching for patterns in how the water rolls in and out. I had just one drink with the gang from work before slipping away early to catch the tram home. If Derek had phoned, or at least sent an email, I would have been in a better mood and stayed on; I'd probably be on my third or fourth drink by now. Undoubtedly he'll phone on Monday to quibble about some minor issue, and I'll have to be nice to him, casual and breezy and not at all like I've been on tenterhooks all weekend . . .

After a while, when I feel that some of my frustration has dissolved into the scene around me, I turn to walk along the promenade towards home. My apartment is on Dalgety Street, a fifteen-minute walk. Thinking about dinner makes me frown again. I don't enjoy cooking; my appetite is fickle at the best of times, and my imagination is drained of ideas on how to create meals that are both healthy and in some way exciting. Whenever possible I eat out, though I know this is a bad habit, expensive and potentially fattening because you never know for sure what restaurants put into their food.

I unlock the door of my apartment to be greeted with eerie silence. Jeanie, my flatmate and friend, is away on business. Jeanie is loud and noisy and very present when she's at home. She's due back sometime next week but with her job the exact day could move either forwards or backwards. Jeanie is a troubleshooter, a problem fixer; sometimes the problems are resolved quicker than expected, other times they take much longer. For the first few days after her frequent departures, I savour the silence. But I always reach a point, like now, when I crave her company and commotion.

Late afternoon sun streams through the balcony doors at the end of the rectangular living area and illuminates the room with hazy light. Two beige sofas with oversized cushions face each other across a low coffee table of dark wood. One of the walls has a plasma TV – Jeanie's – and the other holds a stretched canvas with abstract splashes of red and orange and yellow – mine. A brimming bookshelf and two lamp tables complete the furnishings. The room is comfortable and informal and nothing like my childhood home, where my father's unyielding personality was manifest in the high-backed dining chairs, stiff display cabinets and other meticulous furnishings.

I set down my bag on the wooden floor and kick off my heels then pad to the kitchen, the soles of my feet gathering particles of dirt on the way. The place needs a clean: I will do it tomorrow. I open the fridge and assess its contents. I'm down to bare provisions; tomorrow is shopping day as well as cleaning day. There's a lean rump steak and the makings of a salad; that will do – relatively fast to throw together and with the added benefit of being low in calories.

I'm tearing the lettuce into strips when the phone rings. Wiping one hand with a tea towel, I pick up the handset.

It's Nicola, her voice loud against a cacophony of music and voices. 'Hey, Caitlin, you're missing a great night out!'

'I am?'

'Why did you sneak off so early?'

'I wasn't in the mood.'

Listening to the buoyancy in Nic's voice and the drum of the background noise, I instantly regret my hasty departure. The kitchen feels deathly quiet by comparison.

'Meet me tomorrow night instead,' Nic says. 'We'll go out in St Kilda.'

'Yeah, let's do that. I'll talk to you then.'

I put down the phone and continue to tear the lettuce, albeit more forcefully than before. The steak sizzles away obliviously in the pan. I glance at it and tell myself that I *will* eat it, even though I've lost the little appetite I had. Dinner: steak and salad. But then what? The night stretches out ahead, long and lonely.

The phone rings again early in the morning. Sunshine penetrates the thin curtains and birds twitter outside, adding their chorus to the trill of the phone. I stretch out a heavy arm to pick it up. I know it's my mother. This is her usual time for calling.

'Hi, Mum,' I say over a yawn.

'I've woken you! I'm sorry – I thought you'd be up.'

When I hear her voice, Mum's face appears in my mind, her hair a bright halo around her attractive though somewhat gaunt face.

'It's okay, Mum. I should be up anyway.'

'Are you going somewhere?' Paula is thirsty for details: where I'm going, how I'm getting there, who I'm seeing. She struggles to visualise my life and the colour and nuances of Melbourne. Despite my descriptions and the photos I send, she still doesn't seem to be able to picture what it's like over here.

In the first few months after arriving in Australia, I called Mum from payphones. Those were painful conversations over bad lines, wails of desolation from her, hushed soothing responses from me as I turned my back to the curious suntanned faces waiting in the queue.

'How are you doing this week, Mum?' I'd ask.

She wouldn't reply. Well, at least not with words. Her sobs broke my heart as I stood in the phone booth, traffic revving on the street behind me, perspiration tingling my skin. My mother needed me and I was thousands of miles away, under a hot blue sky which, in her current state, she couldn't begin to imagine.

'It will get better,' I'd promise.

'When?' she'd gasp between sobs. 'When will it get better?'

I couldn't answer because I didn't know. How long did it take to get over a twenty-five-year marriage? What was the ratio of years married to years to recover? Surely it couldn't be one to one; please God, let Mum recover much sooner than that. Paula, so trusting and faithful and true. How could this have happened? What had she done to deserve this on top of everything else?

I blamed myself for not seeing that it was coming. I should have guessed that my departure was yet another crack in our family, a crack it couldn't sustain. Maeve had gone too, to university, leaving Mum alone, with more time on her hands than she knew what to do with, more time to think, to remember, to realise that her husband was distant and unreachable and never there, and that her marriage had disintegrated along with everything else and needed drastic action if it were to survive. Bravely, she'd given her husband an ultimatum, said that he had to choose between her and the support group. He'd promptly chosen the group, the cause, said he couldn't walk away from it, that it was the only thing that kept him going, without understanding at all that *he* was the only thing that kept *her* going.

Paula's hurt ravaged her from the inside out. It spilled down the phone, catching on every word she said. 'How could he do this to me? Discard me like this?'

But although she was bewildered and heartbroken, she was too loyal to speak badly of him for long. 'How are you getting on over there?' she'd ask, trying to gather herself.

'Good, Mum, really good.'

'Have you made any friends?'

'Yes, a few.'

She needed reassurance that I wasn't alone, that there were people around me, people to talk to and socialise with, like a family away from home. But her questions were perfunctory and her concentration poor. I knew that after she hung up she'd think of a detail she hadn't thought to ask about and would stay awake at night worrying.

'Look, Mum, I have to go. There's a huge queue for the phone.'

'Okay. Goodbye, Caitlin. Call again soon, if you can.'

She would sound so lonely and lost that tears would sting my eyes. I'd hang up the phone and step aside for the next person in the queue. Walking down the street, blinking to clear my eyes, sadness and fury churned inside me, the latter directed at my father and usually the predominant emotion. I wanted to take him by the shoulders, to shake him. I wanted to stomp my feet, to yell at him, to force him to listen and take responsibility for the further damage he had caused. There he was, pursuing justice to the detriment of everything else – his wife, his marriage, his family. It was a matter of ethics to him, of right and wrong, of someone being brought to account for the terrible crime that had been committed that day in Clonmegan. But what about the ethics of standing by your wife and family when they needed you most? Did my father, in his crusade for justice, ever stop to think of that?

When I moved from the hostel to my first apartment, I called my mother from the balcony. Five floors up, it was small and windy, the view overtaken by another, too-close apartment block. Out there it didn't matter if I cried after hanging up. It didn't matter if I swore in anger. I could vent as much as I needed to; the wind obliterated it all.

Mum and I fell into a pattern of calling each other on Saturdays, at the end of her week and the start of my weekend. Slowly, month by month, year by year, she has come to terms with the disintegration of her family and she's in a good place now, healed, though still a little sad. She has a man in her life – Tony, a retired teacher – and they go to the cinema and for walks together. She says he's a good companion and she tries to pass off their relationship as platonic, but she doesn't fool me. Besides, Maeve has informed me that Tony stays over in the house a few nights a week.

In the last few years our conversations have become much

easier, more like normal mother–daughter chats you'll hear any-where in the world: exchanging trivial anecdotes about work, the week gone past and other members of the family; the weather, national news, the dismal state of the economy; and to round things off, a nice dollop of motherly fussing.

'When I eventually drag myself out of bed, I'm going to the markets,' I say in answer to Mum's question about what I'm planning to do for the day. 'I need to get some fruit and veg. The cupboards are bare.'

Because she can't see my life, she often takes my words too literally. 'Ach, Caitlin, you shouldn't have empty cupboards, it's not a healthy way to live.'

'Mum, I've eaten, the food is gone, and now I need to go shopping,' I reply dryly. 'It's just the normal weekly cycle. No different from yours!'

A brief silence follows. I pull myself up in the bed and my head starts to fill with thoughts about the day ahead.

'Anything else planned for the weekend, love?' she asks.

'Going out with Nicola tonight. Just for some drinks.'

'In the city?'

'No, we'll go local I think.' Another silence threatens and I hurry to fill it. 'How about you, Mum? Are you doing anything?'

She sounds relieved to be able to answer in the affirmative. 'Maeve is coming home tomorrow. It's mid-term – she's going to stay the week . . .'

Maeve is twenty-seven and still a student. After her bache-lor degree at Queen's, she went on to do a master's and then a PhD. In a few months she'll have a doctorate in modern history: Dr Maeve O'Reilly. I fully expect that she will then promptly find another subject in which to academically excel. God forbid that she should use all that knowledge in any practical way, a job for instance.

'I suppose she's bringing her washing home with her.'

'If she does, then I'll reintroduce her to the washing machine and leave her to it,' Mum retorts.

I stretch and my stomach remembers it's there and rumbles. 'I wish I had one of your roast dinners to look forward to today,' I say without thinking.

'I wish you did too! I worry about you so, so much.'

The sadness that simmers beneath the surface has found a way in. It isn't always so. Sometimes we can have an entire conversation without an opening. But all it needs is a crack, the slightest crack, and we both know it.

She has a catch in her voice. 'You know why I worry, don't you?'

'Yes, Mum, I do.'

'Keep safe, darling. Keep safe until next week.'

'I will. Bye, Mum.'

Chapter 11

I start Monday with a black coffee and the *Financial Review*. There's no sales meeting this week and it's nice not to have to account for myself to Jarrod and the rest of the team, or to have to pinch myself to stay awake as Gary, Chris and Nathan drone on. I skim the headlines of the newspaper, looking for anything that might lead to a sales opportunity. Next door Zoe is doing some filing, humming a strange tune as she slides drawers open and shut. I find myself smiling. Sitting next to Zoe is never dull. She wears clothes in bright, clashing colours that cheerfully defy the all-black protocol. Her sense of humour and views on life and work are pretty off-beat; in fact, she seems to exist, or rather float, in an entirely different orbit to the rest of us. She's good entertainment value, fun to be around, but she works hard too, always on the phone trying to drum up business. In fact, I'm so used to seeing her with her headphones on that she looks a little odd, almost undressed without them as she goes about her filing.

When the clock on my screen turns over to 10 am, I put the paper aside and begin to make my phone calls, judging that those on the receiving end will have drunk their own coffees by now and got over the worst of their Mondayitis. Some of the calls I have to make are cold, others are to people I've spoken to before and made enough progress to follow up with a second call. The first name on my list today is Harry Dixon, the IT director for Net Banc. I haven't spoken to Harry before and I've no idea of his age, personality or what training requirements he might have. All I'm going on is a lead I got last week.

'Harry Dixon speaking,' states the angry-sounding voice at the other end of the phone.

'Oh, hello, Harry. My name is Caitlin O'Reilly from Learning Space –'

'Where?' he barks.

'Learning Space, we –'

'Never heard of them.'

'We provide training –'

'We do our own training!'

'I was speaking to a mutual contact last week and he mentioned that you have a systems upgrade coming up. Maybe we can help with –'

'As I've said, we do our own training,' Harry says curtly and hangs up.

I smile ironically to myself. Now, *that's* a cold call. The client questionnaire form on my desk looks mockingly back at me. Well, I suppose I did glean some information. In clear block capitals I write *CRANKY BASTARD* next to Harry's name and smile again, this time more genuinely. In this job sometimes being childish is the only way to lift your spirits.

I gather myself by looking out the window for a few minutes. Even though this side of my job is often disheartening, it's a necessary part of the sales process and means that there's nothing more rewarding than finally hitting the right person at the right time. It happened like that with Derek. Our first contact was a stilted phone call. It took two months to secure a small-value order and another two years to grow the account to its present size. Thinking of Derek tempts me to call him but I stop myself. It's important to allow him to make the next move. Thankfully, not all my clients are game-players like him.

I take a deep breath, pick up the phone and get on with the rest of my calls. I'm still on the phone, getting nowhere, when Nicola comes around. She sits on the edge of my desk while she waits for me to finish.

'Selling millions?' she enquires with raised, perfectly plucked eyebrows.

'I wish.'

'I'm having a rather extraordinary quiet spell. Want to grab some lunch?'

'Yeah, let's.' I stand up, grateful to leave my desk behind after a fruitless morning. 'Want to come for lunch, Zoe?' Zoe glances up with faraway eyes, smiles and shakes her head. She's obviously in the middle of something important.

It's sunny outside, though maybe not for long because clouds are gathering around the small pocket of blue that's left in the sky. Nicola slides her large designer sunglasses down over her eyes. With her black trousers and shirt and hair and dazzling jewellery, she looks more like a movie star than a floor manager who's often too busy to break for lunch and has to make do with eating her clients' leftovers.

'Where to?' she asks.

I suggest a popular café on Degraves Street. We sit outside. Nicola orders a schnitzel and I get a salad.

'I don't know how you survive on that rabbit food,' she comments disparagingly.

I shrug. 'It's healthy.'

'It's not as if you need to lose weight. If you were any thinner you'd disappear!'

Nicola doesn't know that there was a time in my early teens when I *was* thin enough to virtually disappear, and I hated myself enough to want to. But that was a long time ago and my eating, my health and my self-esteem are more or less under control now. I'm slim, not thin – it's an important distinction but to explain this to Nicola would only draw more attention to my weight.

'Hey, did the guy from Saturday night call you?' Nicola asks.

We met Luke and his friends in a bar on Saturday night. He was a surfer, lithe and a few years younger than me, and that's about all I can remember – I can barely picture his face.

'No.'

'Still, it's only Monday now.'

'I don't think he'll call,' I say dismissively.

I've had many relationships over the last ten years, all of them short-lived. I've discovered the hard way that what I had with Josh was a once-in-a-lifetime thing. At the beginning I would approach each fledgling relationship hopefully, optimistically, only to feel deflated when it became obvious there was no chemistry, or some physical, intellectual or personality flaw that simply couldn't be overcome. These days I've developed a more cynical view. Luke is just another name, another face if I can manage to remember it. If he calls, he calls. If he doesn't call, then it's no big deal. I don't put a lot of thought into who I date; the men are often shallow, conceited, disloyal, and I don't really care. My standards lowered when finally, after dozens of disastrous dates and disappointments, I realised the truth: that love is a fluke. What if Josh hadn't come to my party that night? What if he hadn't cornered Liam into an introduction? Who would have guessed at the outset that we would click so perfectly? Yes, for love to happen once is a fluke; for it to happen twice must be virtually impossible. Holding out for it, hoping against hope, is stupid.

Nicola is just as cynical. She goes through men at a rate of knots, discarding them well before they have the opportunity to discard her. I don't know if Nicola has ever had a significant relationship, if she has ever imagined herself to be in love. Maybe she's living it up here in order to get over someone special back in London. Nicola doesn't say much about her old life and neither do I. Our friendship is based strictly in the present, which seems to suit her every bit as much as it does me.

The waitress brings our food. Nicola's schnitzel looks delicious and I wish it was on my plate instead of the bland salad I have to pretend to be enthusiastic about. My eyes sweep across the café, the tables filled with a cross-section of Melbourne's population, smiling, laughing, gathered together for the purpose of eating good food. It's hard to be on the sidelines, on the outer, unable to fully enjoy what brings such happiness to so many people.

My phone begins to ring in my bag. I fish it out and check the number. 'It's Derek. Sorry, Nic, I have to take this one.' I shoot her a quick, apologetic smile. 'Hello, Derek. How are you?'

He launches straight in. 'I've been through the proposal. It isn't quite there in some respects . . .'

'Tell me where I need to do more work.'

'You haven't demonstrated the capacity of your interstate offices – we have significant staff numbers in Perth and Brisbane and we need to be certain your branches in those cities can adequately cater for our staff.'

'Is there anything else I need to address?' I ask calmly.

He pauses for effect. 'Well, of course, the pricing isn't satisfactory . . .'

'Let's sort out the capacity plan first – then we can meet later in the week to discuss price. In fact, maybe we should lock in a time now.' I'm determined not to let this week finish as inconclusively as the last one.

'Friday. Dinner suits better than lunch.'

'Great. I'll make a reservation.'

I put my phone back in my bag, and take a bite of the uninspiring salad before joking to Nicola, 'Well, at least one man has called me today to make a date!'

Back in the office, I get down to work. If Derek wants a capacity plan, then that's what he'll get: the mother of all capacity plans. Page upon page on each interstate branch, broken down by rooms and weeks and people. For good measure, I add phone and data lines, printers, projectors, even flipcharts. I call staff members in the other branches to check my facts and tweak the spreadsheet to reflect their advice. Then I print out my masterpiece, proofread every word and adjust the font and the colour scheme. I email it to Derek, including details of our dinner reservation in the text of the message.

The rest of the week slips by in a whirl of meetings, client lunches and the usual trivial dramas on the training floor. Finally Derek sends a message to indicate he's satisfied with the capacity plan and now it's all down to price, the simplest and yet the most contentious component of the deal. It's so close now that I can imagine the flourish of his signature on the contract and the thrill as I watch him sign.

At five thirty on Friday I begin to pack up for the weekend.

Zoe takes off her headphones to say goodbye. 'Good luck with Derek tonight.' She winks at me, revealing a peculiar blend of purple and green shadow on her eyelid.

'Thanks.'

'And have a nice, relaxing, *rejuvenating* weekend!'

'You too, Zoe.'

It's another balmy evening and I carry my jacket over my arm for the short walk to the restaurant. Located at the end of Flinders Lane, it's one of Melbourne's most exclusive; Derek wouldn't expect any less. A few of the tables are occupied with early diners, their every need being catered to by a swarm of waiting staff, many of whom are superfluous until the peak-time kicks in.

Derek is sitting on one of the plush couches in the bar area, his bottle of beer missing a few mouthfuls.

'You're early,' I say brightly as I sit down across from him.

'So are you,' he replies with a slight smile.

A waiter appears by my side.

'I'll have a vodka and Diet Coke.' My order taken, I turn my attention back to Derek. 'How was your day?'

'Okay.' He's always like this at the start: stiff and difficult to engage.

'Anything planned for the weekend?'

'Might take the bike for a run . . .' Derek's bike is only a few weeks old and is his favourite toy.

'What make is it again?' I ask with feigned interest.

'BMW K1200.' At last there's a hint of animation in his voice. 'Zero to one hundred in 2.9 seconds – an instant adrenalin hit.'

'I'll take your word for it.' I smile.

'Ever been for a ride?'

'No.'

'You're missing out.'

'If you say so, but I'm happier with the push-pedal variety.'

Last Christmas Jeanie and I bought bikes; the idea came from Jeanie who, a week or two before Christmas, had suddenly realised that she'd never owned a brand-new bike, one that was not handed down, scratched or otherwise defaced by her older sisters, one that had a working set of brakes, not to mention gears. I was instantly taken with the idea and in the new year we'd gone bike shopping. On weekends and some evenings after work during January, Jeanie and I could be found gliding along the foreshore's cycle paths, doing the odd wheelie and sprint-finish. Though the honeymoon period has worn off by now, I still ride my bike most weekends, which happens to be a lot more often than Jeanie rides hers. We keep the bikes in the apartment's carport, in lieu of the car neither of us possesses.

The waiter arrives with my drink and I sip it, trying to think of something to say. It's too soon to talk about what we're here to discuss.

'Where do you usually take the bike?'

'Up into the hills, or out to Torquay or Bells if the weather conforms.'

Derek warms to the topic and the conversation lasts until we're transferred to the dining area, where the wine, food and the comings and goings of the waiter make any subsequent gaps in conversation virtually unnoticeable.

We finish our mains as the restaurant becomes frantically busy. The waiter hovers, whisking our plates away as soon as they are emptied. 'Dessert? Tea or coffee?' His tone suggests that he would rather we leave and free up the table.

Derek clearly doesn't appreciate being hurried. 'Dessert, Caitlin?'

'No, thanks. I'll have tea, though – Irish Breakfast, please.'

Derek orders another beer and the waiter leaves, not bothering to mask his displeasure.

'So, Derek,' I say, and lean forward a little. 'We'd better talk business before we find ourselves out on the street.'

'Yes.' His nod is almost imperceptible.

'You're happy with the capacity plan and everything else now?'

'Yes.'

Our eyes meet and suddenly we've reached it: the point at which we connect. At this mellow stage of the evening, he's more amenable, even slightly attractive. His ego is bearable, his looks darker, sexier. Our differences are hazed over by alcohol and the background atmosphere.

'So, we both know it's down to price,' I say in a low voice.

'Yes, I suppose it is.'

'I've already given you a fifteen per cent discount . . .'

'I want twenty-five.'

'You know I can't go that far.'

'It's what I want, what I *expect* for an order this size.'

'Maybe I can meet you in the middle.' We stare at each other, our eyes flirting, taunting. The air crackles between us.

The waiter returns with our drinks, his outstretched arm sliding between us, severing the connection. By the time he finishes arranging my cup, strainer, teapot and milk jug, the moment is lost. My offer to meet Derek halfway is out there, unanswered, and I wish fervently that I could take it back and reissue it later, at a time when we can't be interrupted.

I sip my tea and Derek his beer. I can feel him slipping away from me. He's not even looking at me now. What can I do to reel him back?

'Take me for a ride,' I blurt out.

'What?'

'Take me for a ride on the bike.'

'Right now?'

'Take me home. Friday night is shocking for taxis.'

He knows what I'm up to, that I'll ultimately do anything to get this deal over the line. I think he knows too that I'm quite scared at the thought of getting on his bike, that I'm making this suggestion purely to reforge a connection, and he's impressed by the extent of my determination.

'Okay.' He grins. 'You're on.'

I slide the helmet over my head and straddle the seat. 'Why doesn't it have a face shield?'

'Because those things can crack your neck,' he says, glancing over his shoulder. 'Ready?'

I put my feet on the pegs. 'What do I hold onto?'

'Me.'

I rest my arms on the cool bulky leather of his jacket.

'Lean with the bike,' he instructs. 'Look over my shoulder. Go with the corners.'

He puts on his own helmet and cranks up the engine. I tighten my grip.

'Okay back there?'

'Slightly petrified,' I'm only half joking, 'but okay other than that.'

'Don't you trust me?'

'No.'

He laughs and takes off with an arrogant burst of speed. I squeeze my eyes shut. My ears fill with the guttural noise of the engine and my nose with the smell of leather and rubber and exhaust fumes. Wind rushes against my neck leaving the rest of my head, cocooned under the helmet, longing for its cool touch. The bike's acceleration lasts only a few seconds. I warily open my eyes and immediately see the reason why he's slowed down: there's a corner coming up. I lean with him and the bike. For a few seconds the ground is dangerously close, and then we straighten.

At some point, my fear dissolves and exhilaration takes its place. Derek, the bike and I are the only things in focus. We're real and surging next to the blurry cars and streetlights. I feel part of the bike, part of him, the flowing road, the enveloping night. We're like scissors, cutting our way out of the city: Spring Street, Wellington Parade, Jolimont Road, then Fitzroy Street, the last stretch, the smell of sea in the air. Derek increases our speed again and I hold on tighter, my fingers biting into the leather of his jacket. I will him to go even faster and, for a few moments, he does. It feels extraordinary, like we're skimming the surface of the road, about to take flight into the night.

But all too soon the race from the city to the bay is over, and we're dropping speed, becoming ordinary again. The road feels solid once more, the streetlights separate and distinct rather than bleeding lines of light. Derek turns into the Esplanade and I automatically lean to take the corner. It happens in slow motion, every second an eternity in itself. The realisation that something is wrong, that the bike isn't coming back up as it should. The screech of tyres, skidding at a precarious angle to the road, Derek swearing and pressing harder on the brakes. The bike jerking and wobbling as he tries to reassert balance, and a moment when it seems as though he might succeed. But then a thud as we hit something – a kerb. I'm thrown from my seat. For a few moments I'm airborne, and then I land on the concrete, dumped unceremoniously, face down.

'Caitlin! Caitlin!' Derek's hand is urgently shaking my shoulder. I'm too shocked to speak.

'Caitlin? *Fuck!* Answer me!'

I roll over slowly and lift myself up on my elbows. He looms over me, his helmet still on. His trousers are shredded at the knees. I can see blood.

'You're bleeding,' I say faintly.

He shrugs and holds out an impatient hand. 'Come on. Get up. We need to get out of here.'

I allow him to pull me up. But it's too soon; I can't keep my balance.

He steadies me, looks me coldly in the eye. 'I need you to hold it together. We need to get out of here. Quickly.'

I look back at him, dazed. What's the rush? What exactly does he mean about holding it together? I think I'm remarkably calm, considering.

'Are you okay over there?'

We both turn towards the voice. It's a girl, the spokesperson of a bigger group, four or five in total.

'Yeah, we're fine,' Derek answers tersely.

'Need help?'

'Could do with a hand lifting the bike.'

He limps towards the bike, two male helpers following him. I'm left with the girls, three of them. They're young, late teens or early twenties, their faces soft and plump.

'We saw it happen from a distance,' one of them says.

I nod and everything around me tilts, just like I'm taking another corner on the bike.

'You need to sit down.'

'You're hurt.'

What they're saying makes sense. I should sit. I'm hurt. I have pain somewhere, but I'm numb too, a rather weird combination. I make a conscious attempt to focus. The pain is coming from my left arm. I twist it and see an angry red gash at the back, matted with the torn fabric of my jacket.

The girls recoil at the sight. 'Oooh.'

Somewhere else is hurting too. I pull back the waistband of my pants and see a mess of blood and gravel on my hip. For a few seconds I'm dizzy again. I realise that the helmet is still weighing heavily on my head. With the help of the girls, I take it off. I shake my hair free and for a second feel better.

Derek has the bike up. He's wheeling it back towards me. Surely he's not expecting me to get back on?

'It's driveable. I'll take it home. You can get a taxi.'

'There's an ambulance coming,' one of the girls tells him. 'We called triple zero.'

'You *what?*' Derek's livid. 'Why the hell did you do that?'

'It looked as though you were both hurt.'

He slams his hand against his forehead. 'Fuck! Fuck!'

I watch him, confused, unable to get my befuddled mind to work. 'What's wrong, Derek?'

He turns on me. 'What's *wrong?* What's wrong is that I might be over the limit, and I might be charged . . .'

'Oh.'

'And if that's not bad enough, my girlfriend will freak out when she inevitably discovers there was another girl on the back of the bike at the time of the accident! That's what's wrong, *Caitlin.*'

The girls swing their eyes to me.

'Sorry,' I mumble, anything else I might have added being cut off by the distant song of sirens.

Derek shakes his head, swears again, and puts his hand on my lower back to propel me to the side. 'Don't tell the ambulance crew we were drinking,' he hisses in my ear.

'I'm not going to lie,' I hiss back.

'This could be disastrous for me.'

'Yeah, just think of yourself, Derek.'

We stare at each other, any attraction from earlier now vanished. I turn away from him and go to sit on the kerb.

One of the girls parks herself next to me. 'Did you know he had a girlfriend?'

'Yes,' I reply, eyes downcast. 'I knew.' I knew that Derek was attached, just as I knew he'd been drinking. What was I thinking?

You weren't thinking, Caitlin. As usual.

It's my father's voice, stern and judgmental, his expression disapproving as he assesses the events of the night, identifying one wrong turn after another. I feel his presence so strongly that he could be standing right here beside me. He's right, absolutely and unequivocally right, even though he's just in my head and not here in person. It hurts, him being right. It hurts more than the gashes on my arm and hip.

Chapter 12

The ambulance arrives in tandem with a police car, their sirens becoming unbearably loud before they mute to rotate in silence. The paramedics, a man and woman, usher Derek and me into the back of the ambulance to be examined.

'What are your names?' the woman asks.

I answer for both Derek and myself.

'You came off a motorbike?'

'Yes. I don't know what happened.'

'How fast were you going?'

'Not very – we were taking a corner.'

'How far were you thrown?'

'I don't know. A few metres.'

'Five? Ten?'

'Three or four, maybe.'

'You weren't wearing any protective clothing?'

I look across at Derek, who doesn't seem inclined to answer any of the paramedic's questions. He stares angrily back at me.

'No,' I say. 'The bike ride wasn't planned.'

The woman grimaces. 'Those kinds of rides are usually the ones that end up like this.'

She's young and attractive. The man, who's treating Derek, is equally good-looking. They look like part of a TV cast rather than real-life paramedics.

Gently, she peels back the fabric from my upper arm.

'Ouch.'

'Sorry. Didn't mean to hurt you. These abrasions are quite deep. They need to be looked at by a doctor.'

'I have to go to hospital?'

'Accident and Emergency. I'll give you some pain relief now. It's going to hurt when the shock wears off.'

I nod. It's already hurting, stabs of pain that have ripple effects in other parts of my body.

'Do you have any allergies?'

'No.'

'Are you taking any other medication?'

I hesitate and glance at Derek again. 'No.'

Through the open doors of the ambulance, I'm aware of the police officers talking to the witnesses and examining the bike. One of the officers comes to the door. He stares at me, his eyes blue and piercing beneath the peak of his hat. 'Everything okay in here?'

The male paramedic replies, 'Yes. We don't think we need collars – no spine or neck injuries as far as we can tell. But both have deep abrasions that may need grafting.'

Grafting? Does he mean Derek or me? Suddenly I feel quite queasy and I clamp my hand over my mouth.

'Are you okay?' It's the officer. He's looking at me as though he can see straight through me.

I nod, breathing deeply until the nausea subsides.

The officer gives me another long stare before flicking his eyes to Derek. 'You were the rider of the bike?'

'Yes,' Derek says abruptly.

'Were you drinking tonight?'

'I had one or two beers.'

'Was it one or two?'

'Two.'

'Anything else?'

'Some wine with dinner.'

'How many glasses?'

'Two.'

The officer's jaw clenches in irritation. 'You know, the risks of motorbike riding are high enough without adding alcohol to the mix.'

Derek doesn't answer.

'You're bloody lucky that your injuries aren't worse.'

Derek's eye twitches, his only reaction.

'The hospital will take a blood sample. I'll speak with both of you later.'

The officer leaves, the ambulance doors shut, and I'm left alone with Derek. His face is grey, his mouth twisted in a grimace, pain evidently wrestling with anger. He refuses to meet my eyes and it's clear he holds me fully responsible for the situation we're in.

Accident and Emergency is in the throes of its Friday night chaos, complete with screaming fevered toddlers, volatile drunks, teenagers with homemade slings and a stressed triage nurse. We wait while everyone is dealt with in order of priority. I glance intermittently at Derek. It feels as though the silence between us is becoming more unbreachable by the minute. I chew on my lip, praying that Derek will realise that it's extremely childish and unfair of him to blame it all on me. Maybe he'll be more reasonable when he's had time to calm down. Maybe he'll feel better, more objective, by Monday.

We wait for close to an hour and then our names are called, Derek's first, mine a few minutes later. We're allocated cubicles on opposite sides of the large treatment room, putting an end to any further opportunity to make amends.

Another wait follows, twenty minutes, before the curtains are swiped back.

'Well, who do I have here?' asks an accented voice.

'This is Caitlin,' a nurse replies from behind me. 'She came off a motorbike tonight.'

'Ah! She was with the other fellow, was she?'

'Yes.'

The doctor looks at me. He's Indian with caramel skin and dark, assessing eyes. 'Well, Caitlin, I would like to know everything that happened,' he says in a bouncy voice. 'How fast you were travelling, how far you were thrown, if you were able to get up straightaway . . .'

I relay the same details I told the paramedic in the ambulance. While I speak, he examines my cuts, his eyes close to the torn skin.

'You are lucky, Caitlin. It is only the superficial layer that is gone. There is no tissue or muscle damage, unlike your friend.'

'You mean Derek?'

'Yes.' His dark eyes flick up to my face. 'He will need some grafts on his knee. The nurse will clean and dress your cuts now and you'll need to visit your GP to have the wounds checked and the dressing changed in a couple of days. I'll give you a script for antibiotics to prevent infection...' He straightens and throws me another assessing look. 'And maybe you will think twice before getting on a motorbike again without appropriate protective clothing!'

I nod, tears clogging my throat.

The nurse begins to clean the wounds, flushing them with water and then dabbing gently, staining the white gauze with blood and dirt and specks of gravel. 'The police want to talk to you,' she says sympathetically. 'I told the officer to wait until I'm finished.' She's a few years younger than me and looks as though she knows what it's like to have a fun night end in disaster. 'What a spunk, though!'

'Who?' I flinch as she uses a brush to remove some stubborn flecks of gravel.

'The officer.' She grins. 'Makes it almost worth it.'

I don't agreee and can't summon even the slightest smile in return.

She bandages my arm and hip with layers of crêpe and stands back to admire her handiwork. 'Okay, you're done! I'll send him in.' She smiles, a soft caring smile, the sort a mother would give. 'Good luck.'

The police officer is the same one who talked to us earlier. Up close, he's big, *very* big, tall and substantial, and I can feel myself shrinking in his presence, becoming even more insignificant than I am. He has his hat off, revealing his features in full: mid-brown hair cut uncompromisingly short, blue eyes set into the deep tan of his face, a symmetrically square jaw which, I already know, clenches when he's annoyed.

'The nurse says you're good to go home.'

'Yes.'

'I'm Sergeant Blake.' He slips a hand into his shirt pocket to extract a card. 'My contact details are here. Now, I need a statement on what happened tonight.'

I take the card from his outstretched hand and hold it without looking at it. His pen is already poised, waiting to make a formal record of everything I've done wrong. I begin to speak, my voice subdued. Once again, I repeat the details of what happened. Some of it he takes down, some not.

'Did you know he'd been drinking?'

I nod.

'Do you know how dangerous motorcycles are? How many fatalities?'

Again, I nod.

He stares down at me, scorn swimming in his blue eyes. 'Pretty stupid thing to do, wasn't it? Getting on the back when you knew the driver had been drinking?'

He's being deliberately provocative, making sure that I've learned my lesson. There's nothing I can say in my defence. I've been incredibly stupid, and as a result I've put the proposal and all my hard work in jeopardy. *Please God, don't let five million dollars have just slid through my fingers!*

'Yes,' I answer him in a small voice. 'It was stupid of me, and clearly the wrong thing to do.'

*

It's after midnight when I get home. I flick on the lights and immediately see Jeanie's plastic futuristic-looking suitcase standing in the hallway. My flatmate is home, for at least a few days until she's required to dash off to the next trouble spot. I'm glad to see the suitcase. I don't want to talk to her right now – I feel too vulnerable and tired – but it's good to know she'll be here in the morning, nursing a coffee and a grin and ready to listen.

I head for the kitchen and gulp a glass of water at the sink. Still thirsty, I down another glass before swaying to the bathroom to brush my teeth and wash my face. My bedroom is as neat and tidy as always, testament in itself to my upbringing. Methodically, I move cushions from the bed to the armchair where they'll spend the night. Then I coax my limbs into a short, sleeveless nightdress. Sitting on the side of the bed, I'm at last able to give my body what it needs. I wince at the sting of the needle: I've hit a bad spot. Still, I welcome the added pain. I'm in control of it. And it's utterly deserved.

Turning off the bedside lamp, I slip gratefully under the covers and fall asleep within minutes.

The next morning I wake to the sound of a poorly tuned radio and Jeanie's singing. I smile sleepily; there's never any mistaking that Jeanie's home – if the radio or telly aren't blaring, then she's usually yakking on the phone or banging and clattering in the kitchen. The noise and bustle that follows her around only seem to accentuate her calm and collected personality.

Jeanie is the Australian equivalent of my childhood friend Mandy. She too comes from a big, noisy family where lots of small things went unnoticed but the big picture turned out remarkably okay. Jeanie candidly describes a house where the radio and TV were kept on all day to drown out the constant squabbling among the eight children, all girls. Disputes often degenerated into fisticuffs, hair yanking and name calling, escalating within minutes, finished and forgotten about just as quickly. Her childhood has given her the perfect grounding for her career. She's unapologetic but never arrogant, calls things as they are and deals with conflict head on, accepting it as part and parcel of life.

I met Jeanie over five years ago when we were both working in the IT industry and I was allocated the workstation next to hers. Our friendship grew from chats over the dividing partition, shared outrage at our impossible quotas, lunch-hour shopping sprees and lots of after-work drinks. Sitting next to Jeanie was not peaceful: she liked to work with the radio on, humming along to the songs and occasionally answering back to the DJ. She never attempted to moderate her voice when she spoke on the phone. Even her typing was noisy!

We worked together for a year before Jeanie moved on to another job. I moved on, too, a few months later. We stayed friends, though, and continued to meet as often as we could after work or on weekends, some nights staying at each other's apartments and bemoaning our respective flatmates until it finally occurred to us that we should get a place together.

I yawn and stretch, the deep ache in my left arm serving as an unnecessary reminder of last night's events. Pulling back the covers, my limbs feel heavy and stiff as I get out of bed. I slip on a warm dressing gown, the material too thick for the time of year but my body yearning for extra padding and comfort.

Jeanie's in the kitchen, standing over the toaster, dressed in a black singlet and grey three-quarter-length pants. Her flaxen hair falls smoothly to her shoulders, and her pale face widens into a grin.

'Top of the mornin'!' she says in a terrible put-on Irish accent.

'G'day,' I reply in an Australian accent that's just as bad.

We kiss and hug, Jeanie's fingers inadvertently knocking against my sore arm.

'Ouch!'

She pulls back. 'What's wrong?'

'It's a long, ugly story.' I sigh. 'Is the kettle warm?'

'Sit. I'll make you one.' Jeanie flicks on the kettle and while it hisses and whistles, takes a cup from the cupboard above. 'What's happened? Have you injured yourself?'

I suck in my breath before admitting, 'I came off Derek's bike.'

'Jesus!' A teabag suspended in one hand, Jeanie turns around to give me her full attention. 'When did that happen?'

'Last night.'

'And you didn't wake me?'

'I just wanted to sleep when I got home – I couldn't face anyone.' I grin weakly. 'Not even you.'

'Have you seen a doctor?'

'I was taken to hospital in an ambulance.'

Jeanie absorbs this for a moment. 'So going by the fact they sent you home, the injuries aren't serious?'

'No. Just sore.'

'How about Derek?'

'He came off worse than me. Last I heard he needs a skin graft on his knee . . .' I finish the rest of the sentence on a sigh. 'And he's in trouble with the police, not to mention his girlfriend.'

Jeanie's thin blonde eyebrows move upwards, the closest she'll come to being judgmental. 'The *police*?'

'He'd had a few drinks.'

'Oh, Caitlin.'

'I know. I was stupid.' I immediately recall the police officer's disapproving blue eyes.

'But why?'

It's a perfectly valid question. The only pity is that my answer is so inadequate.

'We were haggling over a discount and I couldn't quite close it out. I very mistakenly thought the bike ride would seal it.'

'And, of course, walking away wasn't an option . . .' Jeanie's smile softens her tone of voice. She turns back to the counter and pours boiling water into the cup then puts the cup in front of me. 'Here you are, black and tasteless.'

I laugh. One of my favourite stories about Jeanie's family is to do with tea. Her mother always had a pot of tea on the boil, copious quantities of milk and sugar already added, which all the children drank, never questioning the mix. As a young teenager, Jeanie went to a friend's house and was offered tea. Asked how she 'took' it, she was at a loss but eventually, through trial and error, she established that she liked her tea with gallons of milk and three sugars, the closest taste she could get to the 'all-in-the-pot' brew her mother used to make at home.

'So what's the problem with Derek's girlfriend?' Jeanie asks, chewing her toast, surely on the cold side by now.

'Well, he had another girl on the back of his bike – me.'

'Is that a crime?'

'She'd know that he'd been flirting . . .'

'Were you?'

'We always do.'

'I see.'

Jeanie leaves it at that. She doesn't overanalyse or seek out drama. The bike accident has happened, it's unfortunate, but life goes on. I'm instantly reminded of Mandy, who used to be just as matter-of-fact, and her family every bit as big and exuberant as Jeanie's – until one of them was lost.

Jeanie turns up the volume of the radio. 'I like this song,' she says and begins to sing along, her words not quite matching those of the singer.

Sun streams in the window and my face begins to glow from its warmth and from the effects of the hot tea and my heavy dressing gown. The kitchen is cosy and homely and nothing like the deafeningly silent place it is when Jeanie's not around. I'm glad my friend is back, for however long.

Chapter 13

I call Derek a few times over the weekend but his phone rings through to voicemail. I don't leave a message; what I have to say can't be summed up in one or two sentences. I spend a lot of time in bed, resting, reading, and dreading Monday. I rehearse what I'll say to Jarrod, trying to anticipate how the conversation might go, visualising his angriest expression and searching for the right words to soften it. It doesn't help that the biweekly sales meeting is on first thing and Jarrod, along with everyone else, will expect a full update on Telelink.

On Monday I wake to a bright, blue-skyed morning, a good omen I hope. I get out of bed earlier than usual, expecting that my morning routine will take a little longer. My body is stiff and sore and would like a few more days in bed but the rest of me is ready to get the confrontation with Jarrod over and done with, to suffer the inevitable reprimand and then get on with doing whatever is necessary to save the deal.

I wash at the basin, my limbs clumsy and uncoordinated, but my biggest challenge, I quickly find out, is finding something to wear. I pluck a black A-line skirt from my wardrobe, slip it on and begin to search for a top. I try on a few things, fling them across the bed when it becomes apparent they won't work, and yell out for Jeanie's help.

'Nice look,' she comments dryly when she sees me in my bra and skirt.

'Nothing fits over the bandage. Do you have anything?'

'Let's take a look.'

I follow Jeanie to her room, hopeful even though I'm a few sizes smaller and so clothes swapping has never really worked for us before. Like mine, Jeanie's bedroom is a reflection of her upbringing: chaotic. Clothes are strewn across the bed and chair, and shoes are scattered on the floor, presenting a safety hazard that I must negotiate my way through. The laundry hamper overflows onto the floor and the bed is made in such a half-hearted manner that just looking at it gives me the urge to straighten the pillows and quilt.

Ten minutes later, I'm down to two choices: a silver ABBA-style top that's too long in the sleeve and looks more appropriate for a disco than the office, and a white frilly blouse that only someone with Jeanie's unflappable personality could pull off. I decide that the frilly blouse is the lesser of two evils. Substituting my usual heels for black flats, I move as fast as I can out the door and down the stairs. My legs are stiff and the ten-minute walk to the tram takes closer to twenty. A tram hurtles into view and

I breathe a sigh of relief, smiling as the queue shuffles forward a few anticipatory steps. But when I go to get my ticket the smile freezes on my face: in my haste to get out the door, I picked up the wrong handbag.

When I finally get to the office I'm over an hour late. The meeting has already broken up and the sales team, including Jarrod, are back at their desks and perfectly positioned to witness precisely how late I am. I put my bag on the floor – the correct bag, the one that cost me precious time in retracing my steps to the apartment and then back to the tram stop again. I can't tell Jarrod that I'm late because of my handbag; he'll blow a fuse even before I tell him about Friday night.

I flick the switch on my PC, mentally preparing myself while I wait for it to start up. I'll go in there, I resolve, and take it on the chin. I'll agree with everything Jarrod throws at me, be contrite in the extreme, and then I'll set about doing what I can to redeem the situation.

Zoe pops up on the other side of the partition. 'You didn't miss much at the meeting.'

'Good.'

'Jarrod does not have a happy aura today.'

Zoe is rather fascinated with auras. She's been to aura-reading retreats and workshops and finesses her skills on unsuspecting colleagues. From what I gather, auras vary in colour and structure, and reflect one's true nature. But rather confusingly, they can change with time, sometimes very quickly, and thus indicate mood. Given that I can usually read Jarrod's mood directly from his face, I'm not convinced of the need to analyse his aura.

Still, I play along. 'And what colour is Jarrod's aura today?'

'Predominantly black. A sure sign of anger.'

I pull a face. 'I expect his aura will be a lot blacker after I see him.'

Jarrod's door is ajar and he's frowning at his screen, typing with two fingers. I knock, take his glance as an invitation to come in, and shut the door behind me.

'I'm sorry about this morning,' I begin, joining my hands as I walk towards him. 'I have an excuse – but you're not going to like it.'

He says nothing. Jarrod isn't one to prompt, at least not with words; the expression on his face is quite sufficient.

'I was in an accident on Friday night – with Derek Jones from Telelink.'

He's shocked, so shocked that his frown momentarily clears. *'What?'*

'We were in a motorbike accident. Derek was taking me home. We came off the bike.'

Jarrod pushes back his seat from his desk and looks me up and down. 'Were you hurt?'

'We were able to walk away. But we both have cuts. I believe that he might need a skin graft.'

He nods slowly, ominously. 'Friday night? You met him for dinner, didn't you?'

'Yes.'

'Had you been drinking?'

'Not a lot.' I sigh. 'But, yes, we'd both been drinking.'

Fury rushes to fill the blankness on his face. 'Fuck it, Caitlin. What were you thinking?'

'I'm sorry.'

'He's a *client*. You knowingly put yourself and him in danger!'

'All I can say in my defence is that he was close, *so close* to committing . . . I thought the ride would seal it . . .'

It *had* been close. There could have been an order on the fax machine this morning. Jarrod could be slapping me on the back right now.

'That's the problem with you, Caitlin – you don't know where to draw the line.'

'I –'

'You didn't need to be on the bike. If he was going to crash, you didn't need to be there!'

'Yes, but –'

'You don't know how to hold back, do you? Wine them, dine them, get them drunk – you don't seem to know any other way to do business!'

Despite my earlier resolve to take his chiding with good grace, my temper stirs. 'I do what it takes, Jarrod. Sometimes it involves pushing boundaries –'

'Boundaries? You don't know the fucking meaning of boundaries! That's why you'll never go any further in your career, why you'll never become a manager.'

That's unfair, very unfair, and I have to bite down on my lip so that I don't retaliate.

'I don't want you to have any further contact with Telelink or Derek Jones. I will handle the client from today.'

I gasp, the sheer injustice making tears sting my eyes. I've done all the ground work, all the *hard* work, to get to this point and now Jarrod is going to swan in at the eleventh hour and take credit for it all.

'And you can consider this a verbal warning. If you ever blur the lines between business and personal again, you can go and look for a job elsewhere.'

I bite down harder on my lip. Part of me wants to tell him exactly what he can do with his job – and with himself for that matter. But another part, the part that's my father's daughter, knows that I'm getting exactly what I deserve. *An action can be judged by its consequences*, my father would say self-righteously. My actions were unquestionably out of order and the consequence is that my job and everything I've worked so hard to achieve over the last four years is now in jeopardy.

I nod to show him that I understand the warning and then I back out of the room, appropriately chastened. It's my deepest fear, losing my job, a paranoia that goes all the way back to Liam, aimless and chronically bored as he mooched about the house; unworthy and useless, at least in our father's eyes. I can think of nothing, *nothing* worse than losing my job, but nobody on this side of the world, least of all Jarrod, could begin to understand my fear, where it originates from or how deep it goes.

For the rest of the day I keep a low profile. I don't dare to call Derek again but still hope against hope that he will call me and that we can put things right between us; then Jarrod, faced with the evidence that Derek still wants me on the account, will have to back down. Derek doesn't call, however, and by the end of the day the writing's on the wall: my client doesn't want to speak to me and my first multimillion-dollar deal has, as a result of my own stupid actions, spun out of reach. Almost worse, if the deal is somehow salvaged it will be Jarrod who gets the credit and not me.

I visit my GP on my way home from work. When she enquires about the accident, I give her an edited version of events at which she looks up from her examination of my arm, her eyes full of reproach.

'It sounds like you were incredibly lucky.'

I know she's right, but I don't *feel* very lucky.

'I'm going to put on some lighter bandaging,' she continues. 'You can take it off at the end of the week, but come back to see me if the wounds don't seem to be healing or if you have any other concerns. And make sure that you take the full course of antibiotics that were prescribed.'

The phone is ringing inside the apartment as I turn my key in the door. I hurry, kicking the door open with my leg and dropping my bag on the floor inside before dashing to the kitchen.

'Hello.' My voice sounds a little breathless from the rush.

'Caitlin . . .'

For a moment my heart stops beating. Time and distance fall away and it feels as though my father is here, right in front of me, not on the other end of the phone.

'Caitlin, I want to –'

I jab the 'end' button, cutting him off. The few words that he uttered seem to resound in the silent apartment and I resist the infusion of memories they carry. Every few months he does this, phones me. I miss the calls more often than not and only have to deal with the voice messages, his tone familiar and authoritative as he announces himself and asks me to call him back, which I never do. He sends letters too, short ones, a few paragraphs scribed in his exacting handwriting. Contained to paper and thus indirect, the letters are easier to face, and I skim them before throwing them in the bin.

In my bedroom I change into a loose summer dress, the jersey fabric soft against the fresh bandaging. As I pull my hair back from my face, I notice that my hands are shaking. He always has this unnerving effect on me. His timing, as usual, is spot on. How very apt that he should choose today of all days to call. It's as though he can sense the very moment I put a step wrong.

During my first few months in Australia I still maintained some contact with my father. I remember stilted phone conversations, animosity on my end and preoccupation on his, but communication nonetheless. But as my parents' marriage began to unravel, our communication became more and more strained. Over that same phone line I had listened to my mother's despair and heartbreak and I couldn't forgive him for causing it, couldn't forgive him for abandoning her when she needed him the most, when she had already endured so much, for so ruthlessly putting the 'cause' before his own wife and family.

By the time the divorce was finalised, I had severed all contact with him and since then Mum has taken it upon herself to be the mediator between the fragments of what was once a family. Every Saturday morning she keeps me abreast of what's happening, whether or not I want to know. Now, as I loop a band around my hair and slip some thongs on my feet, snippets of old conversations with Mum replay in my head, conversations that bridge the years since I've spoken to my father and form some of the tapestry of our estranged relationship today.

From one such conversation, out on the balcony of the unit in Bondi Junction, I recall Mum blurting in my ear, 'I saw your father during the week.'

'What?'

'We met. We discussed what to do with the house and everything else. It was quite civilised.' She was pretending to be pragmatic but I could hear the unevenness under her efficient tone. 'He said I can stay in the house.'

'That's the least he can do!'

'He's being quite generous. It's his house too, you know.'

'For God's sake, Mum. Fuck his generosity!'

'Don't use that kind of language, please!' Mum's voice had an edge of authority, something I hadn't heard in a long time. 'Your father *is* generous. He's put everything, his heart and soul, into the support group. He and the others in the group have talked to politicians and police on both sides of the border. They've driven up and down the country, had secret meetings with all kinds of shady characters, put their own safety at risk trying to get the names of the men who put that bomb in our town.'

I couldn't find words to formulate an answer, overcome by a variety of emotions: defensiveness, anger, resentment, mostly incredulity. How could she sing his praises like this? How could she act like she had forgiven him, absolved him of everything? She wasn't hoping to get back with him, was she? Surely that wasn't on her agenda.

'He has the names, Caitlin,' Mum said in a gentler voice. 'Your father has the names and he's given them to the police. Those murderers will be brought to justice.'

I stayed out on the balcony for some time after that phone call, feeling disturbed, off kilter, almost as though I was leaning too far over the railing and not sitting safely on one of the deck-chairs. I told myself that I should be happy my parents were on speaking terms again and that Mum was starting to move on. She was sorting out her accommodation and her finances and, in the process, her future. It was all good as long as she didn't do anything stupid like taking Dad back. As I sat deep in thought, the wind whipped up, tossing my hair and bringing goose pimples to my arms. Rain clouds gathered in the slice of sky visible from my seat, and suddenly I didn't feel far away from Ireland, I felt close, frighteningly close.

Leaving that particular memory behind in the bedroom, I pad to the kitchen to make a start on dinner. I extract some vegetables and meat from the fridge and a thick wooden chopping board from under the sink. Methodically, I peel the outer skin from the carrots and chop them into slices, then cubes. Next I deseed and chop a green capsicum into similar-sized pieces, the irony of the orange and green sitting side by side on the chopping board not lost on me. As I slice an onion, another old conversation begins to play in my head, once again my mother the messenger, the go-between. This conversation occurred later on in the piece, around the end of 2001. Mum and Dad had not reconciled. Mum was adamant, though, that she regarded her ex-husband as a friend, a close friend, and she continued to tell me of his achievements and challenges, defending him fiercely whenever I dissented.

'It's been a big week here in Clonmegan, Caitlin,' Mum had said in opening.

'Why? What happened?'

'There was an important report published. Have you seen anything about it in the news over there?'

'No, Mum, I haven't.' I didn't admit that I rarely watched the news. Too often it brought on flashbacks of my younger self standing in my room at the Elms, practising sign language from *News for the Deaf*, a memory from what seemed like a lifetime ago but was so easily and readily retrieved.

'The report was from the police ombudsman,' Paula continued, her voice threaded with an emotion that I couldn't quite identify. Was it nervousness, or a sense of excitement? 'The ombudsman criticised how things were handled on the day of the bombing. She said that had the authorities acted with more urgency and transparency things could have turned out differently, and that there at least wouldn't have been so many fatalities.'

I was silent. I didn't want to hear this kind of news. The notion that the fatalities could have been prevented was too unsettling and confronting. If I thought about it for any length of time, it could tear me apart, destroy me.

'Now, it doesn't change the fact that the terrorists who planned and executed the bombing were the ones really responsible. We all know that.'

The terrorists. Those faceless men who lurked in the recesses of my mind. I thought of them randomly, like when I was grocery shopping or sitting in a café or on the tram. I imagined them going about their daily lives, shopping for milk and bread, stuck in gridlocked traffic, drinking mugs of tea, just like me. I imagined their routine being disrupted by their sudden arrest, their hands cuffed as they were walked away from their families and everything they held dear. It was just a dream, though. In real life only one of them had been arrested and tried, and there were already rumours of a mistrial. A conviction, if I read between the lines of what my mother had previously reported back, seemed unlikely.

'This formal acknowledgment by the police ombudsman that things weren't handled the right way has brought great comfort to the town.' Mum hesitated for a fraction of a second. When she spoke again I was able to identify the emotion that had been present in her voice from the outset. It was pride. Exhilarated and unadulterated pride. 'Your father made this come about, Caitlin. He and the others in the group. They have been pressing and pushing and pleading. They've not let up.'

'Good for him.'

'You should be proud of him, too.'

'Well, funny how I'm not,' I retorted like a sullen teenager.

I hung up the phone, fresh anger and hurt snarling inside me. I couldn't begin to fathom that my mother had forgiven my father so far as to be *proud* of him. He'd done nothing to deserve such a civilised relationship with his ex-wife. He didn't deserve to be forgiven or to receive accolades for his supposed achievements. I could *never* be proud of him, not after what he did to our family.

In the years since that particular phone call, my father has continued to lecture at Queen's, drilling his students on ethics and values. In every spare moment, he pursues justice for the bomb victims and their families. The list of names that seemed so promising at the start has come to nothing but he still continues to do battle, with the police, the politicians, the media, in the vain hope that someone will eventually be brought to justice.

A few years back, frustrated by the lack of progress with the criminal system, the support group began civil action of their own against the individuals on the list. Had I been talking to my father, I would have advised him that this was taking things too far, that it was time to stop his crusade, to put the past to rest and move on.

I tip the diced meat into the wok and it lands with a hiss against the hot metal. I stir for a few minutes before adding the vegetables. Jeanie will be home soon and I'll have the stir-fry ready as a surprise. Jeanie is the closest thing I have to family in Australia. It's like having another sister, or at least all the positive aspects of a sister, such as dependability in a crisis, familiarity, no need for pretence, and without any of the negative aspects, like sibling rivalry, teasing, grudges that go back to when you were kids. Though I'm not confiding by nature, I have involuntarily revealed a lot of myself to Jeanie over the years. I've told her about the controlled environment in which I grew up, my father preaching and hammering values into us from a young age only to throw aside many of those values – along with his wife and family – in the pursuit of 'justice' and his personal goals. I've laughed at Jeanie's tales about her seven sisters, the fighting, one-upmanship, conniving and ever-changing allegiances, and in turn shared the odd anecdote about Liam and Maeve, including how much I miss them. I've even told Jeanie little things about Josh – songs he liked, aspects of his personality, the things he cared about – and once, when I was rather drunk, I admitted to feeling him with me, on a different plane but there nonetheless. Jeanie has taken my confidences on board, filed them away in her oh-so-logical mind, and never takes them out for reassessment without my instigation. Jeanie isn't about wanting to change the world or other people. She's practical and accepting, and if I don't want to talk, which is usually the case, then that's perfectly okay with her. Whenever I do want to talk, she's there to listen.

The phone begins to ring over the hissing sound coming from the wok. I eye it warily. It could be Jeanie announcing that she's either delayed or on her way, but I don't risk answering it. My father is persistent if nothing else. For the last eleven years he has doggedly pursued those terrorists to the detriment of everything else. When I'm at my most negative, I liken him to them. They too believe in a higher cause, blur the lines between right and wrong, and convince themselves that the end justifies the means.

'My round.' Jeanie slides off her stool. 'Same again?'

'Yeah, thanks.'

As she saunters towards the bar, I glance around. Only a few patrons are sitting down like me; most are standing, clutching glasses, their conversation and laughter rising into the canopy of stars and black sky. It's surprisingly busy for a Tuesday night: Coldplay thumping from the sound system, girls dancing provocatively, men sizing them up through slightly bloodshot eyes, bouncers prowling in black suits and white shirts, soberly scanning the outdoor scene.

'One vodka and Diet Coke for you,' Jeanie puts a glass in front of me a few minutes later, 'and one big pint of beer for me.' She sits down, tucks her blonde hair pragmatically behind one ear, and takes a swig of beer. She doesn't have a preferred brand: beer is beer, and as far as she's concerned all the various brands taste just as good.

'It's getting quite rowdy over there,' she comments, glancing over my shoulder.

I swivel in my seat to take another look. Two bouncers are having an exchange with a group of men at a neighbouring table. The music swallows their voices but it's obvious the men are being asked to leave.

I turn back to Jeanie. 'Yeah, it's getting to that point in the night. Might go after this, okay?'

'Sure.' Jeanie takes another swig of beer. 'Not like you to be the one to call it a night.'

'I shouldn't even be drinking,' I say wryly. 'I'm still on antibiotics until tomorrow.'

'I'd forgotten about that.' Jeanie frowns and looks at my drink as though she'd like to take it back.

'Besides,' I add, 'Tuesday night's a school night and maybe the last few days have taught me the error of my ways.'

I'm not joking. I have, in fact, done a lot of self-examination since the accident. I've replayed what everyone said: the police officer, the paramedic, the doctor, Jeanie and, of course, Jarrod. They're right, all of them. I went too far. If Derek didn't want to negotiate, I should have stepped back. If I had bided my time, the accident wouldn't have happened. It's that simple. Of course, Derek was in the wrong too. He should have turned me down, knowing that he was a relatively inexperienced rider and that his reflexes could be affected by the alcohol. But that's almost beside the point.

I sip my drink. The Diet Coke is flat and reflects exactly how

I feel. 'Jarrod says I'll never go any further in my career, that I'll never become a manager.'

Jeanie shrugs. 'Jarrod's pissed off with you and so he's not being very nice.'

'He also insinuated that the only way I know how to make a sale is by wining and dining my clients – with the emphasis on wining.'

'As I said, he's pissed off.' Jeanie is matter-of-fact to the point of being snappy. It would be interesting to see her up against Jarrod in a conflict situation. Or a scenario, like my own, where Jeanie had done something wrong and was in a position of disadvantage. I'm quite sure that Jeanie would come off the better of such an exchange. Not only is she strong and direct with her opinions, she somehow still manages to be warm and endearing, which has a very disarming effect. There's a lot I could learn from Jeanie.

I swirl the drink in my glass. 'He said that I don't know the meaning of boundaries. I don't think that's true or particularly fair . . .'

Jeanie considers this at more length. 'I would say that your true nature is to be compliant and very respectful of boundaries and such,' she muses, cocking her head to one side as she looks at me. 'But there's also this rule-breaking streak in you – it's like there are two very different Caitlin O'Reillys.'

'You're making me sound schizophrenic!'

Jeanie grins in response. 'You said it, love. Though I do think that this wild streak goes against your true nature and that in your heart of hearts you're more of a good girl than a party animal.'

'And what about being a hard worker, super-intelligent and a good friend?'

'Oh, I'd say all that too,' Jeanie replies in a tone that suggests the opposite.

I pull a face. Even though Jeanie's succeeded in making me laugh, I'm still extremely peeved with Jarrod and the comments he made about my career.

'Party girl, smarty girl, what difference does it make?' Jeanie asks, seeing the shift in my mood.

'Party girls don't get promoted.'

'Ah. I see.' Jeanie is suddenly distracted by something over my shoulder. 'Hey! The cops are here!'

I turn in my seat and see two police officers walking towards the group of men who were asked to leave earlier but obviously haven't budged. My eyes are instantly drawn to one of the officers. He's tall and broad with a distinctive square jaw and blue, blue eyes.

I turn back to Jeanie, my face bright red. 'I don't believe it! That's the officer – I mean, the *sergeant* – who was there on Friday night.'

'Really? Which one?'

'The taller one.'

'A fine, strapping fellow,' Jeanie states in her woeful Irish accent.

'What's happening?' I ask urgently, afraid to look over my shoulder again should the officer see and recognise me.

'Looks like they're all willing to go home except for one of them. He's talking back. Uh-oh . . .'

I swing around, curiosity getting the better of me. The man

Jeanie mentioned has sprung forward, his friends holding him back by his arms while he snarls his displeasure. He's dressed respectably enough but is drunk to the point of being obnoxious and abusive. The sergeant nods calmly, as if taking the man's viewpoint on board, and says a few words before jerking his head towards the exit.

'He's going,' Jeanie breathes.

But just as his well-meaning friends loosen their grip, the man lurches forward again, burrowing his head into the sergeant's midriff, taking him down along with a table of drinks.

Jeanie scarpers from her seat. 'Get out of the way, Caitlin!'

I get up more slowly, my eyes transfixed by the rolling bodies on the ground. Another table goes down in a ruckus of shattering glass and spraying liquid. Onlookers gasp. Some barstools are the next casualties, toppling down and bouncing off the ground, the legs dislodging on impact. The bodies on the floor twist through the debris, the sergeant on top then under the drunk, and then on top again. He somehow manages to get the drunk in a head-lock and soon it's over, and the man is being handcuffed by the other officer. Both policemen pull him to his feet and, taking an elbow each, march him outside. Bouncers usher spectators back from the scene and bar staff move in to begin the cleanup.

'Fight over,' says Jeanie, gulping the last of her beer. 'Let's get out of here.'

'Just a minute.' Picking my way through the broken glass, the ground wet and sticky against the soles of my shoes, I retrieve the sergeant's hat from under one of the toppled tables. It's soaked through and smells like a brewery, but I assume that he wants it back.

Outside, the drunk is already in the paddy wagon, screaming abuse as he kicks and pounds the back door, the vehicle rocking from side to side with the onslaught. The sergeant stands close by, notebook in hand as he takes a statement from one of the bouncers. A cocktail of spilt drinks splotches his shirt and glistens in his hair. He looks up as I approach and I notice a small cut over one of his eyebrows.

'Excuse me . . .' I begin.

'Yes?'

'You lost this.' I hold out the hat, my heart beating erratically and a little too hard. The intensity of his gaze is unnerving.

Blue eyes flick from my face to the sodden hat in my hand. 'Thanks.'

'I'm Caitlin. You probably don't remember me –'

'I do remember. The motorbike, wasn't it?'

'Yes.' I'm acutely conscious of the bouncer and Jeanie looking on, but there's something I have to say. 'Look, I just wanted you to know that I'm not usually that stupid.'

'I'm glad to hear it.'

'Well, goodbye . . .' I turn to go.

'How are your injuries?'

Surprised at the question, I turn back to him. 'Much better today, thanks.'

'Good.'

I take a step back, attempt another goodbye. 'Bye . . . officer.'

'Matthew.'

'Excuse me?'

'Matthew. That's my name.' A smile sparkles into his eyes. 'Bye, Caitlin. See you around.'

Chapter 14

The rest of the week crawls by, punctuated by a few insignificant orders from other clients (not Telelink), a breakfast seminar, some boring meetings and far too much thumb twiddling for my liking. I clear my inbox, catch up on some filing, make cups of tea and coffee I don't finish and read *The Age* from front to back. I'm at a loose end and can't disguise it no matter how many trivial tasks I try to busy myself with. Telelink is my biggest account and their daily small, high-volume orders usually form the backbone of my work schedule. Those orders belong to Jarrod now, along with the one-off multimillion-dollar deal I cultivated and priced, if Jarrod manages to save it. All incoming calls and emails from Telelink are being diverted to his office. It feels as though I've been fired, except for the fact I'm still sitting at my desk with more time than I have work.

'Enjoy it while it lasts,' Zoe advises when I complain.

'I can't,' I wail. 'I need to be busy.'

She nods sagely. 'No urgency, no motivation.'

'Want to go out for a long lunch?' I ask beseechingly.

'Sorry, can't do today. I'm meeting a friend to do some lunch-time meditation. Of course, you're welcome to join us.'

'Thanks but no thanks. I've had more than enough "quiet" time today, I think!' Next I phone Nicola. 'Fancy a bite to eat?'

'Can't. The modems in one of the training rooms are acting up. Need to stick around to make sure the tech guys fix them properly.'

Jo in reception has another commitment and can't go to lunch either and so I leave the office without a companion. Outside the sky is picture-perfect blue, the kind of blue that would usually make me happy just to look at it. Not today, though. Instead of going straight to get something to eat, I find myself heading towards Bourke Street Mall. I veer in and out of a few clothes shops, glancing at the garments on the racks but not caring enough to pick up anything for closer examination. I feel aimless, demotivated and superfluous among the lunchtime bustle. My job is like my access card to this city, but now Jarrod has watered it down to the mundane, to something that doesn't have enough substance to give me purpose. If he continues to punish me, do I have the courage to resign, to go out into the market and find something else? Up until now I've loved working at Learning Space – for the flexibility, the autonomy, and because my qualifications, or lack thereof, don't seem to matter. Once I start going for interviews, it will matter a lot.

'Why didn't you finish your degree?' the recruiters will ask.

Now there's a question I don't care to answer.

I wander into one of the shopping arcades and stop at a jewellery stall. The pieces are eye-catching and unusual, made of silver and patterned glass. I pick up a necklace; it feels heavy in my hand, substantial, and for some reason I think of Maeve. I imagine that she would like the eclectic design, even though I know little about what my sister likes or dislikes these days. Maeve has twice come to visit me, making Melbourne a stop on the backpacking trips she sandwiched between her degrees. Though she had friends in tow on both occasions, I really enjoyed the time we spent together. It was lovely to see a face I'd known all my life, to savour the freshness and yet the deep familiarity of her voice and her gentle, girlish laugh. My last image of Maeve is at Melbourne airport. I remember what she was wearing as she said goodbye – a red tank top, loose white cotton pants, Jerusalem sandals – her plaits of light brown hair and the straps of her backpack resting on her shoulders. She was twenty-three then and looked much younger than her age. From what Mum tells me, it sounds like Maeve hasn't changed at all since the last time I saw her; she still leads a student lifestyle and seems to have retained a teenage perspective on the world, including an aversion to responsibility. I send my sister books and CDs for birthdays and Christmas, but I'm never sure if they're to her taste. As I stand in the middle of the arcade, the assistant hovering close by and the silver and glass weighing in my hand, it feels like too much time has elapsed since I bought Maeve an impulsive gift, where I thought of her before I thought of a reason for buying her something.

I extract some money from my purse to pay for the necklace, deciding that I will send it as an early congratulations for achieving her PhD. At the register there's a small display of gift cards and I choose one with a glossy pink orchid on a white background. By the time I pay and my purchases are sealed in a paper bag, I feel quite light-headed. I will have to eat, and afterwards I will go to the post office and send the necklace and card to Maeve. Then back to work, though I can't imagine how I'm going to fill the rest of the afternoon.

Luke, the twenty-four-year-old surfer I met when I was out with Nicola, phones on Thursday, almost two weeks after taking my number. He asks if I want to meet for a drink, his tone so casual it borders on indifferent. I should say 'thanks but no thanks'. Instead I arrange to meet him.

The Elephant is busy, a live band setting up on stage, testing microphones and instruments and tweaking the sound system. I sit at the bar and I've half finished my drink before Luke makes an appearance. I recognise him immediately, which is a relief considering I haven't been able to clearly picture his face. He wears a blue Billabong T-shirt and ripped jeans, his snowy blond hair ruffled with gel. Girls pay attention as he sashays in my direction. He's very aware of the effect he's having.

'Hi.' His smile is apparently the only apology I'm going to get. He nods at my drink. 'Fancy another one of those?'

'Yes, please. Vodka and Diet Coke.'

Luke catches the barman's eye. 'A bottle of Crown and a vodka and Coke, mate.'

'*Diet* Coke.'

'That's Diet Coke,' he relays my correction to the barman. Once the order is placed, his eyes glance to the stage. 'Who's playing?'

I shrug. 'Don't know yet.'

'How was work today?' It's a perfunctory question.

'Okay,' I reply, equally superficial. 'You?'

'Yeah, it was all right.'

We have nothing in common, no shared interests, and I wonder what I'm doing here. If I analyse it past the current moment I know the reason. Men like Luke are hard to get, impossible to keep, and there's no chance of a relationship developing. I know where I stand with him and in that way he makes for a 'safe' date, though I'm well aware that most women would regard him in quite the opposite way.

I finish off my drink to make way for the new one. The band finally gets it together and starts to play, throaty voices and acoustic guitars filling the air. I like their sound and lyrics, and for the first few songs I almost forget that I'm with Luke. When I finally look his way, he's leaning against the bar, his heavily lashed eyes surveying the room. He looks bored, with the music, the venue, with life in general. I wonder again what I'm doing here and realise that I'm here for exactly the same reason as him: in some vain attempt to keep boredom at bay.

An attractive girl walks in with her friends and Luke openly looks her up and down, his mouth curling in appreciation. On another night I might not have cared, but tonight I do. I'm not pretty enough or interesting enough for Luke. Really, it's better to be bored than to sit here feeling so utterly inadequate.

I gulp some of my drink and stand up to leave. 'This wasn't such a good idea.'

Luke looks momentarily confused. 'You're going?'

'Yes, yes, I am.'

He moves his shoulders up and down in a shrug that's both offhand and insulting. He clearly couldn't care less if I leave now or later. He wouldn't have cared if I hadn't turned up at all tonight. But, in fairness, I more or less knew this from the outset.

I push my way towards the exit and pause outside the pub, the cool breeze from the bay chilling the skin on my arms.

'Hey, Caitlin.'

I look around to find myself the focus of blue eyes that seem strangely familiar. The face beyond them also looks familiar, albeit somewhat out of context. It's the sergeant, Matthew. He's not in uniform, and this is what threw me.

'Oh, it's you – again!'

He grins a little self-consciously. 'Well, St Kilda's a relatively small place.'

I take a moment to readjust to this disconcertingly casual version of him. He's wearing a white shirt, loose over faded jeans. The shirt accentuates the breadth of his shoulders, so wide and muscled that he looks like he belongs on the back line of a rugby team. His hair is cut too short and his eyes glitter against the tan of his skin. He seems even taller than I remembered, six foot three or four, yet, stripped of the authority that comes with his uniform, there's something oddly vulnerable about him standing with his hands sunk into the pockets of his jeans and that hint of self-consciousness in his expression.

'Getting some fresh air?' he asks.

'No, going home.'

'Seems a bit early for that.'

'I had a date that went wrong.' He looks immediately

concerned and I feel compelled to reassure him. 'It was just a bad case of incompatibility, that's all.'

There's an awkward silence, into which I should say goodbye and go not-so-merrily on my way. Instead I scan the vicinity, looking for someone I have so far failed to notice that Matthew might be here with. 'You're on your own?'

'I have some friends who went in ahead of me.'

'Police officers?'

'Yes,' he answers with a sheepish smile. 'Off duty, though. Like me.'

A pause follows. It's less awkward than the one before.

'Have you always worked in the St Kilda area?' I ask.

'No, only in the last six months.'

'Where were you before then?' I seem to be unable to look away from his eyes, and I can feel my face heating up in response.

'My home town, Deniliquin.'

I've heard of Deniliquin; it's located somewhere between Melbourne and Sydney, though I'm unsure which state it falls into, Victoria or New South Wales.

'Ah, a country boy.'

'And you?'

'I've been in St Kilda, or at least the general area, for the last seven years. Before that I frittered away a few years in Sydney and Brisbane.'

'And before that?'

'Ireland.'

His mouth lifts in another smile. 'Well, that's quite obvious. I meant what part of Ireland.'

I feel the usual twinge this question evokes. 'The North.'

'Belfast?'

'No. A small town inland from Belfast.' The twinge deepens before it eases, and suddenly I feel silly standing here, chatting to this virtual stranger. 'Well, I'd better get going. I guess I'll see you around.'

Matthew surprises me by putting his hand on my arm, preventing me from moving away. 'Caitlin, wait. Do you want to have a drink before you go home?'

I look back at him, confused.

'I mean, we don't have to go in here.' He indicates the doorway behind my back. 'We can go somewhere else if you like.'

I feel so bemused that I can't begin to formulate an answer. As the silence grows, I can't help but notice a deeper colour creep across his face. He's embarrassed, sorry that he asked and put us both in this excruciatingly awkward situation. This knowledge, that I've managed to embarrass him, throws me even further off kilter.

'Thanks for asking,' I eventually manage, 'but I think I'll just go home.'

I walk away, along the street and towards home, my arms hugged around my body, keeping out the cold breeze, and keeping in my conflicting emotions. I should have answered him more quickly; it would have been much less embarrassing if I hadn't hesitated for so long. In my defence, I didn't see it coming: it doesn't seem that long since he was glowering at me and calling me stupid for getting on the back of Derek's bike.

I make it all the way home and into bed before I acknowledge there was a split second when I actually considered it: having a drink with Matthew Blake. I was right to turn him down, though. He's nice, really nice in fact, but he's not my type. He's a police officer, and for some reason I can't quite pin down, this bothers me.

I chew the top of my pen as I read the newspaper article. The headline is inconspicuous, the font small and narrow as though the journalist wasn't confident enough to make a bolder statement: *Net Banc circling Metro*.

Both Net Banc and Metro have refused to comment on a possible acquisition and the article lacks hard evidence. Still, the journalist, Joe McFaddon, has regular pieces in the business section and they're usually well researched and written. My instincts tell me that Joe is onto something with this alleged acquisition; he obviously doesn't have all the facts but I'm sure that he's sniffing in the right direction. I flick through my filing cabinet, searching for the client questionnaire form I used last time I called Harry Dixon. I locate it and laugh to myself when I see *CRANKY BASTARD* written after his name. Dialling the number, I mentally brace myself for another curt reception.

'Harry Dixon.'

'Hello, Harry, this is Caitlin O'Reilly from Learning Space.'

'Where?'

'Learning Space,' I say pleasantly. 'We provide training –'

'We do our own training!'

'Yes, I know. But I've just read the article in *The Age* about Metro –'

'Net Banc will not comment on that article.'

'Yes, of course,' I say, keeping my tone light. 'I'm not looking for a comment. I just wanted to let you know that if something does happen, Learning Space may be able to –'

'As I said, I have no comment!' he roars and crashes down the phone.

Rubbing my ear, I put the receiver back in its cradle and neatly print *VERY* before *CRANKY BASTARD*. Then I cut out the newspaper article and attach it to the back of the form with a paperclip. After returning everything to the filing cabinet, I make a diary note to send Harry some marketing material in a week's time. By then he will have hopefully forgotten this last conversation and realised that any acquisition will involve significant systems change and training.

With nothing else of interest in the newspaper, I once again find myself at a loose end. It's at least an hour before I can legitimately go to lunch, and another six hours before I can call the working week over. I hate clock-watching like this. For the want of something to do, I go on the internet and google Deniliquin. The town is in New South Wales, three hours' drive from Melbourne and eight from Sydney, set on the fringes of the Riverine Plain and a vast redgum forest. The tourism website describes the area as 'an oasis of green', a haven for fishermen, kayakers, bird-watchers and bushwalkers. It looks like Matthew grew up in a nice place.

Next, before I can question my motives too closely, I google Matthew himself. The results line up one after the other on my screen.

Sergeant Matthew Blake praises rescue efforts.

Sergeant Blake of St Kilda Police says bail decision will be appealed.

Local sergeant warns of crackdown on antisocial behaviour.

Apparently, and quite understandably given his position in the community, Matthew is someone journalists seek out when they want a comment, and a considered opinion. He probably stands in front of the police station looking solemn and righteous in the same way my father used to stand in front of the university when he was being interviewed by the media.

This is what bothered me about Matthew last night, though at the time I couldn't pinpoint my reservations. Now, thanks to Google, I can.

The Mitre Tavern is our local, and Learning Space people congregate there most nights of the week, not just Fridays. I like the Mitre; it reminds me of the old traditional pubs at home: nooks and crannies, rustic tables and chairs, quirky artefacts on the walls and behind the bar, a certain smell that I like to think of as the scent of history. In the alleyway outside there's a beer garden and in summer people prefer it to the dim interior – pavers under their feet, the open sky overhead. This is where I go with Nicola when my terminally long working week is finally over.

'Here.' Nicola slips a drink into my right hand, even though the glass I'm holding in my left is still three-quarters full.

I regard the drink suspiciously. 'Are you trying to get me drunk?'

She screws up her face. 'Trying to get myself drunk.' Apparently it's been a hard week on the training floor.

'Well, no need to take me down with you.' I laugh. Truth be told, I already feel quite tipsy.

I throw back the old drink and set down the empty glass on a nearby table. Once my hand is free, I turn my wrist to glance at my watch: 8 pm. A waitress passes by, plates lined along her forearm, steam rising from them, the smell of grilled steak and hot chips whetting my usually erratic appetite.

'Should we get something to eat?'

'Let's hold off until it's quieter.' Nicola twirls the stem of her glass, her eyes sweeping across the crowd.

'See anything of interest?'

'Maybe. Left wall. Halfway down. The one with the black hair.'

I follow her gaze. The man in question has slicked-back dark hair, an arrogant set to his face and glinting cufflinks on his designer shirt. 'He looks like an investment banker. Just your type.' Nicola's taste in men runs to smooth, handsome, rich and, more by consequence than design, shallow.

'He's seen you staring,' she hisses.

I grin unrepentantly. 'Well, at least now you're on his radar.'

'Face this way,' she instructs urgently, moving so that he's no longer in her direct line of vision.

I turn sideways with a long-suffering sigh, my view now truncated by the back wall. My eyes swoop upwards. The sky is murky, dusk smudging the brightness from the blue that was there the last time I looked. Noise bubbles around me: conversation, laughter, clinking glasses, the rumbling of a truck going down Collins Street. I raise my glass, still looking up at the sky, and drink until the ice rushes forward to kiss my lips.

'This is going to be my last,' I slur to Nicola.

'Don't be so boring – it's still early.'

I wag my finger. 'You are a bad, bad influence.' A little unsteady on my feet, I go inside and add my body to those pressed around the bar, waiting for service.

I come back outside to find that Mr Slick has made his move on Nicola.

'I'm David,' he introduces himself to me with a confident, practised smile.

'Caitlin,' I return.

Like Nicola he has glossy hair and tanned skin; they could be brother and sister.

'So, you work with Nicola?'

'Yes, I'm in sales. What about you?'

He mentions an investment bank on William Street, confirming my earlier guess. His friends, still huddled by the wall, obviously hail from the same industry.

Nicola nudges me. 'Checking out his friends?' she asks in a stage whisper.

'Not really.'

'Come on . . .'

'No, seriously not interested.' I sip my drink and realise I'm quite full up. 'Think I'll go home.'

'Hey, don't leave.' Nicola looks distressed.

I smile to indicate that I'm not leaving because I feel like a spare wheel; I actually *want* to go home. 'Have fun. Don't do anything I wouldn't do.'

I make my way down the alleyway, the voices and music fading behind me. My head is swimming nicely, my feet blurred as one goes in front of the other. I'm drunk. I should have eaten. Bloody Nicola! I always have too much to drink when I'm out with her. My father would call her an 'unsuitable friend'. I burst into a fit of giggles.

Emerging onto Collins Street, I look up and down in search of a taxi. Seeing one in the distance I raise my hand. Fortunately, it stops. 'St Kilda,' I say as I slide in the back. The driver nods and glides away from the kerb.

My handbag sits uncomfortably on my knees. I move it to the seat, next to my thigh. My eyes keep darting back and forth to it. Finally, I give in to the urge to extract my phone, along with the card, *his* card: Sergeant M. Blake. Before I can think twice, I dial the number on it.

He answers on the first ring, his voice at once hesitant and authoritative. 'Hello.'

I could pass this off as an act of spontaneity, fuelled by too many drinks on an empty stomach. But the truth is that he's been on my mind all day. The sergeant: crisp uniform, bulging forearms and that cool blue stare. Then his alter ego, Matthew: faded jeans, hands in his pockets, disarmingly shy. Despite what Google revealed about certain, disturbingly familiar aspects of his job, I still can't seem to dismiss him from my thoughts.

'Hi, Matthew. It's Caitlin.'

His voice becomes wary. 'Hello, Caitlin.'

There's a pause. A long pause.

'I still have your card, in case you're wondering how I got your number . . .'

'I wasn't wondering, but thank you for explaining.' Now he sounds like he's teasing me. Maybe it would be best to stop focusing so hard on the tone of his voice and say what I want to say.

'I just wanted to apologise for last night. It wasn't a good time . . .'

'No worries.'

The taxi is closing in on St Kilda. Soon I'll have to give the driver directions. If I'm going to do this, I have to be quick.

'Look, Matthew, I was . . . I was wondering if you'd still like to go for a drink sometime . . .'

Chapter 15

I wake up, the inside of my mouth like cardboard and the inside of my head equally dry and dull. It takes me a few moments to determine what day it is – Saturday – and another few to figure out why I feel so bad. Bloody Nicola! My mind flits through disjointed memories of last night: the beer garden and darkening sky overhead, the steak and chips I didn't eat, Mr Slick and his diamond cufflinks, the taxi ride home. Then I jolt in the bed, squint my eyes to sharpen my recollection. The taxi. Sitting in the back. My phone in one hand, his card in the other. I didn't, did I?

Oh, Jesus. Please don't tell me that I rang Matthew Blake and asked him out!

Even as I ask the question, I know that I did, and I sit up in bed with a loud groan. I asked a police officer on a date. And if my sluggish memory serves me right, he said yes. I'm meeting him tonight, for dinner. I cover my face with my hands. What a huge mistake! I will absolutely have to cancel.

Getting out of bed, I test to see if I can function vertically before slowly making my way to the bathroom. I turn on the shower, shivering while I wait for the water to warm up. The water courses over my face, cleansing the residue of yesterday's makeup from my sticky skin, soaking my hair, gushing over the red, stinging skin on my arm and hip, the bandaging now removed. Steam rises around me. Feeling dizzy, I flatten my hand against the shower wall to steady myself. I have to stop doing this. Drinking too much, not eating enough.

I step out of the shower and wrap a thick white towel around myself. Rubbing some of the excess water from my hair, I rake through its length with a wide-tooth comb. Back in my room, I sit on the edge of my bed. A few moments later a small drop of blood pools on my finger. Bright, glistening, vibrant; it's hard to believe something so beautiful comes from me. Sometimes, on days when my self-esteem is really low, I fantasise about extending the cut down the length of my finger, slitting it open, but I don't seem to hate myself enough today to indulge in such a fantasy.

The kitchen serves as another reminder of last night, a slimy black banana skin and a half-empty packet of crackers sitting on the table. Too little, too late.

I fill the kettle and pop two slices of wholegrain bread in the toaster. The coffee eases my hangover and the toast fills the craving in my stomach while I strive to clearly recall the conversation with Matthew. He sounded guarded at first, I remember, but once he relaxed, he seemed pleased to hear from me. If I ring now to cancel, he won't think much of me at all. I'm not sure why, but I don't want him to think badly of me.

The phone rings and I answer, thinking that it'll be Mum with her regular Saturday morning call.

'Caitlin – it's Matthew.'

'Oh, hello.' My face blushes bright red and I'm hugely grateful that he can't see.

'I hope you don't mind me calling your home number – your mobile doesn't seem to be working.'

'Oh, the battery must be flat.' I attempt a joke. 'Lucky you have all my details in that notebook of yours!'

'Yeah, lucky.' He sounds as nervous as I do. 'Look, about tonight . . .'

He's going to cancel. He's taking the problem out of my hands. Relief and disappointment combine to form a tightness in my chest.

'Yes?' I prompt.

'I'm sorry, but I have to work. Two of my officers have called in sick.'

'No problem,' I say, my voice shaking a little.

'Maybe I can call you during the week to organise something else?'

'Yeah, sure,' I manage, trying to be casual.

There's a pause. This is where he'll say goodbye.

'Sorry to let you down.' He doesn't seem to be ready to hang up just yet. 'Hope it's not too late for you to make other plans.'

'Don't worry about it,' I reassure him. 'I think a quiet night at home is in order.'

Nicola will be going out tonight but I'm not sure I can take two of those kinds of nights in a row. Jeanie's in Sydney visiting family and so it will be a genuinely quiet night in.

We talk for another few minutes, though when I hang up the phone I'm hard-pressed to remember what we spoke about. Afterwards I sit and sip my coffee and try to comprehend my seesawing reactions to him. Though he's easy to talk to, I could hear a certain reticence in his voice, the same underlying shyness that was evident when I met him the other night, and I find it hard to marry this side of his personality to the police sergeant who gives such confident, opinionated quotes to the media.

My head aches. I'm far too hungover to figure him out.

The phone rings again. This time it is Mum. 'Hello, love.'

'Hi, Mum.'

'You're up?'

'Yes, just having a nice wholesome breakfast.'

'I'm glad that you're eating well.' Lucky she doesn't know I skipped dinner last night. 'Is Jeanie there with you?'

'No. She's up in Sydney.'

'With the family?'

'Yes. Boarding at the lunatic asylum – her words, not mine.'

Mum chuckles. She likes to talk about Jeanie as though she's met her, which of course she hasn't. The closest she gets is a friendly chat on the occasions Jeanie answers the phone. Mum deeply appreciates these chats and the chance to become acquainted with one of my friends even on a limited level.

'I'm so happy that you have a good friend staying with you,' she often says. 'I hate the thought of you living with virtual strangers, or, even worse, on your own.'

I know exactly where she's coming from. I hate the thought of her being on her own too, rattling around a house that was once home to a family of five. I'm really glad that she has Tony in her life, and that he stays over some nights and absorbs some of the empty space in the house. One day I will tell her this.

'And how are things with you, Mum?' I ask now, setting down my coffee mug and directing all of my concentration, and love, down the line.

'Caitlin!' Jarrod calls from the doorway of his office. He stays long enough to ascertain that his summons has been heard before disappearing back inside.

Zoe sighs perplexedly as she stares in the direction of his office. 'Such a beautiful morning! The sun is shining. Birds are singing. And Jarrod, he is unaware.' Zoe's positivity is always at its height on Monday mornings after a weekend of candle-lighting, meditation and aura alignments.

'Can't hear any birds in here.' I grin, getting up from my seat.

Jarrod is back behind his desk. 'Close the door, please, Caitlin.'

Being asked to close the door isn't unusual; Jarrod likes to have his conversations in private. But there's something different about his tone: it doesn't have its usual stern edge.

'Sit.'

I suddenly feel sick to my stomach. He isn't going to fire me, is he? Sitting, I stare at him. He shifts his eyes away.

'Caitlin, the thing with Telelink –'

'I'm sorry, Jarrod. It won't happen again, I promise. And you were right, I need to learn when to stop, where to draw the line –'

'Caitlin!' He cuts across my babbling. 'Look, taking the

account off you has been hard, on you and on me, and I'm realising that maybe I was too hasty . . .'

I swallow the lump of fear in my throat. 'You are?'

'I can't handle the day-to-day account, I was naive about the sheer volume and so I'm going to hand it back to you.'

'Okay.' I nod, too relieved to be smug. 'What about the proposal?'

'I still believe it's for the best that I'm the main interface on the new deal.'

I nod again. The proposal is the butter icing, the day-to-day orders the rather bland cake beneath. Still, at least I'm back in.

'Thanks, Jarrod. I'm sorry again about what happened.' I stand up to leave but the expression on his face tells me that he isn't quite finished.

'All week I've fielded questions from the Telelink people about you. "Where's Caitlin? Why isn't Caitlin taking our orders? Caitlin knows about this . . ." I got a strong sense of the various relationships you've built, Caitlin. Not everyone has that ability to reach people on all levels of an organisation. It's one of your strengths.'

Praise. From Jarrod. A rare thing. I acknowledge it with a modest smile and leave his office feeling anchored. Jarrod needs me. That's good, because I need this job. More than he could ever know.

Before returning to my desk, I take a detour via the training rooms where I find Nicola reading the riot act to one of the technicians.

'Change it!' she orders, using her foot to point to the tangle of cables on the floor.

The technician, a boy who looks too young to be in the work-force, drops mutely to his knees, his blunt fingers unpicking the cables.

'What's wrong?' I ask Nicola as we walk towards the break-out area.

'He used a blue cable!' She throws up her hands in a gesture that reveals her Greek roots. 'Our protocol is white. Bloody colour blind!' Nicola is a perfectionist. One blue cable in a roomful of white ones is enough to make her want to strangle the guilty technician with the offending cable.

At the kitchen bar, I take two rainbow-coloured coffee mugs down from the shelf. 'Now, tell me *all* about Friday night.'

She instantly looks coy. 'What about Friday night?'

I press the hot-water dispenser and fill the first of the mugs. 'What happened with Mr Slick?'

'Don't call him that!' Nicola gives me a little push in protest. Then, realising she could have scalded me, she claps her hand over her mouth. 'Sorry.'

'Feeling a little tense, are we?' I can't resist teasing her further. 'Waiting for a certain someone to call, perhaps?'

She shrugs.

I finish filling the second mug and add coffee and milk before leading the way to an empty sofa seat. 'Well?' I prompt again when Nicola doesn't volunteer information of her own accord.

'Well, what?'

'God! This is like drawing blood from a stone.'

'We left the pub shortly after you . . . Went for a walk . . . talked.'

'Talked?'

'Actually, yes.'

'And?'

'As a matter of fact, he called yesterday. We met in St Kilda and went for an ice cream.' She sees me trying to hide a smirk. 'What's so funny?'

'Nothing,' I answer, almost deadpan.

She looks at me suspiciously before deciding to change the subject. 'What did *you* do over the weekend?'

'Nothing much at all.'

'You should have called me!'

'To be honest, I was still suffering the effects of Friday night,' I raise my coffee mug to take a small sip, 'and I wasn't up to another big night out on Saturday. I did manage a bike ride yesterday, all the way from St Kilda to Brighton. Now I wish I'd thought to stop off for an *ice cream* on the way back!'

Nicola stands up, her face darkening with temper. 'Oh, I'm sorry that I told you *anything*!' She stomps away, which is easier said than done in stilettos. I hope, for the technician's sake, that the blue cable has been removed and put somewhere safely out of sight.

Returning to my desk, I have a quick chat with Zoe before getting down to work. An hour later, my inbox is clear and my admin completely up to date. The rest of the day stretches in front of me, peppered with small, unsatisfying tasks. Thank God Jarrod has come round. The operational orders, once they're filtered my way again, will bolster my workload and sense of purpose. I'd go out of my mind if I had to put down another week like the last one.

My phone rings and I pick it up eagerly.

'Caitlin, this is Tanya McManus.'

'Hello, Tanya.' I envisage Tanya in my mind, her wide torso behind a fragile-by-comparison desk, her pouting mouth emitting breathy sentences down the phone.

'I need to *meet* you to discuss some *changes* at Chambers.'

'What changes?'

'I'd rather not say over the phone,' Tanya replies in a hushed voice.

'Let's meet for lunch,' I say, stifling a sigh. Tanya loves to be taken out for a meal and is much more amenable on a full stomach. Sitting on the other side of the table from her is not a pleasant experience, though, as she consumes voluminous quantities of food; it makes me feel a little queasy. 'Can you do today?'

'No, it will have to be next week. There's too much going on at the moment.'

We agree on a time and place and hang up. I turn from the phone to the window, where the sunny start to the day has been obliterated by multiplying clouds and a wind that swishes the hair and clothes of those walking along the pavement. Clients like Chambers and the Roads and Transport Board are steady accounts; business trickles in all year round with no major surges or fall-offs. 'Changes' are something to be nervous about.

The tram rattles along under the grey-black sky, doing its best to get people home before the clouds fulfil their threat. I get off at my usual stop and, ignoring the droplets of rain in the wind, walk towards the bay instead of heading home. When it comes into view, the water is grey and swollen, just like Belfast Harbour. Needing to get closer, I walk to the tide line, and sit down on the last of the soft sand, my legs pulled up and crossed at the ankles. The wind roars in my ears and homesickness washes over me with the same ferocity. Days like this – the heavy grey sky, the cruel wind – fill me with yearning. To see Mum, divorced, recovered, a new man in her life. To see Maeve, books under her arm, preoccupied with the next assignment. To see Liam. God, what I wouldn't give to see my brother! I scoop up some sand and watch it trickle between my fingers. What would Liam make of Melbourne? The city, the buzz, the way of life. The diverse ethnic influences, the vast sporting facilities, the opportunities every which way one turns.

Sorry, Liam. Sorry, sorry, sorry.

I have the money to go home. I wouldn't have to stay long, a flying visit, just enough to satiate the yearning and fill the pit of loneliness inside of me. But the problem about going back is that I'd see my father, too. I can picture Mum producing him with a flourish and standing back, expecting a heart-tugging reunion. She simply refuses to accept how much I despise him.

The sand has disappeared through my fingers, leaving a fine layer of grit on my skin, and I wipe my hands against each other to get rid of the residue. In fairness, Mum never puts pressure on me to go home: she hasn't once asked me to, even though I've not been back, not once in ten years. As far as she's concerned, I'm safer in Australia. She has no desire for her family to walk the streets of Clonmegan; she hardly goes into town herself. Apparently she's not alone in that respect: many of the locals have a deep-rooted fear of their own town.

The drops of rain are heavier now, though still sporadic. From the depths of my handbag, my phone begins to ring. I should go, make a run for it before the rain starts in earnest. But I'm lonely, so achingly lonely that I need to hear a voice.

'Hello?' The wind is whistling around me and I have to press the phone firmly against my ear to block it out.

'Caitlin, it's Matthew. Can you hear me?'

'Just about,' I breathe, immediately feeling less desolate. Another gust of wind fills the pause that stretches down the line.

'I was wondering if you'd like to have dinner on Friday night?'

'Yes, I'd like that,' I hear myself answer.

Rain pelts down, suddenly ferocious, and I hurriedly get to my feet and run for shelter, the phone still to my ear. 'It's pouring.' For some strange reason I'm laughing, in total contrast to the despair I felt only moments ago. 'I'm getting *soaked*.'

He laughs too. 'Are you in the city?'

'No, on the beachfront.' I find shelter under the eaves of a nearby building. The beach and surrounds have cleared within seconds and many people are in the same position as me, standing under shelter and peering at the black sky for clues as to when the deluge will ease.

'Hello? Are you still there?' Matthew asks on the other end of the phone.

'Yes, still here. God, that certainly woke me up!'

He laughs again and then he mentions a restaurant on Acland Street, a place I've walked past countless times but never gone into.

'Yes, I know the one.' I nod, gazing at the rain angling in from the bay and bouncing off the promenade.

'Is eight okay?'

'Yes, fine. I'll see you then, Matthew. Bye.'

After a few minutes it becomes apparent that the rain is in for the long haul, there's no waiting it out. I put my head down and make a dash for it. The rain lashes against my shoulders and arms, cold and unforgiving, indeed very like the rain in Ireland. Yet for some reason I'm smiling as I run towards home.

Chapter 16

Summer seems to have died a sudden death. I surge forward against the wind and rain, holding my umbrella close. The restaurant is a mere ten-minute walk but the wind resistance is turning it into much more. The umbrella inverts as the erratic wind changes direction once again; I swear and turn to catch a fresh gust to pop it back into place. When it's right side up, I fold it down and jog the remaining distance, rain cascading on my bare head.

The restaurant's outdoor area is shielded from the elements by thick plastic sheeting and indoor gas heaters. I smooth the rain from my hair and scan the half-empty tables. Matthew, sitting on the far side, raises his hand to catch my eye. My stomach does a little turn. Ever since I agreed to this date I've been contemplating pulling out, telling myself that I was lonely when he phoned, not thinking straight, and it was impossible to say no. I've already decided I won't see him again after tonight.

'I'm joining that table over there,' I say to the maître d' when he sails my way.

He nods imperiously and holds out his arm. 'I'll take your jacket and put it somewhere to dry.'

I slip off the jacket. Underneath I'm wearing a plain black top and navy-blue jeans, knee-high boots keeping my calves warm and snug, protecting them from the wet denim.

Matthew stands up from his seat as I approach. His smile is unmistakably self-conscious, and again I find his shyness endearing if somewhat perplexing. How can he present so differently at times? Then again, I realise, if he were to see *me* at work, he might be equally confused, finding it difficult to equate the reckless girl from the motorbike accident with the composed professional at her desk, typing decisively and talking business jargon on the phone.

'Hello, Caitlin.'

'Hello.'

He's wearing a casual shirt and jeans, similar to the last time I saw him, which suggests that his wardrobe is basic and unfussy. This, too, I find quite appealing. I see suits and ties and sharp dressers in the office every day, and hordes of ultra-trendy surfy types at the weekends. Matthew falls into neither category.

He grins. 'You got caught in the rain again?'

I smile in return. 'Whatever happened to the summer?'

He waits until I'm seated before sitting down again himself. 'Would you like something to drink?'

'Yes, definitely! Vodka and Diet Coke, please.'

As he relays my order to the waiter, I hear him emphasise the 'Diet'. Matthew Blake knows how to listen.

'How was your week?' he asks when the waiter has gone.

'It was quiet. I much prefer when it's busy. How about you? How was work?'

'Okay. Quiet too.'

I cock my head to one side as though I don't quite believe him. 'No fights? No drinks poured over your head?'

He smiles the slow smile I'm beginning to recognise, the one that shows the small gap between his front teeth and makes his eyes sparkle. 'Not this week.'

The waiter returns and sets down my drink on the white tablecloth. I pick it up. 'Well, if it would make your week complete, I could always do the honours with this . . .'

He laughs. 'No, it's okay, really. Better that you drink it.'

I raise the glass to my lips and sip from the mix of fizz and ice. 'Yes, better in me than on your head! While we're on the subject, what's the worst injury you've had on the job?'

He spaces his fingers out on the table. 'I've broken a few of these.' The crooked knuckles seem to fit his large hands. 'I've dislocated my shoulder more than once. And cuts, bruises and verbal abuse are par for the course.'

I lift one eyebrow. 'No bullets?'

'Sorry to be boring.'

A waiter, different from the first one, positions himself next to us. 'Ready to order?'

Matthew looks at me. I nod and he waits for me to order first. His manners are impeccable; not that I haven't dated well-mannered men, but Matthew is different, almost old-fashioned.

'I'll have the Thai beef salad, please,' I say, glancing up at the waiter.

'Anything to start?'

'No thanks.'

Matthew takes his cue from me and doesn't order a starter. The waiter removes the redundant cutlery and departs in the direction of the kitchen.

'Where were we?' asks Matthew.

'Talking about work safety, or lack of.' I smile.

'How about you? Any hazards where you work?'

I tell him about the food embezzlement on the training floor, Jarrod's dangerous lack of humour and some of my clients' bull-dozing behaviour (I'm thinking specifically of Tanya McManus, though of course I don't name her).

He laughs again. I'm trying to stay detached because of my decision not to see him again, but he's making it hard. His laughter is warm and inclusive, his smiles frequent and uncomplicated, like invisible cords drawing me closer.

'Do you like your job?'

'Yes,' I reply, because I do. I like figuring out what my clients need and then delivering beyond their expectations. I even get a kick out of trying to please difficult clients like Tanya. Matthew asks more questions and I find myself expanding on what my job entails. Now I not only like the way he laughs and smiles, I also like that he seems genuinely interested in what I do. My job is a big part of who I am – sometimes I think it's the only worthwhile thing about me – and I've never been on a date where I've felt free to talk about it this much. It's as though Matthew knows what's at the heart of me.

Our food arrives. Matthew, I notice, eats nicely, his mouth shut, seeming to enjoy the food but not shovelling it in at a rate of knots like some men.

'So, are all the family back in Ireland?' he asks between bites.
'Yes.'

'Brothers and sisters?'

'One of each,' I respond shortly.

For the first time since I sat down, there's silence. It sits awkwardly between us, testament that we don't know each other and that some things are out of bounds.

'How about you?' I ask after a while. 'Do you have any family close by?'

'My sister lives here in Melbourne, in Carlton, with my nephew, who's four going on forty! The rest of the family – my parents and two brothers – are in Deniliquin. Mum and Dad have a farm about twenty kilometres outside the town.'

'What kind of farm?'

'Bit of everything. Livestock, dairying, a few crops . . .'

'So you're a country boy through and through!' It fits with what I know of him so far. The nice manners, the shyness, the rough and tumble of his job.

The waiter comes to take our empty plates and tempt us with dessert. I decline and so does Matthew, but we order coffee and talk more about the farm and his family and then, somehow, it's nearly eleven and the staff are starting to close up for the night.

Standing under the canopy outside the restaurant, we survey the rain as it pings off the pavement and the road beyond.

'Where do you live?' he asks.

'Ten minutes' walk . . . Far enough to get soaked through, but I don't fancy my chances with a taxi.' The road is empty of all kinds of traffic, not to mention taxis.

'Excuse me a minute . . .' He takes his mobile from his pocket and uses his large but surprisingly nimble thumb to press the keys. 'Hey, Karen, it's me.' His voice is quiet and distinct. 'Any cars close to Acland? Yeah, would appreciate a lift.'

I gape at him. 'Please don't tell me that our taxi is a police car!'

He grins. 'Desperate times . . .'

I grin back. This is a surprising end to what has been a surprising night. 'Let's just hope I don't meet anyone I know!'

The car pulls up a few minutes later. Matthew takes my hand and we run through the rain, diving for cover into the back seat.

The driver shoots a friendly grin over his shoulder. 'Hey, Sarge. Where to?'

Matthew looks at me.

'Dalgety Street,' I supply.

Matthew and the driver, whose name is Will, talk easily as the car splashes through the saturated streets.

'Quiet night?'

'Yeah, Sarge. Hooligans don't like the wet weather!' Though they're clearly on friendly terms, I can hear respect in Will's voice.

'Who's back at base?'

'Annie and Max. Jamie and Tom are at a domestic on Lock Street, and Caroline and Dan are at a minor car accident on the intersection of Princes and Fitzroy.'

Will parks outside my apartment block. I pull my jacket tighter, hitch my bag over my shoulder and thank him for being my stand-in taxi.

'I'll walk you in.' Matthew swings the door open. 'Won't be long,' he adds to Will.

Once more we dash through the rain, and we're both slightly out of breath by the time we reach the shelter outside the main door of the building.

'Well, goodnight,' I say awkwardly.

'Goodnight, Caitlin.'

He lingers. A few seconds pass, measured by the beat of the rain against the perspex of the shelter.

'I'm working nights for the next couple of days,' Matthew says finally. 'I'll call you as soon as I know the roster for next week.'

'Okay.'

His hand, wet and cold, trails along the line of my jaw. It's a tentative gesture, profoundly tender, and it suffuses me with warmth. He leans down, and just as I'm wondering if he's about to kiss me, I feel his lips brushing my forehead.

'I'd better go,' I hear him say.

'Okay.' I'm too disorientated to expand my vocabulary.

Then he's gone, head hunched, darting through the deluge. The car door slams shut and the tail-lights disappear down the street.

Inside, the apartment is silent, hollow, aching for Jeanie's return. I carry out my bedtime routine, removing makeup and moisturising, brushing my teeth, all the while trying to ignore the butterflies dancing in my stomach. When I'm clean and scrubbed, I pause in front of the mirror and look critically at my face. A flush spreads across my cheekbones and my eyes are brighter than usual. When Matthew touched me I felt a tingle, an undeniable feeling of attraction. Would he have kissed me properly, on the mouth, if Will wasn't waiting in the car? My face goes a shade redder at the thought. I stare harder at the mirror, my eyes narrowing with familiar self-hatred. What does Matthew see in me anyway? Wouldn't he prefer dark skin and eyes? A girl with more curves, who isn't so skinny, who doesn't have so many defects, so many imperfections that no amount of gym workouts or makeup or trendy clothes can fix. I shake my head to dispel the negative thoughts. Though I can identify the self-hatred as it happens and try to hold it in check, I can't seem to stop it from coming to the surface in the first place and tainting everything, just like now.

I turn out all the lights and climb into bed. Rain drums against the guttering outside and I snuggle into the bedclothes. My stomach continues to dance, though, not at all ready to settle down. Matthew. Matthew Blake. Sergeant Matthew Blake. Why is he single? Don't women find doctors and policemen fatally attractive? Shouldn't he have a beautiful wife or girlfriend in the wings? Is there a reason he doesn't, some annoying personality trait that will eventually be revealed? Is Matthew Blake a little too good to be true?

The big question, however, is whether he will call. The answer: of course. Matthew Blake doesn't say anything he doesn't mean – I know this instinctively. And when he calls I'll have to find a polite way of turning him down. Aside from how indisputably attractive he is, he's interesting, polite and very easy to talk to. He'd make a good friend, but he's not boyfriend material. When it comes down to it, Matthew Blake is of the same ilk as my father: the police officer and the ethics professor, both driven by very definite notions of right and wrong, delusions of safety and a dogged overriding belief in justice. I left all that propaganda behind me in Ireland. The last thing I need is to start it all over again.

Chapter 17

At the sales meeting Jarrod brims with Monday morning purpose. I sit up straighter in my seat, trying to convey that I'm also feeling purposeful; in reality, I'm still in weekend mode.

'Good morning, all.' Jarrod's greeting comes out sounding like a reprimand. I sit even straighter. 'Let's shake up the order this morning. Zoe, you can go first.'

On hearing her name, Zoe shuffles her papers and softly clears her throat. 'Good morning,' she begins, her voice gentle and floaty and infinitely more pleasant than Jarrod's. 'This week is going to be a busy one for me. I have a number of client meetings and I'm quietly confident that I can move them all to a better place . . .'

Zoe is still getting to know her clients and she clearly enjoys this stage: finding out what they need, building trust and respect.

'I have a wonderful surprise for my clients this week. I've booked a three-minute angel.'

'A *what*?' Jarrod splutters.

'A three-minute angel.' She smiles beguilingly. 'The angel massages the neck and shoulders for three minutes, easing tension and stress from the muscles.'

Zoe's sales tactics are far too intangible for Jarrod's liking. For someone who's supposed to be so in tune with auras, she seems quite oblivious to the scepticism written on his face.

'After the lovely massage, my clients will be much more receptive and malleable when I speak to them about their training needs.'

Jarrod's expression remains thoroughly unconvinced.

The other sales reps, Gary, Chris and Nathan, follow Zoe in turn, flat and unsmiling. In fact, they're so interchangeable that if I close my eyes, which I'm very tempted to do, it would be hard to tell which one of my male colleagues is speaking. My thoughts drift back to Friday night, the feeling of Matthew's cold, wet hand on my face and his lips as they brushed my forehead, such small gestures that seem to have become oddly enhanced by the fact I can't stop thinking of them. Matthew phoned me on Saturday, and on Sunday too. Though our conversations disclosed nothing significant, I can't seem to stop thinking of them either.

'What are your plans for today?' he'd asked.

'Nothing much. Some chores. Might go for a ride on my bike – if the rain stops. How about you?'

'Just getting ready for an eight-hour shift,' he replied wryly. 'Very antisocial, I'm afraid.'

I pictured him in his uniform, the tan of his skin against the fresh blue fabric, the complementing shimmer of his eyes, and felt an instant wave of something that could very well have been lust.

'Do you have to work many weekends?'

'A fair share of them.'

'Do you mind?'

'I guess I'm used to it.'

And so though nothing monumental was revealed, I gained snippets, mainly about his work and how committed he is to it. This should turn me off him, because again it has echoes of my father, but it doesn't. He's wrong for me, I know this for a fact – it's just that whenever I hear his voice or as much as think of those eyes, I instantly seem to forget it. The only saving grace is that he doesn't have his roster worked out yet and so he hasn't asked me on another date and I haven't had to turn him down.

Nathan is talking now; like the others he seems to revel in reporting tedious details the rest of us have no real need to know about. I would much rather be at my desk doing something semi-constructive than sitting here listening to him droning on about the technical, cash-flow and location challenges of a deal that, now I've listened properly, doesn't seem worth pursuing. I contain my boredom with an inward sigh – or maybe not so inward, because Zoe blinks in my direction.

I'm last to speak and Jarrod is glancing at the clock, which suits me: I don't have a lot to say. Unfortunately my sales pipeline sums up to very little, and I don't want to mention my concerns about Chambers until I know the facts.

'I've got some leads to follow up on,' I finish my status report with false brightness, 'so hopefully I'll have something more exciting to talk about at the next meeting!'

I glance at Jarrod, who looks even more cynical than when Zoe described her three-minute angels.

With a flick of his hand, the waiter whisks the napkin from the table to my lap. He repeats the exercise with Tanya, who is wearing a low-cut top revealing an expanse of cleavage that seems quite inappropriate for a respectable restaurant in the middle of the day. The waiter's gaze becomes momentarily lost in her bosom before he averts his eyes and stares steadfastly at me. 'Drinks, madam?'

'Water for me, please. Tanya?'

'I think some wine . . . Red, to go with the *sudden* change of season . . . Something warm and full-bodied . . .' She winks flirtatiously at the waiter. 'I'll let *you* choose for me.'

His face reddens. 'A selection of bread to start?' he squeaks.

Tanya nods emphatically. 'Yes.'

He leaves, with visible relief, to dispatch the order, his steps short and tight.

Tanya presses her heavily ringed fingers against her mouth as she clears her throat. 'Pity all the good-looking ones are gay,' she says chirpily. 'Still, no harm trying, is there?'

I smile, nod and refrain from commenting.

Tanya doesn't waste any further time on preliminaries. 'Well, Caitlin, Chambers has just finalised *budgets* and the year ahead is tough, very tough. The global credit squeeze is hurting us, as it is all other financial institutions.'

Tanya becomes distracted by the arrival of the bread basket, set on the table by the waiter who is gone before we can thank him. She helps herself to a slice, layers it thickly with butter, and demolishes it in two large bites. Some crumbs land unnoticed in her cleavage. She reaches for another slice, this time speaking as she butters. 'As usual in hard times like this, learning and development is impacted the most. Our budget has been *slashed* by thirty per cent.' She pops the bread in her mouth, chewing vigorously. 'I'm sorry to say that I will have to make a few people in my department redundant, and that our training program will be cut back to bare bones. I feel it's only fair to alert you in advance that our use of your training facilities will drop *significantly*.' She eyes the bread basket again. 'Aren't you having any?'

I put on my auto-smile. 'No. But you go ahead.'

Tanya doesn't need to be told twice. I ponder the situation while she polishes off the remainder of the bread. It's quite depressing, really. I have no other prospects on the horizon to make up for this significant drop in business. 'When do you expect the changes to take effect?'

She swallows a mouthful. 'Within the next two weeks.'

The main course arrives. I pick at the food while Tanya stuffs in as much as she possibly can. Before she devours dessert, she has another crack at flirting with the waiter. It's mortifying to watch.

I get back to work late in the afternoon. Jarrod's in his office, talking on the phone. I hang by his door until he's free.

He nods as he puts down the phone, beckoning me to enter. 'What's up?'

'I just had lunch with Tanya. She announced that she'll be reverting to minimum contract levels.'

'When?'

'In the next few weeks.'

Jarrod takes the news in silence, his hand cupping the lower half of his face.

'The thing that worries me is that it's not just Chambers,' I continue. 'Business is quiet, *really* quiet. I think the GFC is finally heading our way.'

When Jarrod speaks, his words are measured and I realise he's been aware of the situation for a while. 'Yes, things are quiet. The Australian market is definitely slowing but everyone is still at denial stage. It won't be long before we can no longer ignore the obvious and there'll be a rush of drastic cutbacks, probably more than is really needed.'

'So what do we do?'

'We look harder for business,' he replies pragmatically. 'It's not going to come to us – we have to seek it out, intelligently and strategically. And obviously we'll have to cut back our costs too.'

Jarrod has a master's degree in economics. His certificate is framed on the wall and I often find myself looking at it when I can't quite face looking at him. Its gilt frame and embossed cursive print reminds me of my own unfinished degree. When I can't bear to look at it any longer, I'm ready to turn my eyes back to him.

We talk a little further on Chambers and what we can do to minimise the impact, but he doesn't mention his cost-cutting plans again. Will he, like Tanya, have to make some people redundant? It doesn't bear thinking about.

Maeve phones on Wednesday night. I haven't spoken to my sister for a few months. Usually we're better at keeping in contact, every few weeks emailing or ringing, more the former than the latter.

'Sorry I haven't been in touch,' she begins.

'I'm sorry, too.'

'I've been busy with the PhD – trying to get everything in before the deadline.'

'Well, you're nearly there now. How does it feel to be on the last stretch?'

'Exhausting!'

The pause that follows is long, even for us.

'Is something wrong?' I ask, suddenly anxious.

'Nothing's wrong,' she replies quickly. 'I was just ringing to thank you for the necklace.'

'Of course. The necklace. I'd forgotten.'

'Sorry, I didn't mean to give you a fright.'

'Don't be sorry. I'd just forgotten about it, that's all. Do you like it?'

'I love it. I'm wearing it now. It was very thoughtful of you.'

I smile into the phone, glad that I made the effort to send the gift. 'It's my pleasure. I'm thrilled that you like it.'

There's another pause. When we speak on the phone it's always like this: full of awkward pauses, long gaps laden with thoughts and memories. Sometimes it's the same with Mum, but not as often. Over the years Mum and I have learned how to keep the conversation going, how to disregard what we're really thinking and maintain our dialogue on a different level. But Maeve and I don't talk frequently enough to have developed such a technique. The pauses are gaping, so big that sometimes I feel as though I could go hurtling through them.

'So, the PhD is almost done . . .' I revert to where the conversation began.

'Yes. Just another two months now.'

'And what then?'

'Well, actually, I'm considering law.' Maeve's voice trails away.

'*Law?*' Incredulity sharpens my tone.

'Yes. I've always been interested in it.'

'So why, exactly, have you spent the last four years doing a PhD in modern history?'

'I'm allowed to be interested in more than one thing, aren't I?' Her tone is light but I can hear the defensiveness underneath.

'Yes, but you don't have to do a degree on every single subject that takes your fancy!'

'You make it sound like I'm collecting degrees,' she cries.

'Are you?' I can't help but ask.

'Of course I'm not.'

'Don't you think that this is a good point in your life to look for a job?'

Maeve responds with a blatant change of subject. 'How about you? How are things at *your* work?'

I hesitate. I want to pin Maeve down, tell her that she needs to get out into the workforce and stop hiding behind academia. But it's a hard conversation to conduct over the phone. Face to face would be easier, less harsh and less likely to come across as criticism. I don't want to be judgmental – that would make me no better than my father – but at the same time I'm not sure I can stand back and watch Maeve become so overqualified that she's virtually unemployable.

Maybe I can ask Mum to talk to her? Mum would handle it

more gently than me. She'd sit Maeve down and quietly remind her how soul-destroying it was for Liam when he couldn't get a job, and point out that Maeve wouldn't want the same thing to happen to her. Yes, that's a better way to go about it. I've said enough for now. I'll ask Mum to take it from here.

'My work's just same old, same old,' I say, feeling slightly embarrassed at how non-committal I sound.

My client's making people redundant and I'm worried that Jarrod might be too, I could have replied. It would have been a more truthful response, and might even have eased the niggling feeling I've had since Monday. But such a response would necessitate an explanation of who Tanya and Jarrod are. I would have to provide details, descriptions, history. Maeve knows next to nothing about my job and what I do all day, and it seems like a mammoth task to bring her up to date.

'Anything else going on? Any man on the scene?' Maeve asks.

'No.' Matthew isn't exactly on the scene. Yes, he called again yesterday and sent a few text messages but that's hardly significant enough to tell my sister. 'How about you?'

'Nothing serious . . . How's the weather there? Beautiful?'

'Not quite! It's been raining solidly for more than a week now.'

'Sounds just like here.'

The conversation is at its end. We've both kept our distance. Nothing worthwhile has been shared, other than Maeve's crazy notion of doing law.

'I wish you'd call Dad,' she says suddenly.

I don't answer.

'He'd love to hear from you.'

This is why emails work better: the messages are warm and chatty without any agonising pauses or last-minute pleas on my father's behalf.

'Well, thanks for calling,' I say, feeling like I've failed but at a loss as to how I could have managed the conversation differently.

'And thanks again for the necklace,' Maeve replies softly and hangs up.

Though it's early, not yet nine o'clock, I start to get ready for bed. In the bathroom mirror I examine my not-pretty-enough face. Then I turn to the left to reveal the angry flesh on my arm and hip. The GP said I'd be left with some minor scarring. Is this what life is about? A collection of scars? Fresh shiny scars alongside aged dull ones, new scars layered over old ones in particularly painful spots. Never knowing if the blemish will eventually disappear, or if it's there for keeps.

I walk around the apartment, turning off the lights and checking the doors. Jeanie's in Asia, first China then onto India and Singapore, the trip ending with a quick stop in Sydney to see her family. She's not due back in Melbourne for at least another week.

Satisfied that everything's secure, I climb into bed. Sleep quickly overcomes me. My dreams are absurd. Maeve's in Australia, in St Kilda, wearing her school uniform and her hair in pigtails as she drinks beer in the Elephant.

'You need to grow up!' I tell her firmly.

Maeve looks put out. 'I *am* grown up,' she declares, twirling a pigtail around her finger. 'Anyway, what have you got against me doing law?'

Matthew walks in before I can answer and all I can think

about is how to avoid introducing him to Maeve and, as a direct consequence, my past. At the last moment, just before he sees me, he becomes embroiled in a brawl. Suddenly he's rolling on the ground, knocking over tables of drinks and smashing stools. I wonder idly if he'll lose his hat again. Maeve watches the fight for a few moments before turning back to me, her eyes glassy and unfocused, and asking once again what I have against law. I'm torn between a long-overdue intervention in her life and a fear for Matthew who is still rolling on the ground, and who I now know isn't as tough as his size would suggest.

The dream ends without me telling Maeve that it isn't law in itself that I have a problem with, more that she seems to be frozen at a certain stage in time, unable to mature past the schoolgirl she was when the bomb shattered all our lives.

Chapter 18

The rain hangs around for the rest of the week, the trams overcrowded and running behind time. The city is drenched, footpaths splotched with enormous puddles, water rushing down gutters, disappearing into roaring drains. I'm wearing a trench coat with a wide belt tied tightly at my waist. Rain lashes the hand I'm using to hold the umbrella, trickling inside my sleeve, leaving a cold, shivery trail along the skin on the underside of my arm, rather like the effect of an unpleasant memory.

'Your aura is different today,' Zoe greets me.

'Even wetter than yesterday?' I suggest wryly, removing my sodden coat and hanging it on the coat stand in the corner.

'Auras don't get wet, silly.' She tilts her head as she looks me up and down. 'No, it has a tinge of anticipation, I would say.'

I feel a blush spreading across my face. I'm annoyed at both my transparency to Zoe and the ridiculous fluttering that's been going on in my stomach since Matthew texted late last night.

Roster sorted out at last. Are you free on Sunday? Sorry for texting so late. Hope I didn't wake you up. Will call tomorrow.

He did, in fact, wake me up, and I felt a strange sense of fulfilment as I read his message, as though something that had been missing from my day had finally happened and thus made it complete. I seem to have very quickly got to a stage where I need to hear from him, in some way or another, every day of the week. This excites and worries me in equal measure.

'Enough about auras!' I say to Zoe in a mock businesslike tone. 'Don't you have any work to do?'

She lowers her voice. 'Just between you and me, I don't have that much work at all. I'm trying hard but nobody's biting.'

Zoe's phone rings and she answers it, her confession left out there unanalysed. It combines with what Tanya and Jarrod intimated about the economy and leaves me with a sudden feeling of panic about Zoe's job and my own.

I open my inbox and deal with what's new. I type one-line replies, accept meeting invitations and process some minor orders. As I'm working, an email comes through from Jarrod: *US market fallen by another five points overnight. Financial sector impacted the most.*

I stop what I'm doing and log onto the internet where I find a more comprehensive account of this latest hit to the US market. I read that America is getting deeper and deeper into recession, that every day more jobs are being lost and more companies are folding. The banks were giving credit too cheaply and easily and now they're flailing, hands raised, begging to be rescued, to be bought out.

I stare at the article, mulling over its key points: recession, panic, cutbacks, *takeovers and acquisitions*. For every company that's bought out, there's the company taking it over, and for every takeover there are training requirements, as the acquiring company seeks to integrate the acquisition into their 'superior' way of doing things.

My mobile rings mid-morning and my heartrate increases when I see Matthew's name on the caller ID.

'Hi, Caitlin.' His voice is becoming familiar to me: quiet, polite, a little shy but still commanding in its own way. An image of his face swims into my mind, the glitter of his eyes, the movement of his mouth as he smiles. 'How's your day going?'

'Okayish.'

'Are you busy? Should I call back later?'

That would mean more waiting. 'No – I can have a quick chat now.'

'Great. So, about Sunday . . .'

'Yes, I'm free.' Somewhere along the line, amid all the texts and phone calls and an awful lot of daydreaming about that kiss, of sorts, under the shelter, I seem to have completely abandoned my resolve not to see him again.

We agree to meet at noon outside the Pavilion. Good. It'll be broad daylight; no darkness, alcohol or stormy weather to conjure up false chemistry. This date will surely put an end to the silly butterflies I've had all week.

I spend the rest of the morning on the internet, researching the financial institutions that have been affected in the US and their ties to Australia. Then I look at the local retail and investment banks and mortgage lenders. Despite the turmoil in the overseas markets, the impact in Australia appears to be somewhat contained. But how long can we remain relatively immune? Is this slowdown of recent weeks a warning of worse things to come? And – putting on my sales hat again – who will be the winners and losers if a serious recession befalls this side of the world?

Saturday passes with the usual fare: a half-hearted attempt at cleaning the apartment, shopping for groceries, preceded by the routine wake-up call from my mother.

'Mum, has Maeve said anything to you about doing law?' I ask carefully.

'No. Why?'

'I was talking to her during the week and she mentioned something.'

'It's the first I've heard of it!' Mum is clearly surprised.

'We can't let her start another degree, Mum. Another three or four years of studying – it's ridiculous!'

'Well, I don't know . . .'

'She's twenty-seven and she's never had a proper job.'

'It's not as though she's been idle, Caitlin.' Mum's protective instincts are roused. 'She's been studying, learning . . .'

'And now it's high time for her to stop *learning* and start *doing*. She's already dangerously overqualified. Employers will be daunted by her. And she doesn't have any practical skills. You need to talk to her, to explain this.'

Mum is silent as she processes what I'm saying. I let the silence continue.

'I'll ask your father to talk to her,' she says eventually. 'He knows more than me about being overqualified – if there is such a thing.'

This is not turning out how I planned. 'Dad will only lecture her . . .'

'Maeve listens to your father. They get on quite well.'

I haven't seen them together in years, so I'm unable to refute this. 'Okay,' I say, though it's not okay at all. I'm uneasy leaving this matter in my father's hands. He does not have a good track record in this area.

That evening I meet Nicola for a drink. She's still being rather coy about Mr Slick, whom she insists I call David. I know he phoned during the week and that they've been on another date. Judging by the frequent beeps emitting from her phone, and her smile as she reads the messages, things are progressing nicely.

For my part, I don't mention Matthew at all, but even though we both keep a lot to ourselves, it's still an enjoyable evening. As usual when I'm with Nicola, I end up having more drinks than I should. I get home after midnight, feeling fuzzy around the edges, and fall into bed.

I wake at dawn the next morning, my head woolly and my mouth dry, not quite sure what day of the week it is. Once I establish it's Sunday, I ease back into sleep and don't wake again until ten, feeling much better. My phone rings and I reach out to pick it up from the bedside unit.

'Hi, Caitlin.' It's Matthew.

'Hi,' I reply hesitantly. Is this another last-minute cancellation?

'You sound sleepy.'

'I only woke up a few minutes ago.' Sitting up in the bed I draw my knees in towards my chin. 'I should point out that I'm not usually this lazy.'

He laughs and then, in a more serious tone, adds, 'Hey, I have a little problem with later . . .'

'What?' I ask warily.

'I have my nephew with me today. It wasn't planned, obviously, just one of those things I couldn't avoid. Anyway, if you're not allergic to children, I thought we could still meet. But I perfectly understand if you'd rather give it a miss.'

'He's four, isn't he?' I'm so looking forward to seeing Matthew that he could tell me he had to mind an axe-murderer for the day and I still wouldn't be deterred.

'Yeah, but he acts like he's been around before!'

'What's his name?'

'Ben. He's a good kid. It's completely up to you, though.'

'Let's go ahead.' I smile into the phone. 'We can always abort if it's a disaster.'

Outside the day is sunny; the rain has finally gone, leaving everything looking cleaner and greener in its wake. The crowds around St Kilda are smiling and upbeat, grateful that summer isn't over after all. Matthew and Ben are waiting. Ben is taller than I expected, with tousled brown hair and big, serious eyes.

'What age are you?' he asks by way of greeting.

'Me?' I feel myself go red. A four-year-old is making me blush! 'I'm twenty-nine.'

'Uncle Matt is thirty-one.'

I glance at Matthew, who shrugs sheepishly. He's wearing a soft blue T-shirt, almost the same colour as his jeans. Blue is his colour, I decide. It enhances his eyes, his tan. It's part of the reason why he looks so good in uniform.

'Where's your mum and dad?' Ben looks past me with a puzzled expression on his pale face, as if he can't believe I've been let out on my own.

'In Ireland.'

'Where's that?'

'It's a wee country on the other side of the world.'

His eyes widen. 'And you're here all on your own? Without your mum and dad?'

'Well, yes,' I reply disconcertedly.

'My mum's asleep. She's having a bad day. She –'

Matthew steps in and diverts the conversation, taking Ben's hand. 'What do you think, buddy, time for an ice cream?'

Ben doesn't need to be asked twice. 'Chocolate!'

Matthew shakes his head. 'Nice try but too rich for a young bloke like you. Vanilla or strawberry?'

'Strawberry.'

'Caitlin?' Matthew turns to look at me. 'Ice cream?'

'Chocolate?' I joke.

'It'll make you sick!' he says in mock warning.

'I'll pass, so.'

'Sure?'

'Yes – I don't actually eat ice cream.'

Matthew joins the queue at the kiosk and Ben resumes question time. 'You really don't eat ice cream?'

'No.'

'*Really?*'

I shake my head.

'Why?'

'It's too sugary for me.'

Without missing a beat, he changes tack. 'Where's your house?'

'Not far from here. Actually, it's not a house, it's an apartment.'

'Me and Mum are in an apartment.' His tone is solemn. 'Dad's in another apartment.'

'Oh.'

'Does your dad live somewhere different to your mum?'

'Well, yes, he does.'

He nods wisely. 'Some families are like that, aren't they?'

'Yes. Yes, they are.'

Matthew comes back with two ice creams. I smile to myself as I recall Nic's first date with David, and how huffy she got when I teased her about it. Hopefully the two of them won't get it into their heads to go for an ice cream at the beach today – if Nic met me right now, she'd have a field day in revenge.

'Ben asks lots of questions,' I say *sotto voce* as we stroll towards the beach.

'Yeah, he does. He's had a lot of change in his young life, and questions seem to help him measure things and normalise what he's going through.'

'I've gathered his parents are separated.'

'Yes. It happened a few months ago, but it's still very raw.' We sit on the sand and look out at the water as it shimmers under the sun.

Matthew finishes his ice cream and licks his fingers. 'That was good.'

Ben's still hard at work, so occupied catching drips with his tongue that he seems oblivious to everything else.

Matthew smiles at him indulgently, asking me, 'Do you have any nieces or nephews?'

'No.'

'Do you go back to Ireland often?'

'No,' I say again, feeling the dull ache of homesickness. 'I've not been home at all.' There's a pause. I feel Matthew's eyes on me, waiting for me to elaborate. 'The family situation there is a bit fractured. My father, well, he . . . he had an affair.'

Even as I say it, I'm stunned. I have no idea what made me blurt this out; it's something I try not to think of, let alone talk about.

Matthew's still looking at me, waiting for me to carry on, and for some reason I do. 'Mum and Dad were having a break at the time, trying to work out their priorities, and he went and had an affair . . . Of course there was no fixing anything after that.'

The affair destroyed our family. The hardest thing for me to accept was that this atrocity wasn't perpetrated by strangers, like the bomb. The decimation of our family was single-handedly caused by someone I knew and trusted, a hypocrite if ever there was one: my father.

'He had an affair with his *secretary*, how pathetic and unimaginative is that? It didn't last long, just enough to wreck the marriage completely. The divorce was devastating – for all of us.'

Matthew nods, as though he understands some of what I feel. 'Sophie, my sister, is pretty devastated about her marriage break-up, as are the rest of us.' His voice is deliberately low.

Even though Ben is presently preoccupied, Matthew obviously doesn't want to risk him overhearing. 'Her husband had an affair too.'

'Do you still talk to him? Your brother-in-law?'

'Steve? Of course I do. I meet him for a drink every now and then.'

'Really? But what about the impact of his actions on Ben?' My tone, though muted like his, is harsher than I intend. 'How can you forgive that so easily?'

'I don't condone what he did,' Matthew replies, taking a fistful of sand into his large hand and watching it sift through his crooked fingers. 'He's damaged Ben and Sophie – they'll never trust anyone unequivocally again. But he doesn't deserve to be completely ostracised.'

'I don't see it like that. Trust is more important than anything.'

'What's most important is keeping the people you love safe,' Matthew looks up and holds my gaze, 'not hurting them physically, or doing things that put them in danger.'

I wait, expecting him to continue, to put forward arguments to justify his point of view, but he doesn't. In his own quiet way, he's said all that he's going to say.

I smile. 'I think, because of your profession, you see things differently to me – more leniently, which is kind of surprising, really.'

He smiles back. 'Yes, I suppose I do.'

Ben finishes his ice cream and looks up, a big pink circle around his grinning, satisfied mouth. Matthew uses a napkin to clean him up. 'Want to take a walk, mate? Look for some shells?'

'Yes.'

'Stand still a second – I'll take off your sandals.'

As soon as his footwear is removed, Ben makes a beeline for the water, dancing along the edge, leaving small footprints that are quickly removed by the incoming tide. Matthew and I follow him at a more leisurely pace, shoes swinging from our fingers.

'Ouch, it's cold.' I wince when a wave laps over my toes.

'Chicken.' He grins and takes my hand in his.

We walk along, Ben veering in and out of the water ahead of us, lost in his own little world. My hand feels awkward in Matthew's, like an intimacy I'm not quite ready for, a closeness and warmth that don't fit with a mere second date. But I get used to it. Just like I get used to the water, which isn't that cold at all after a while.

That night, in bed, I toss and turn and try to make sense of it. If there's one thing more sanctimonious than an ethics professor, it's a police officer. On that level alone it doesn't make any sense that I'm attracted to Matthew Blake. Throw in his gentle personality, his steadiness, his overall *niceness*, so different to the men I've dated in recent years, and it becomes even harder to understand – not to mention the fact that I've had the most extraordinarily intimate and revealing day despite the presence of his four-year-old nephew!

Unable to figure it out, I punch my pillows and determinedly close my eyes. But Matthew's face is there, his blue eyes looking through me, seeing into my soul. My father's affair obliterated everything I believed in: my parents' marriage; my own already fragile self-worth; not forgetting all the values around which we lived our lives, like honesty, respect for others and keeping promises. Telling Matthew has revived some of the hurt, betrayal and anger. Maybe that's why I can't sleep.

Chapter 19

The training floor seems remarkably calm for a Tuesday morning. I find Nicola at her desk, a place she rarely frequents.

'Hey, Nic. All well at the coalface?'

'You should have been here an hour ago!' She grimaces. 'But the mob is locked away in the rooms now, being trained to death.'

I laugh. 'Got time for a chat?'

'Yeah. What's up?'

I sit on the edge of her desk. 'What bank does David work for again?'

'National. Why?'

'I'm just wondering how they're faring in the financial crisis . . .'

Nicola looks thoughtful. 'I don't know. David doesn't talk much about work.'

'What *does* he talk about?' I can't resist teasing her a little.

'Never you mind.'

'Still keeping her cards close to her chest . . .'

'Stop talking about me in the third person!'

'Where was I?'

'Something about the financial crisis?'

'Oh, yes. Actually, I was wondering if I could talk to David –
sound him out about the industry in general.'

'I'm not his keeper,' Nicola responds tartly. 'You don't have to
ask my permission.'

'Why are you being so touchy?' I say, grinning.

'I'm not *touchy*!' Snatching a post-it pad from her desk, she
writes down some numbers, her handwriting heavy and slanted.
'Here, work and mobile numbers.'

'Thank you.'

I call David as soon as I get back to my desk. Though he sounds
surprised to hear from me, he agrees without too many questions
to meet for a coffee later in the week. I put down the phone
and jump when I realise Jarrod has been listening in. 'Jesus! You
gave me a fright.'

'Sorry,' he replies, not sounding sorry at all. 'Just letting you
know that Derek and another Telelink executive are coming in
at eleven. I want you to keep a low profile while they're here.'

'How low?'

'Go out for a while.'

'Okay, if you think that's necessary.'

'It is.' He turns to walk away. 'At least until I get the order in
the bag,' he offers over his shoulder.

It's *my* order. If anyone should be getting it 'in the bag', it's
me! Smarting, I begin to type, hitting the keys with unnecessary

force, missing some and backspacing to correct the errors. I invested months of groundwork in that deal and now I'm being excluded, being asked to leave the building no less. Anger blurs my vision of the few words I've managed to type. Anger with Jarrod and Derek. And, most of all, with myself.

I sweep mascara along my lashes, leaving a thick black coat, instantly transforming my eyes, making them look bigger, darker, more striking than they really are. Outlining my lips with pencil, I fill them in with cherry-coloured gloss and decide to leave it at that: mascara and lip gloss, jeans and a dark purple cotton top, casual, perfect for a night at the movies and my third date with Matthew.

The phone rings just as I'm leaving. Pausing, I calculate the time difference, and deduce that it's possibly my father, sitting upright behind his office desk, fitting in a phone call to his estranged daughter before his official lectures commence for the day. I close the door behind me and descend the stairs, the ringing becoming fainter and fainter until I can no longer hear it.

Walking along the street outside, I will the calmness of the evening to settle over me, trying not to think about Jarrod and Derek, or about the other matter that's been occupying my thoughts all day: whether Matthew will kiss me tonight. There'll be no obvious reason not to – no colleague waiting in the car, no four-year-old nephew tagging along – and this is making me feel irrationally nervous.

As I approach, I scan the outside of the cinema for his large, distinctive figure. When I don't immediately locate him, I instantly assume the worst: that he's stood me up. Just as my heart begins to plummet and everything about my life feels instantly and overwhelmingly hopeless, he emerges from inside the building and waves to catch my attention.

'What's on?' My nervousness manifests as a show of briskness.

'I was just checking that,' he replies and gives a run-down of the films that are showing. 'What would you like to see?'

I turn the question back on him. 'What would *you* like to see?' Conscious that I sound even more abrupt than before, I tell myself, firmly, to relax.

'I'd like to see something light. I think I need a laugh.'

Looking at him more closely, I see lines of weariness on his face. 'Not a good day?'

'No.'

'What happened?'

'A teenager beaten up for the amusement of other bored teenagers. He's having brain surgery as we speak, to remove a massive clot, and if he survives the operation it's quite likely that he'll be brain damaged.'

My problems with Jarrod and Derek are swiftly put into perspective. 'I'm sorry. That's awful. The poor boy. His poor family.'

I instinctively reach for Matthew's hand, but once I have it in mine it doesn't seem enough and so I hug him instead. We stand there, my cheek pressed against his shoulder, my hands spanning his back as though they're quite used to hugging him like this, the bustle around us distant and irrelevant.

'Do you want to just give the movie a miss?'

'No.' He steps back from me. 'It will take my mind off things.'

And so we go inside and agree on a romantic comedy. Matthew

buys the tickets and I insist on buying drinks, bottled water and the obligatory popcorn.

The movie is surprisingly good – funny, cynical and satisfyingly unpredictable – and when it's over and we're leaving the cinema, I feel like I've been away somewhere for an extended time. Outside the calm evening has transformed into an equally serene night.

'Do you want to go for a drink?' Matthew asks, pausing outside one of the half-empty bars.

I can see from his face that he's exhausted and, while the movie has undoubtedly eased some of the stress from his day, I'm sure he'd rather call it a night. Maybe he won't kiss me after all. Maybe, after such a bad day at work, he'll deposit me outside my apartment and that will be that.

'No, thanks. You're clearly very tired – and I've an early meeting in the morning.'

The meeting is with Jarrod: he wants me to talk him through the pricing models for Telelink. Just thinking about it makes me feel angry all over again and I have to make a conscious effort to put it out of my mind. I'm with Matthew now. Is he going to end this date with a kiss? Or is the timing not quite right this time too?

Matthew holds my hand firmly in his as we leave the main strip behind. The side streets are deserted, it's just the two of us, our footsteps echoing and our voices hushed and intimate as we chat about our favourite films. It isn't long before we reach my apartment block and suddenly the conversation ceases. I know then that he will. Kiss me, that is. He looks as nervous as I feel.

Once again he touches my face with his hand. And again the tenderness of his touch is surprising, totally at odds with the sheer size of his hand, the size of him. He lowers his head and I instinctively tilt mine back. My first impression is that it feels awkward, my neck is strained: he's too tall for me. As though reading my mind, he sits down on the low retaining wall that borders the front garden and manoeuvres me gently onto his lap. His thighs feel solid and muscular beneath me and I experience a strong physical reaction even before my mouth opens under his. It's immediately obvious that Matthew Blake is a good kisser. His lips are at once tentative and firm, edging me towards a state of sweet, sharp arousal. His big hands burrow in my hair, encasing my head, and the kiss deepens further. How long it goes on I'm not sure, but when it finally comes to an end we're both breathing hard.

'I feel like a teenager, pashing in the front garden.' He smiles, his lips still very close to mine.

'In Ireland we would say "snogging" but I know what you mean!' My voice comes out husky and disjointed. I sound as though I've been well and truly kissed, which I have.

My apartment is upstairs, tantalisingly close, and I have to stop myself inviting him up. I don't want to rush things with Matthew. I need to get used to each new stage before I can proceed to the next. I don't know why I feel like this, but it seems to be intuitive.

We start to kiss again and once more it builds to a point where I'm hardly aware that we're sitting in full public view. His hard thighs on which I'm still seated, the warm strength of his arm, supporting my lower back, his mouth pressing, retreating, pressing again are all I'm conscious of until reality intrudes, in the form of someone slamming shut the front door. It takes all my willpower to pull away and disengage myself from his lap.

'I should go . . .' I feel a little wobbly on my feet. 'That meeting in the morning . . .'

He also gets to his feet. 'Yes, I should be going too. I'll call you tomorrow.'

'Okay. Good luck with the boy. I hope he comes through the surgery okay.'

His face clouds over. 'I think the best I can hope for is to catch the kids who did it to him.'

He leans his head down for one last kiss, a stand-up variety, definitely not as good as the sit-down ones, but still very nice all the same, and then says goodnight.

When I get inside, the light on the phone is flashing. I warily press the button, but it isn't my father after all. It's Jeanie, sounding vexed.

'Caitlin, Jeanie here. I've been calling all evening. Why don't you ever answer the bloody phone? Anyway, I've lost my mobile, but wanted to let you know I'll be home on Friday. I'll see you then.'

I'm sorry now that I didn't pick up the phone when it rang before I went out. Poor Jeanie! All those contact details lost with her phone. On the positive side, she'll be back soon. This trip seems to have gone on forever, and a lot has happened since she went away. For one thing, Matthew Blake has happened.

I climb into bed and my thoughts revert to Matthew, which is becoming somewhat of a bedtime habit. My lips curve in an involuntary smile as I relive the feeling of his mouth moving over mine, his hands gathering up my hair, the words and glances and details that made up the evening. His list of attributes is growing steadily: handsome, strong, well-mannered, good with kids, excellent taste in films, brilliant kisser.

If Matthew has a major personality flaw, it has yet to reveal itself. Even his profession, initially a sticking point, seems to matter less and less. He doesn't preach, lay down rules or force his opinions on others; in fact, now that I know him better, I can safely say that he isn't of the same ilk as my father at all.

David is late. Nearly twenty minutes so. Still, when he eventually turns up at the bistro where we arranged to meet, he seems genuinely apologetic.

'Sorry,' he says, scraping out a seat and sitting down. 'I had a meeting that went over.'

'Oh well, at least you're here now.' I smile, pretending not to mind.

He raises his hand, signalling to the waiting staff that he's arrived and expects immediate service. I notice his cufflinks, mini clocks that seem, from my quick glance, to keep the correct time.

'No chance of losing time with those.'

He smiles. 'Unfortunately not!'

The waiter comes promptly. David orders a latte and I ask for a long black. Then David clasps his hands and leans forward in his seat. 'Well, Caitlin, what's this all about?'

'I'm hoping you can help me second guess the effects of the GFC on the Australian financial sector.'

He raises his eyebrows. 'That's a tall order.'

'Isn't that what you guys do every day? Make educated guesses?'

'Usually about other industries, not our own!'

'What's so hard about your own?'

'It's harder to predict. And there's this scary phenomenon called the self-fulfilling prophecy.'

'That's if you say something will happen, the market blindly believes it and involuntarily makes it happen?'

'That's right.'

'Well, just between us, and not for the market's ears,' I slip my notebook across the table, 'I have a list of financial institutions here, and I'm trying to determine who's the strongest, the most likely to acquire – that's assuming there are acquisitions to be made.'

David glances down at the notebook, then back up at me. 'Can I ask why you care?'

I shrug. 'Because acquisitions, at the end of the day, mean training.'

'I see.' He lifts the notebook and studies it closely, then quickly reels off a number of organisations missing from the list. By the time his latte arrives, he's slashing lines across the page, drawing arrows up and down and generally rearranging the list to his satisfaction.

I peer across at his handiwork, trying to read it upside down. 'So you think Chambers is strong?'

'Chambers is rock solid. They'll cut back but they'll never go down.'

'And Net Banc?'

'Net Banc is carnivorous – they like to eat other banks. In times like this, all the smaller institutions will be potential fodder.'

Suddenly David startles, checks his watch and exclaims that he has to be somewhere else. He returns the notebook to me, slips his Cartier pen back into his shirt pocket and drains his latte.

'Thanks,' I say. 'That was really informative.'

'My pleasure.'

He walks away, his dark skin and hair striking against the white of his shirt, his stride that of a man who knows exactly where he's going, albeit a little late. I'm beginning to understand what Nicola finds attractive about him.

Jeanie returns late on Friday. Her keys jangle in the lock, her suitcase lands with a thud on the floor and the door bangs shut behind her.

'Hi, stranger.' I stand up from the sofa where I've been watching TV.

'Hellooooo,' she replies, elongating the word until it descends into a sigh. 'What a week!'

'Did you find your phone?'

'No.' She sighs again and moves away from the doorway and further into the room. 'Didn't think you'd be home.'

'I had a few drinks with Nic after work, but left early to be part of your welcome-home committee.'

'Some committee!'

'Want a drink?'

Jeanie flops down on the couch. 'I think it might be a matter of *need* rather than *want*.'

I go to the fridge and extract a bottle of beer, using the hem of my T-shirt to twist off the lid. 'Here.' I hand it to her. 'Anything else madam would like? Vegemite sandwich? Cheese and crackers? Or perhaps a bar of chocolate?'

Jeanie slugs the beer. 'No, thanks. This is all that's required.'

I return to the kitchen to fix my own drink: the usual vodka and Diet Coke, the only variant being the number of ice cubes. Holding the glass in my hand, I curl up on the sofa across from Jeanie. 'Other than the missing phone, how was the trip?'

'Harder than usual. Complex problem and, worse, complex personalities.' Jeanie takes another long drink, the bottle in her hand already half-empty. 'How about you? Anything new?'

Matthew Blake is new – and complex too, at least in how he makes me feel. 'Nothing much. Only that Nic has a new boyfriend.'

Jeanie raises her eyebrows. 'Her usual type?'

I nod. 'Investment banker, slick from head to toe . . .'

We all have types. Jeanie's is rough and ready, men who talk and laugh in loud voices, a line of dirt under their fingernails evidencing an honest day's work. My type is, or at least was, surfy and irreverent; men who flaunt the sea and any kind of authority. Matthew's nothing like my usual type, but I'm not ready to dissect this deviation and so I continue to talk about David instead.

'He seems okay, though,' I say. 'I met him yesterday for a coffee.'

Jeanie cocks her head. 'You did? Why?'

'I wanted to pick his brains about the economy,' I reply with a shrug. 'Have *you* noticed the slowdown?'

'It's impossible not to notice.' Jeanie rubs her forehead as if struck with a sudden headache. 'When business slows, people look around for reasons: systems, processes, any recent changes to how things are done. That's what made this last job so difficult. The general manager would not accept that the drop in online orders was only partly due to the glitch in the system.' She puts down her empty bottle and stands up, her arms extended above her in a long stretch. 'Geez, I'm whacked. All I want to do is go to bed. I'll move my suitcase in the morning, okay?'

'No worries. 'Night, Jeanie.'

The apartment descends into quiet, though the empty bottle on the coffee table and the abandoned suitcase at the door promise that the silence will only last the night.

Chapter 20

'Take the bean bag and cradle it in the palm of your hand. With your elbows close to your sides and your arms extended at about waist height, toss the ball repeatedly from one hand to the other. Each throw should peak at about eye level, with the throw coming from slightly towards the centre of the body and the catch slightly towards the outside.'

As instructed, I throw my red bean bag with one hand and catch it jerkily in the other.

Nicola, throwing and catching adeptly, rolls her eyes. 'I thought this was a business skills development class, not a crash course for clowns!'

Jarrod overhears, as Nicola intended him to. 'This . . . is to . . . show us . . . how learning new skills . . . can be . . . fun . . .' He says through gritted teeth, his expression not conveying the fun he's supposed to be experiencing.

The instructor joins in on the conversation. 'Juggling is not only fun, it's good for stress relief, problem solving and developing a flexible attitude to work and life in general. It also teaches us how to handle failure – there will be times when you drop the balls in front of an audience and you have to learn how to handle it!'

'Speaking of balls, why are we using bean bags?' Nicola asks.

'Because balls roll when you drop them,' he replies dryly, 'which can be very irritating when you're learning.'

As though on cue, I drop my bean bag. Nicola sniggers and I elbow her in the ribs. She bellows in pretend pain but still doesn't lose her rhythm: it's already obvious that she will be the star pupil today.

The instructor stands behind me and takes my hands in his to demonstrate. 'As you make each catch, let the ball fall into your hand, cushioning its landing, and in the same circular motion send it on its way again. It's important to get this technique right, as it's the same technique that's used for three, four or however many balls you juggle.'

After a few more minutes of practice, we progress to step two of the lesson which involves adding a second bean bag, green this time.

'Using the same technique we learned in step one, throw one of the balls to the other hand. Now, this is the tricky bit: the hand the ball is heading towards is already occupied, so before we make the catch we must make space for it! Here's how it's done. At the point when the first ball reaches its peak and starts its descent, throw the second ball just inside the arc of the first one. You should find that the balls land in your hands one after the other and that they have exchanged places.'

Everyone has a go and red and green bean bags shower the ground amid much laughter.

'It's very important that you throw *both* balls to the same height – this is the most common error.'

Nicola executes it perfectly, a smug grin on her face.

'Have you done this before?' I ask suspiciously.

'No. I'm just good with my hands.'

'Show-off!'

Zoe is the next to get it right and eventually the whole group has it mastered, even Jarrod – everyone except me. The instructor patiently repeats the steps, telling me that the most important thing is to relax and not to panic so much when the balls are in the air. But no matter how hard I try, my timing isn't right and the most I can manage are a few erratic exchanges before one or both bean bags plop to the ground. The instructor has no choice but to leave me behind as he moves to the next stage of the lesson.

'Now, let's try juggling three balls . . .'

I continue with two balls while the rest of the group practises with three. 'I guess there's a hopeless case in every class,' I say conversationally to the instructor.

'*Everyone* can juggle,' he assures me, his tone distinctly condescending. 'And once you learn this skill you'll also gain the confidence to try other things you thought beyond you.'

Behind his back Nicola sticks out her tongue at me and I feel like giving her another elbow in the ribs. Come to think of it, I wouldn't mind inflicting some pain on the patronising instructor too!

I'm relieved when the juggling session is over and we sit back at our desks to learn about some *real* business skills.

I meet Matthew after work and we get takeaway to eat at his house. I'm nervous at the thought of seeing where and how he lives, but excited too. His house is in Elwood, a three-bedroom Edwardian cottage on a street with a friendly feel to it. I'm immediately impressed with the leadlight windows, parquetry floors and high ceilings.

'This is beautiful,' I exclaim as he shows me around. 'It's got such character.'

Matthew smiles shyly. 'Well, the kitchen and bathrooms need updating and the walls could do with a lick of paint, but other than that it's great.'

I look out the kitchen window into the dusk and onto the compact, well-maintained back garden. 'Do you own it?'

'No – I rent along with two mates from work. But when I buy a house, hopefully in the next year or so, I want something exactly like this.'

After the tour, we sit outside on the terracotta-tiled patio where he sets us up for dinner, fetching two bottles of ice-cold beer. A citronella lamp flickers on the small wrought-iron table as the last of the daylight eases from the sky.

'That teenage boy who was attacked – how is he doing now?' I ask.

Matthew's face tightens. 'He had the clot removed along with some of his skull to relieve the pressure. The swelling on his brain is still very prominent and he's in a critical condition.'

I raise my beer bottle to my lips and take a small sip. It's been a long time since I last drank beer. It tastes nice, simple and refreshing, rather like how it feels to be here with Matthew at his house. 'And any luck with finding out who did it?'

'We have some CCTV footage but it's not very good quality. We put a plea for witnesses to come forward in last Thursday's *Leader* and again today.'

'How's his family?'

'They're devastated, especially the mother. From what I can tell he was a great kid, good at school and sport, a real all-rounder. It's sickening to see this happen to a perfectly healthy boy who had the best part of his life in front of him.'

Before meeting Matthew, I held the vague assumption that police officers, doctors and other people in confronting professions eventually became hardened to tragedy and wasted lives. I now know how wrong and ignorant such an assumption was. Matthew may well have appeared professional and detached while dealing with the boy's family, but tonight, out of uniform and with more time to dwell on the injustice and senselessness of the attack, he's clearly very affected by this case.

I reach for his hand. He interlocks his fingers with mine and takes a long slug of his beer. 'Enough about me. What did you get up to today?'

'Errr . . . I spent a good portion of the day trying to learn how to juggle.'

He grins. 'Really? What for?'

'Good question! Apparently, juggling is good for you, and anyone can do it – except me, that is. The instructor had the cheek to insinuate that I'm not open to trying new things. Nicola got it straightaway and thought she was too cool for school. Even Jarrod was better than me! We were meant to be doing a course on business skills and we spent more time on juggling than we did on communication and negotiation. I don't need to be able to juggle to do my job. It was a ridiculous waste of time and energy.'

'You've convinced me.' Matthew laughs.

'I wouldn't mind, but later on, when the course was over and we were back at work, they were all still at it. Every time I looked up there were bean bags flying in the air. It was so annoying!'

I'm smiling, rather enjoying exaggerating how annoying it was, and Matthew laughs again. An easy silence falls as we finish eating. Then Matthew clears the table.

When he returns from the kitchen, he sits and takes my hand again, his thumb drawing circles on the soft skin of my inner wrist while he uses his other hand to lift his beer to his lips. Suddenly I can't focus on anything else but that very slight movement of his thumb, and a shiver of excitement runs down my back.

'Are you cold?' he asks.

'No.' My voice is whispery.

He puts down his beer bottle and I know that he's going to kiss me. I've been waiting for this moment all evening, wondering if it'll be as good as the last time. It is. Better, even. His lips are less tentative, more confident, as are his hands, which slide across my shoulders to hold me tightly against him. I love the wave effect he creates with his lips – soft, firm, soft again – and the way his hands are now entangled in my hair, pressing me deeper and deeper into the kiss until I lose all sense of time and place.

Afterwards, when I've been once again thoroughly kissed by Matthew Blake, he nuzzles my face, his eyes dark in the shadows and showing no hint of their usual brilliant blue. 'What are you doing over Easter?' he enquires unexpectedly.

I attempt to straighten my hair, clothes and thoughts all at the same time. 'Easter?'

'Easter – you know, Stations of the Cross, egg hunts, bunny ears, coming to town this very weekend . . .'

'Ah, that Easter! I've nothing definite planned yet.'

Nicola is going away with David, a promising step forward in their relationship, and Jeanie's going to Sydney again to visit her indomitable family. Her regular family get-togethers never pass off without at least one row and she's already speculating which sister will start the argument.

'I'm having lunch on Sunday with Sophie and Ben.' His breath is warm against my face. It makes me want to kiss him again. 'Normally we'd go back to the farm at Easter but I'm working on the weekend and Sophie doesn't want to go home without me. Anyway, this lunch is pretty casual – I'll just be throwing a few snags on the barbecue – and you're very welcome to join us.'

'I don't know.' I'm aware that I sound every bit as reluctant as I feel. I'm still only getting used to the idea of this relationship and it doesn't feel right to draw other people into it just yet. Neither Jeanie nor Nicola knows that Matthew exists; meeting his sister would, in the spirit of fairness, necessitate telling my own friends and family and I'm not ready for that.

'Just say no if you're not into it.' Matthew shrugs, sitting back in his seat and picking up his almost-empty beer bottle. 'I know it's early to meet my family – I just thought I'd mention it in case you didn't have anything to do.'

He sounds quite relaxed about it, as if it's no big deal, and so it's easy to be honest with him. 'Actually, it does feel kind of early. Maybe we could meet for a drink afterwards instead?'

'Sure.'

Matthew finishes his beer; I've lost interest in mine. After a short, charged silence, it feels perfectly natural to start kissing again. Finding it imperative to get closer to him, I move from my seat to his lap and loop my arms around his neck. I can feel a heightened urgency in his mouth, and I respond accordingly, kissing him rather wildly. Lust washes through my body and I know that my resolve not to rush things is about to be tested. His mouth strays to the curve of my neck, hot against my cool-by-comparison skin, and I tremble in response. It lowers further, to the line of my top. Just as I'm trying to summon the will to stop him, he restlessly moves it again, to my hands, kissing each finger, chaste and yet somehow erotic. But then, suddenly, he stops.

'Did you cut yourself?' he asks, examining the small scabs on the tips of my fingers.

I pull away from his scrutiny. 'I just pricked my hand . . .'

'On what?'

'Can't remember,' I lie.

'Did it hurt?'

'No.'

Not ready for this conversation and where it will lead, I direct his mouth back to mine and kiss any further questions away. Some indefinable length of time later we're interrupted by the slam of the screen door and a booming voice. We jump back from each other, as guilty as teenagers caught in the act by parents arriving home unexpectedly; grinning sheepishly, Matthew introduces me to Pete, one of his colleagues and housemates. Unperturbed, Pete sits down and joins us, Matthew procures another round of beers from the fridge, and the three of us talk until I look at my watch and realise how late it is.

'I'll call you a taxi,' Matthew offers. 'Or I can see if we have a car nearby . . .'

'A taxi will do fine, thanks,' I assure him primly. One ride home in a police car is more than enough to be going with!

Ten minutes later, I'm once again kissing Matthew, this time outside the front of the cottage. 'Now that I know where you live I can cycle here,' I murmur.

'I like that idea.' He puts on an official voice. 'Make sure you wear a helmet, madam, and cycle responsibly!'

'Of course, officer.'

Matthew kisses me one last time. 'I'll see you on Sunday.'

'See you then.'

'Phone me if you change your mind about lunch. I know you'll like Sophie and she'll like you.' He opens the back door of the taxi and I get inside.

'Okay,' I say, but I know that I won't change my mind.

On Thursday, just in time for Easter, Jarrod announces that Telelink have signed on the dotted line. He delivers the news in a specially convened sales meeting. The rollout will start a month later than planned, commencing in June rather than May, and will run for eight weeks. Jarrod's very pleased, so pleased that he comes dangerously close to smiling. He hardly looks at me, let alone acknowledges my part in the deal, and I sit through the meeting feeling jealous, indignant and completely invisible.

'You should have heard him,' I say crossly to Jeanie later that night. 'You would swear he had done it all himself.'

'Well, he was the one who managed to get Derek to sign in the end, wasn't he?'

'But I did all the legwork . . .'

'Including nearly killing Derek and yourself!'

'That was as much Derek's fault as it was mine,' I retort.

Jeanie isn't interested in discussing it further; she's too busy entering contact details into her new phone. 'What's your work number again?' she asks, her forehead creased in concentration.

Obligingly, I reel it off. She then asks for the number of a mutual friend.

'Thanks.' She sighs, her shiny new phone held in both hands as she looks across at me. 'To be honest, I think I'd rather stay here this Easter than going all the way up to Sydney.'

'You don't mean that.'

'I do. I saw them all last week and it feels far too soon to see them again. I've been away a lot recently, I'm tired, and spending four consecutive days with my dearest sisters isn't exactly relaxing.'

'Your sisters are fabulous!'

'Fabulous in small doses. Plus, Mum will see that I'm in a mood and she'll give me a hard time. She always says there's no room for moods in our house – it's too packed as it is.'

I chuckle, always enjoying Jeanie's stories about her family: the quick, fierce arguments, the unpredictability of all those personalities thrown in together, the guaranteed laughter at the end of the day, so unlike my own ordered and painfully measured upbringing.

'It's not funny,' Jeanie says tersely. 'Honestly, if my airfare wasn't non-refundable, I'd cancel.'

'It'll be fine,' I assure her. 'You'll be glad that you went in the end. Your family is wonderful.'

Jeanie shoots me a dark look. 'Why do you always think my family is so great? It isn't, you know.'

I shrug. 'At least your parents allowed you all to develop your own character.' I hear the bitterness in my voice, but I can't manage to temper it. 'At least they weren't always trying to mould you into their ideal of a perfect child.'

'Trust me, my sisters could have done with some moulding!' she retorts. 'They ran wild – Mum didn't know where they were half the time.'

I don't say anything further. Jeanie is too grumpy to reason with tonight. Instead I scroll down through the contacts in my phone, and helpfully call out some more numbers that she might need.

Chapter 21

I'm awake well before my mother's call on Saturday morning. The flat is totally silent, as is the street outside. I only ever notice the silence when Jeanie's away, and I know it wouldn't seem so quiet if she was sound asleep in the room next door. Yesterday was deathly quiet too, all the shops, restaurants and bars closed, and nothing to do other than take a bike ride along the largely deserted cycle paths and roads and then come home to finish the book I was reading. I don't like Good Friday. In fact, I'm not that keen on Easter as a whole. It brings back too many memories: the sombre religious services in the parish church we attended as a family; cracking open my egg after mass on Easter Sunday, gorging myself on chocolate but still trying not to eat any faster than Liam or Maeve; the Easter I spent with Josh, holding his hand as we voted for the peace agreement, blissfully unaware of what was to come.

I pounce on the phone when it rings and the sound of my mother's voice immediately eases the loneliness I've been feeling since the start of the long weekend.

'Hi, Mum.'

'Hello, love. You sound bright and chirpy.'

It's troubling how easily I can fool my mother over the phone. 'I woke early.'

'Are you off somewhere for the day?'

'Nowhere in particular.'

'You're not on your own for Easter, are you?' Mum sounds worried now.

'No. Nicola's around. I'll see her.' It's easier to lie than to have her worry about me being alone at such a family-focused time of year. 'Is Maeve home for the weekend?'

'Yes, she is. Well, she dropped her bags here at least – she's been off visiting her friends since. I'm waiting for my turn!'

'Did Dad talk to her about getting a job?'

'They've discussed it. From what I understand, she wasn't overly receptive but he's going to let her think about what he said before he mentions it again.'

There's a small silence in which I imagine Maeve having a heart to heart with my father in his office, or maybe in the university canteen, sitting among the overcrowded tables and drinking milky cups of tea. The image makes me feel uncomfortable on a number of levels.

'Oh, I nearly forgot to tell you!' Mum exclaims suddenly. 'You won't believe who I bumped into. I was in town, you know I don't go in there very often, but I had a few things to get at the supermarket and I met an old friend of yours . . .'

'Who?'

'Mandy. She lives in the south now, in Dundalk, but she's home for Easter.'

I feel an instant pang of guilt. 'How is she?'

'She looks great, hardly a day older than when I last saw her. She has two children, one about six months old – he was asleep in the buggy, a bonnie-looking child. The other one, another boy, was hiding behind her leg, obviously a different personality to his mother. Mandy was never shy!'

I'd heard that Mandy got married, not to Brendan, her old boyfriend, but to someone else. It's weird to think of her as a married woman, even weirder that I wasn't at her wedding and haven't even met her husband. The fact that she has children and is a mother seems stranger still.

'She gave me her email address and her phone number,' Mum goes on chattily. 'She said she would love it if you got in touch.'

I'm assailed with a sharper, fiercer pang of guilt. During my first year in Australia, Mandy wrote copious letters but my responses were half-hearted. As a result the letters, and the friendship, fizzled out and I've always felt sorry that I didn't do more to keep it alive. The problem was that thinking of Mandy brought back a rush of memories and I couldn't bear to be reminded of all the times we'd 'borrowed' her sister's clothes and makeup without her permission, the nights out with Brendan and Josh in Belfast and how well the four of us had got on together, and seeing my own grief and shock reflected on Mandy's face that awful day at the sports complex. I still think of Mandy quite often. Maybe I have no right to, but I still consider her my friend.

*

I'm early for my date with Matthew, despite the fact that I took an inordinate length of time to get ready, styling my hair and experimenting with eyeshadow and lipstick, changing my outfit a total of four times before settling on a tight-fitting pair of jeans and a black sleeveless top.

He comes through the door and I'm grateful that he's early, too. I feel a stirring of happiness, the first in this memory-logged weekend.

'Hi.' I can't help but smile when I see him.

'Hi, yourself.' He leans down, his mouth covering mine in a short kiss that tastes of the air outside, and then he sits on the bar stool next to me.

'I'll get you a drink.' I beckon the barman, ordering Matthew a beer. 'How was the barbecue?'

'Good, though Sophie was a bit subdued. She finds family occasions hard – that's when she misses Steve the most.'

'And Ben?'

'Ben was his usual chatterbox self – five thousand questions a minute.'

I laugh, picturing Ben with his serious, questioning eyes. 'Did they mind you leaving to come here?'

'No, I don't think so. I got the third degree from Ben, though!'

'Not from Sophie?'

'Not as much. She can't really think beyond her current situation.'

'Mum was like that,' I reveal, surprising myself. 'It took almost a year before she could talk to me on the phone without crying.'

'I'm sure Sophie will eventually be okay, too.' Matthew's beer arrives and he pauses to take a sip. 'Are your parents on good terms now?'

'Mum claims that Dad's her closest friend.' The words feel acidic in my mouth.

Matthew's eyes fix on me as he waits for me to expand on the topic. Instead I change the subject. 'Do you play pool?'

I've noticed a free table at the far end of the bar, the electric-blue cloth luminous under the suspended light fitting overhead, and I feel the sudden urge to crack a cue stick against a ball.

'Yes.' He follows my gaze. 'Do you want a game?'

'Yeah, I'd love a game.'

Drinks in hand, we make our way towards the table. Matthew delves in his pocket for some coins. The balls rumble down the chute and I crouch to gather them up.

'Do you want to break?'

'Ladies first.' He throws me a cue.

I chalk the tip, lean over the table to take aim and forcefully strike the white, which careers into the top of the triangle, dispersing the balls evenly, one disappearing into the bottom right pocket. Walking around the table, I survey the lie of the remaining balls before potting the red in the middle pocket, the white pulling back nicely to set up the brown. After the brown goes down, I sink the purple from long range.

'I didn't realise I was playing a pro.' Matthew watches me with folded arms.

'You didn't ask.'

'Who taught you to play like that?'

'My brother. And Josh, my first boyfriend.'

I don't know whether it's mentioning their names or just that my aim is slightly askew, but I stuff up the next shot, hitting it too far to the right and causing it to bounce back up the table.

Matthew steps up to take his turn. The cue wedged between his fingers, he pots his first ball with ease. His next ball, which is in a rather awkward spot, goes in just as fluidly.

'You're not too bad yourself,' I comment. 'Where did *you* learn to play?'

'We had a table in the back barn. I spent many happy hours being thrashed by my older brother.'

Matthew pots two more balls before missing an ambitious ricochet shot off the side. I take my turn eagerly and send down a series of balls to close out the game. He looks slightly bemused.

'What's wrong?' I ask.

'I've just realised there's nothing as sexy as a girl who can polish off a game of pool in the manner that you did just there!'

I laugh and blush at the same time. 'Another game?'

'You set up while I get us some more drinks. Same again?'

'Yeah, thanks.'

Matthew disappears into the growing crowd while I set up the table. I feel happy, unfathomably happy considering how down in the dumps I've been all weekend.

While Matthew's at the bar, I get a text message from Jeanie. *It was me! I was the one who started the row this time.*

I smile and text back: *Must have been your turn! Hope you're not in too much trouble with your mum.*

Jeanie's response is quick. *Wish I was somewhere else. Where are you? Are you out?*

Matthew returns from the bar and kisses me before taking his cue.

'Your turn to break,' I remind him.

I reply to Jeanie while he lines up his shot. *Yes, I'm out. See you tomorrow.*

Matthew wins the next game and we decide to play best out of five. I enjoy watching him play every bit as much as I enjoy taking my own turn at the table. For someone so big, he's remarkably good with his hands, careful, precise, dextrous. I find him sexy too, his skilfulness with the cue, the way he looks up at me before taking a shot, the taste of beer from his lips when he kisses me, which is increasingly often. We get a new round of drinks to complement each game and I'm buzzing from the alcohol, the game, the chemistry between us. Eventually we reach a point where we've sated our desire to play pool, where it's impossible to concentrate on what's happening on the table; we can hardly keep our hands off each other. And so I decide that this is the right time, that to sleep with him now would not be 'rushing things' at all, and that I'm more than ready to go to this next stage.

'I think we should go somewhere more private,' I suggest, breaking away from one of his kisses.

'Sophie and Ben are sleeping over at my place, just as a novelty for Ben. I'm sorry, but it won't be very private there . . .'

'It's okay,' I whisper. 'My flatmate's away for the weekend.'

Outside on the street, voices and music billow from the restaurants and bars. Traffic and pedestrians are thick as we walk towards my apartment, hands held tightly. I have no clear plan for when we get there, I don't know if I will show him around or offer him a drink or put on some music. But the moment, when it comes, is not staged in any way. Once inside the door, I turn into his arms as though it's the most natural thing in the world to do, and within moments we're lying on my bed, hands and mouths sweeping warm, bare skin. The curtains are open and the room has borrowed some light from the street outside. Matthew is a shadow, a large tender shadow moving over me. He's gentle and thorough with my body, tracing its outline with his fingers, using his mouth for deeper exploration. No part goes untouched. I feel as though I'm melting, dissolving into the bed, becoming nothing but a jumble of sensations. I explore him too, the muscles knotted across his shoulders, the taut skin on his back, the jut of his hips and the part of him that will go inside me. Impatient now, I writhe beneath him. I've been ready for a long time, well before tonight, and cannot wait another moment longer.

I wake in the early hours. Dawn has infused the room. Birds squawk outside, their calls loud and intrusive in the otherwise peaceful morning. Matthew lies flat on his back beside me, his head turned slightly to one side, his body naked beneath the white cotton sheet. I feel a tingle at the thought of last night, his hands on my skin, how his body felt against mine. The sex was hot, intense, meaningful. I gaze at his face, boyish in repose, his mouth slightly open. Taking in the breadth of his shoulders, the light hair on his upper chest, the sheet making it necessary to use last night's recollection for the rest of him. I feel incredible tenderness towards this huge man in my bed. I haven't felt this way about anyone for a long time. Not since Josh.

Thinking about Josh ruins the good feeling. Suddenly I'm

scared that Matthew will hurt me or I'll hurt him. Or that fate will take us from each other, just like it did with Josh. Matthew's job is dangerous – he could get involved in a random fight at any time of the day or night. Or someone holding a grudge could attack him in a premeditated way, injuring or even killing him . . .

I'm getting ahead of myself. It's still only early days with Matthew, and this panicked feeling is unwarranted. Taking some deep breaths to calm myself, I shimmy closer to him in the bed. Heat radiates from his body. Feeling instantly safer I close my eyes.

When I wake the second time Matthew is sitting on the side of the bed, dressed to the waist. 'Good morning.' He smiles down at me.

I smile drowsily in reply.

'Sleep okay?' he asks.

'Very nicely, thank you. And you?'

'Excellent. Very comfortable bed and very beautiful bed companion.'

I blush. 'Well, I'm glad you're satisfied . . .'

'More than satisfied,' he says with a mock leer and I laugh. 'I just need to use your bathroom . . .'

'Go ahead. It isn't hard to find.'

He kisses my forehead. 'I'll be back.'

I stretch in the bed while I wait. More memories of last night circle in my head. Matthew's hands stroking my breasts, his mouth and tongue on my nipples. His hands caressing the velvet skin on my stomach, my inner thigh, his mouth following again. I feel aroused just thinking about it. I hear the flush of the toilet and then the running of the tap. He'll be back soon. I hope he isn't rushing off somewhere, that he can come back into bed.

He is slower to return than I expected, and instead of getting into bed with me, he stands near the door, his face solemn. 'What's going on, Caitlin?'

'What do you mean?'

'I opened your fridge to see if there was some cold water. It looks like a mini pharmacy in there!'

Last night's glow is quickly extinguished. 'Oh.'

'You have those scabs on your fingers and last night I noticed some bruising on your stomach . . .'

I sit up in the bed and open my mouth only to close it again. I've told him about my father's affair and the divorce; I've gone as far as mentioning Josh's name; but this is of a completely different magnitude. All my insecurities, the cracks in my self-image, the loathing I feel for my body emanates from this one thing.

'You're always so conscious of your diet – no dessert after dinner, no ice cream that day with Ben, Diet Coke as a mixer . . .'

From the expression on his face I can tell that he's already worked it out. He wants to hear it from me, though. It's hard to say it, to admit that my body, the one he made love to last night, is so dysfunctional, so imperfect.

'The fridge is like a pharmacy because I keep insulin in there,' I reply finally, my voice sounding more like that of a child than a grown woman. 'My diet needs to be healthy, low in sugar and fat, and I shouldn't miss meals. The scabs on my fingers are from the glucometer, which I use every day to test my blood. I inject the insulin into my stomach and sometimes, if the needle is blunt, I bruise. I'm a Type 1 diabetic.'

My announcement is met with a long, loaded silence.

Finally he reacts, moving from the doorway to sit heavily on the bed. 'Why didn't you tell me this weeks ago?'

I shrug, and I'm sure the gesture looks every bit as defensive as it feels but I can't help it. 'Don't most people want to show their better side? Hide all their faults and weaknesses until later on in the relationship?'

He looks at me with that stare of his that sees everything. 'This isn't any old fault or weakness, Caitlin. It's a matter of your health, and safety, too. What if something had happened any of those times you were out with me? How could I help, get medical assistance or whatever, if I didn't even know you were a diabetic?'

I didn't expect this. At best, I expected him to spout reassurances that it didn't matter, that it didn't change things between us, that he still liked me. But he seems to have leapfrogged past this stage, as if it's a given, and is instead concerned about how he can protect me, keep me safe. In surprise and shock, something inside me breaks open and suddenly the teenage me is speaking, venting her sorrow and frustration.

'I hate it! I hate that my body won't do what it's meant to do. I hate that everything I put into it must be considered and later on measured and adjusted, taking all the joy out of eating and drinking. I hate that I always need to have insulin pens and snacks in my handbag, and that if I ever pick up the wrong bag for work it's imperative that I turn back to get the right one. I hate that it's easier, safer and healthier to stick to the same boring low-fat diet, the same boring sugar-free vodka and Diet Coke, and that any impulsiveness and experimentation are not worth the ensuing game of Russian roulette with the insulin. I *hate* being like this, Matthew! I know there are people worse off than me, with much more serious illnesses and problems, but that doesn't stop me detesting this part of me that just won't work as it should.'

I bury my face in my hands as my outburst meets with another long silence. This self-hatred, this sense of inadequacy, dogged my teenage years until I met Josh and realised how perfect he was despite his physical defect. I've learned to keep it under control and in perspective, but sometimes, when I feel vulnerable and unsure of myself, it spirals back up to its former prominence. I suppose it will always be there, like a nondescript colour on a painter's palette, a primer for the other colours even if it's not the main hue itself.

After a few moments, I feel his arms circle around me, both heavy and reassuring.

'All right, I get the picture – you hate it. But let's not ignore it. It's there. It's part of you, and I need to know about it as much as I need to know about the rest of you. Okay?'

'Okay,' I agree, my voice muffled and reluctant from behind my hands.

His voice holds a smile as he says, 'You know, I can't kiss you properly if you don't take your hands away.'

I remember that I'm stark naked under the sheet at the very same moment I realise that Matthew Blake has every intention of getting back into bed with me.

Chapter 22

June 2009

I read the headline with immense frustration: *Net Banc completes successful takeover of Metro.*

The journalist's predictions three months ago were on the mark, as was David when he said that Net Banc was carnivorous, but given that I've not managed to break into the account both the headline and the fact I guessed this was coming are maddeningly irrelevant.

I pop my head over the partition and see that Zoe is also reading the paper. 'Zoe, what do you do with people who have cranky auras?'

'Pardon?'

'You know, what's the best way to handle cranky bastards?'

'You mean Jarrod?'

'No. Harry Dixon – the man's in a completely different league to Jarrod.'

'Really?' She seems unfazed.

'Yes, *really*. He must be pulling out his hair at the thought of merging all the systems and I could make his life so much easier, if only he would listen.'

'Firstly, you need to be calm,' she advises. 'You're giving off all the wrong signals.'

I shrug with disheartenment. 'It's just that I have so little else on, and I know that this account would be great for both me *and* him.'

'And don't call him a cranky bastard. You shouldn't label people like that.'

'I know, I know. But every time I phone he bites my head off – I can't seem to get past first base.'

'Maybe you should try a different medium?'

The problem with asking Zoe for advice is that her solution is often slightly bizarre. 'What?'

'Verbal clearly isn't his thing. He might respond better to the written word.'

'Oh. You mean write him a letter?'

'Maybe. At the very least you'll feel like you're doing something constructive.'

Well, that's not too bizarre at all. Zoe's obviously feeling quite conventional today. As I sit back down my phone beeps with a text. It's from Matthew.

See you tonight. Your place or mine?

Mine! I send back. Jeanie's away on business and it's a perfect time to have him over.

Hope you're not working too hard, he adds.

Chance would be a fine thing. I've hit the odd lull with work before but none lasting this long. Is it me? Have I lost my touch? Or is it the impact of the global financial crisis, as Jeanie, Jarrod and the media would have me believe? I sigh. All I know is that I can only spend so much time in the day reading the newspaper. I open a Word document and begin to type a short letter to Harry, congratulating him on the takeover and reminding him that I'm here if he needs me. Funnily enough, Zoe is right: it does make me feel like I'm doing something both positive and productive.

That night, curled up against Matthew on the sofa watching a legal drama on TV, I find my thoughts wandering back to the situation at work. I can't help but wonder how long Jarrod can hold out. Australian businesses have started to shed employees, it's in the papers every day. How much extra must Zoe and I and the rest of the team sell in order to make our jobs safe?

'Are you okay?' Matthew asks, perhaps sensing my abstraction.

'Just worried about work – or the lack of it.'

'Things are quiet?'

'That's pretty much an understatement.'

'Are you going to look for something else?'

I really don't want to entertain the possibility. 'I've so much invested with Learning Space . . . I don't think I could get such a good position with another company.'

'So you're going to ride it out.'

Matthew's attention is totally fixed on me. If there's something wrong, he always wants to know what it is; he never puts a TV show or anything else trivial first. He cares about me, *really* cares; it's evident by how much he worries. He scolds me, gently but

consistently, if I drink too much or eat too little, and for refus-
ing to wear a diabetic identity bracelet. Having witnessed how
I weave between cars and zoom through orange traffic lights
when we're cycling, he's begged me to stick to bike-paths where
my supposedly reckless riding is less likely to get me killed. I'm
touched that he worries; it's like having a warm blanket wrapped
around me. And I worry about him too: affectionate, mild, normal worry – when I can manage to contain it.

Tonight Matthew's tiredness is showing around his eyes and I
realise that his day wasn't so great either.

'You seem to be pretty quiet tonight as well.'

'Ah, just a frustrating day at work. None of the kids will talk.
It's obvious they know who did it, but they're too scared to say . . .'

Matthew is still working on the same case. Other things have
come and gone in the months in between – a sexual assault, a fatal
car accident, a messy and protracted case of domestic abuse – but
this case with the brain-damaged teenager is always there in the
background, the injustice and unfairness niggling away at him.

'I don't want to wreck the lives of the kids who did it. I just
want them to suffer some consequences, enough to make them
stop and think if they're ever in that situation again. If it was my
kid, I'd rather he was caught and faced the music. I'd hate it if he
got away with something so violent and unprovoked.'

When I first met Matthew I spent many quiet moments wondering why he was single, why he hadn't been snatched up and
if he had a major flaw that had yet to reveal itself. I've since
learned that he doesn't have a flaw, at least not in himself. His
job is his flaw: the unsociable hours, the unpredictability, the bad
days which cause him to worry when he should be relaxing in

front of the TV and to toss and turn in bed at night. It's his job that turns women off, not Matthew himself.

I snuggle closer to him. I'm more resilient than other women. I can work around the long hours and last-minute changes of plan. I can handle his bad days at work and he has already demonstrated many times that he can handle mine. He hugs me closer and I ignore the stab of fear that always follows any feelings of happiness or contentment: fear that this relationship won't last; fear that fate, once more, has something terrible in store.

Standing in the reception area, Nicola is juggling; she has apparently graduated from bean bags to balls and she's demonstrating her proficiency to all those who care enough to watch, which is a surprising number of people.

'Don't you have any work to do?' I ask a little sourly.

'Yes,' her eyes are cast upwards, 'but I'm just taking a moment to de-stress.'

'You're showing off – stop passing it off as something else.'

She allows the balls to fall into her hands. 'Want to have a go?' she asks provocatively.

'Don't make me swear at you!'

She grins as though she's won some imaginary battle.

I haven't seen much of Nicola socially in the past few months. She continues to keep her cards close to her chest on David but it's clear they're spending the majority of their free time together. I do manage to catch up with them both in the Mitre after work on Fridays and I've come to like David. He's certainly overly conscious of his image, but he isn't as shallow as first impressions suggest. He's keenly intelligent, funny in his own droll way and surprisingly obliging; all Nicola has to do is raise one of her black eyebrows and David's already at the bar buying a new round of drinks.

'Is it a social visit to the training floor this morning?' she asks.

'Actually, I'm here to get the Telelink feedback surveys for Jarrod.'

'Ah, so you're Jarrod's lackey now?'

I shrug in reply. The Telelink implementation has been running for a week and I'm assisting in small ways, though staying firmly in the background. To be honest, I'm grateful to Jarrod for allowing me to be involved at any level. 'I've been –'

I stop short at the sight of a familiar figure making his way in our direction: Derek. He isn't limping, at least not noticeably, and this brings me an instant measure of relief. I raise my head, poised to deliver a civilised greeting, one that will leave the way open for warmer exchanges in the future but won't ask too much of this first meeting since the accident.

He looks through me. 'Nicola, we're having technical issues in room three . . .'

Nicola moves quickly and Derek follows without so much as a glance at me.

When I get back to my desk, all I can do is sit and fume: I'm so furious I can't pretend to work. Derek snubbed me. Derek, who I've wined and dined and danced attendance on for the last two years, has just treated me as though I'm some lowly employee he hasn't even met.

My phone rings. I swallow a lump of fury before picking it up. 'Caitlin O'Reilly speaking.'

'This is Harry Dixon,' says the clipped voice at the end of the line. 'So, it's training facilities that you provide . . .'

'Yes, yes it is.' I try to collect myself, to put Derek out of my mind and focus on this very unexpected call. 'We specialise –'

'I read through the brochures you sent. You have some very high-profile clients.'

'Yes, we do, across –'

'And the case studies make interesting reading.'

'Yes, I –'

'What I need to know is if you can handle big numbers?' he demands.

'We have three thousand Telelink employees going through here at the moment.' Finally I'm allowed to finish a sentence, and I get a satisfying sense of revenge from dropping Telelink's name without Derek's knowledge – it's nice to use him, for a change.

'You'd better come in and see me, then.'

Smiling triumphantly, I put down the phone after arranging a time to meet. I promptly decide to channel all my thoughts and energy towards Harry Dixon, and to do my best to forget about Derek and the immature, vindictive manner in which he snubbed me.

Matthew's sister looks little like him. Sophie is small-boned with a delicate face, her dark hair tied back in a ponytail. Her eyes are blue, but softer, not as intense as Matthew's. She wears jeans and a peasant-style top, her feet clad in silver thongs and her toenails painted with dark-purple varnish.

I've been apprehensive about this meeting, making excuses to put it off until now. From Ben's and Matthew's descriptions, I expected someone older, sadder, but Sophie doesn't look old enough to have a four-year-old son. She also seems genuinely pleased to see me.

'It's so nice to meet you at last.' She smiles warmly, squeezing my hands in hers. 'Come through. I thought we'd eat on the balcony – the kitchen is too tiny. Can I get you a drink, Caitlin? A glass of wine? Oh, I almost forgot – you have to be careful about what you drink, don't you?'

'I can eat or drink most things in moderation, I just have to adjust the insulin accordingly,' I reply, trying to make my tone light and not display how awkward I find it to talk about my diabetes. 'I'd love a glass of wine, thanks.'

The whole apartment is tiny, not just the kitchen. It's neat and well presented but the lack of space makes it feel constricting and a little dark. The living area, where we're standing, has a small dining table, a two-seater sofa and a TV stand, the furniture plain and inexpensive.

Ben tugs at my arm. 'Come and see my bedroom.'

I share a smile with Matthew before allowing Ben to pull me away.

'So, this is where you hang out.' I take in the single bed with the Spider-Man duvet, the bookshelf holding books and toys, and the grey, industrial-looking blinds on the window. 'It's very tidy in here – much tidier than my room when I was a kid. I shared with my sister, Maeve, and she was very messy.'

'Mum made me clean up because you were coming,' he admits earnestly. 'She's been cleaning all morning. For you!'

'Oh.' I don't know how to respond to such honesty.

Thankfully, Ben's thoughts have already moved elsewhere. 'Do you want to play something?'

'Err . . . what do you want to play?'

'Car stunts . . . or meat-eating dinosaurs . . . or Lego.'

Lego sounds the most harmless. Ben slides out a big tub from under his bed and up-ends it at my feet. Suddenly the room doesn't look quite so tidy and I hope Sophie won't be cross.

'What will we build?'

'Let's build a city,' I suggest, getting down on my knees.

We spend a few quiet minutes constructing high-rise buildings on the Lego mat, before Matthew comes to the door with my glass of wine.

'I see that you've been sucked in.' He smirks.

'Uncle Matt, can you make a police car for our city?' Ben looks up with big, imploring eyes.

'Speaking of getting sucked in . . .' Matthew puts my glass on the bookshelf and joins us down on the floor. He builds a police car and an ambulance, and I build an emergency services headquarters. All three of us are quite absorbed until Sophie calls out that lunch is ready.

The balcony is a decent size and has a pleasant outlook on some nearby Victorian terraces. The pale winter sun is already at the back of the apartment block and it's a little cold, but I imagine it would be lovely sitting out here in summer.

'I hope the food is okay,' Sophie frets, tucking an escaped wisp of dark hair behind her ear. 'I didn't know what you could eat, Caitlin, so I kept it light and simple.'

'It's perfect.' I smile.

Lunch is a salad – chicken, walnut and pear – with an accompanying bowl of chat potatoes. Sophie seems to have given a lot of thought to my dietary requirements as well as, it soon transpires, other aspects of my diabetes.

'I've noticed that you don't wear an identity bracelet or necklace,' she comments during the meal. 'If anything happened, how would people know that you're diabetic?'

'Hear, hear!' Matthew interjects. 'My concerns exactly.'

I give him a fond look of exasperation before turning to Sophie. 'As I keep pointing out to Matthew, the negatives of wearing that kind of jewellery far outweigh the benefits.'

'Why?' Ben enquires, as though he fully understands the conversation.

'The main problem is work,' I explain. 'Every workplace wants fit, healthy employees and management gets nervous with illness or health issues of any kind. If my boss knew I was diabetic, he would notice every single sick day, every morning I was slightly late for work. He would worry about me checking my blood and disposing of needles in the bathroom, and he would be constantly on the watch for ways that the disease is affecting my work, when in fact it doesn't affect it at all. In case of emergencies, I carry an ID card in my wallet.'

I'm not used to discussing the everyday realities of diabetes, and the social and work challenges that come with the disease. I'm still uncomfortable even with Matthew, who's quite determined to talk about it openly and frequently, and to fully understand its impact on my life. And it's not just my diabetes he wants to understand, it's everything about me: my work, my childhood, my family. I don't always answer his questions.

Thankfully, the conversation moves on after my little speech. Sophie and Matthew begin discussing their other siblings. They're clearly a close-knit family, and I soon learn that meeting Sophie is not an end in itself but a first step.

'Mum can't wait to meet you, Caitlin.' Sophie has a mischievous glint in her eye. 'She's instructed me to report back to her after lunch today.'

Matthew shoots me a glance. 'Hopefully we can get up there for a weekend sometime soon.'

He's mentioned the idea of going to Deniliquin a few times now but I've managed to sidestep the conversation whenever it comes up. I know I have to go at some stage; I just need to work my way up to it, like I did with meeting Sophie. I can't help this reluctance, my instinctive resistance towards each level of involvement as it comes. I'm aware that my reluctance stems from a sense of self-protection, in case our relationship doesn't last. But Matthew has no such reservations. He assumes that our relationship is permanent, that nothing can destroy it, that I will meet all of his family and he will eventually meet all of mine.

It's after five when we leave. I thank Sophie and Ben and promise that I will come again soon – and I mean it. I think.

'You were right. I do like your sister,' I tell Matthew as we walk down the stairs.

He smiles over his shoulder. 'I could say I told you so.'

'She seemed really happy and upbeat. She's obviously come to terms with things now.'

'Not fully.' Matthew opens the heavy door at the bottom of the stairs and stands back for me to go through first. 'Sophie puts up a good front. She's great most of the time. It's just when she's alone, or lets her guard down.'

My thoughts jump to Steve, Sophie's cheating ex-husband, the one who broke her heart, and Ben's. 'Don't you feel furious at Steve for causing all this pain?'

'Yeah, I'm angry with him. But at the end of the day he's a good dad. He cares about Ben – he makes sure he has everything he needs.'

'Doesn't Ben need a father who's there for him morning and night? Isn't that the most fundamental need of all?'

Matthew fires me a look: he's obviously guessed that I'm drawing parallels with my own father. 'Ideally, yes. But in the absence of the ideal scenario where both parents live together, a father can still be there for his child. As long as the child knows he's cared for, that he's loved, and if anything goes wrong, Dad will try to fix it . . . Given the domestic situations I see every day at work, that counts for a lot.' He leans down to seal his point of view with a kiss. 'By the way, you were great with Ben.'

'So were you.'

'Well, I'm his uncle – it's part of my job description!' He kisses me again, his lips lingering this time.

'Should we go to yours?' I murmur.

'Pete and Phil are having a few people over. Can we go to yours instead?'

'Let me just ring Jeanie to see what time she's coming home.' I break away from his embrace to locate my phone.

'Does it make a difference if she's there?' His tone has a slight edge to it.

'It's nicer to have the place to ourselves.' I dial Jeanie's number. 'Hey, it's me. What time are you getting in tonight?'

'Who is this?' asks a strange voice.

'It's Caitlin. Who's this?'

'Kim.'

'Sorry, I was looking for Jeanie –' The dial tone cuts me off. 'I just rang Jeanie's old number by mistake,' I explain to Matthew as I check my phone for the new number. 'Someone called Kim has the number now. I'll just try her again.'

This time I'm successful. Jeanie's killing time in an airport lounge in Adelaide. She'll arrive in Melbourne at seven, provided her flight is called soon and there are no other delays. It doesn't leave enough time.

'Let's just go to yours,' I say to Matthew as I tuck my phone back in my bag. 'Otherwise Jeanie might walk in on us.'

'Am I ever going to meet this elusive flatmate of yours?'

'Of course you are.' I laugh uneasily and hook my arm through his.

Chapter 23

Net Banc's headquarters are located in one of the most prestig-
ious buildings in the city, the décor in the foyer ultra-modern,
red leather couches, black and white patterned ottomans and
large colourful pieces of art set against stark white walls. Harry
Dixon's office is equally modern and the man himself younger
and less stern than I'd envisaged. He shakes my hand briskly
and we both sit down on retro-style armchairs, positioned near
the window to maximise the spectacular view of the city. I sneak
a quick glimpse down at the grid of streets, splashes of greenery
and the Yarra River splitting the view in two, before I take his
file from my briefcase and rest it on my knees.

'Thanks for seeing me, Harry. I can only imagine how busy
you are at the moment.'

He nods, his hands clasped as he stares steadily across at me.

He doesn't offer any information and, from the brief silence, I assume he wants me to take the lead.

'How many extra staff do you have coming in through the merger?'

'Two thousand. Approximately fifteen hundred in operations and the remainder in corporate services.'

I go to write down the details on my form and suddenly, in a moment of horror, notice what's written after Harry's name: *VERY CRANKY BASTARD.* As discreetly as possible, I scratch over the damning, deal-breaking words with my pen.

'And what's the most immediate training challenge?' I ask, hoping he hasn't noticed anything untoward.

'To train the new operations staff in our computer system.'

'Do you already have training materials for the system?'

'Yes. We had an upgrade a few months back and all the material is current.'

'Great. And do you have experienced trainers in-house?'

'Yes, but perhaps not enough of them.'

'Is there a plan for how and when you might run the training?'

'We're building a plan and a budget at the moment.'

'And what's your decision-making process when the plan's complete?'

'You're looking at it: me.' He looks slightly amused. 'I'm the decision-maker here!'

Though most deals involve a protracted fact-finding stage before pricing is as much as mentioned, my instincts are telling me to jump in now and not let this exceptional opportunity pass me by.

'I can do some preliminary pricing based on the number of employees,' I offer, looking up from my notes. 'And I would really like you to come and visit our premises, Harry, so you can see our state-of-the-art facilities first-hand.'

He blinks and rises to his feet. 'Let me introduce you to a few key people first. Then we'll see if we can organise a date to suit everyone.'

I can hardly keep the smile off my face. In one monumental leap I've gone flying past first base, and probably second and third base too. *Whooosh*. Progress at last.

I take my laptop home with me. It's been a long day and if I stop to think about it I should be tired, but adrenalin has kicked in and I know I won't sleep until I've at least constructed the basis of the Net Banc proposal. Jeanie's also catching up on some admin and so there's a rather industrious atmosphere in the apartment.

'Bills, bills, and more bills,' she moans, going through the mail that accumulated during her last trip away. 'There's not one nice thing in here. No letters, no exciting invitations, just demands for money!'

'That's the problem with technology,' I offer as I type some data into a spreadsheet. 'Everything is done by email these days. The only time anything nice comes in the post is Christmas and birthdays.'

Jeanie doesn't respond. I glance her way and see that she's staring incredulously at a piece of paper that looks, from this distance, like a phone bill.

'What's wrong?'

'This is wrong!' she squeaks. 'It says that I owe five hundred and fifty-two dollars – for my lost phone!'

'Your lost phone?' I cast her a long hard look. 'Don't tell me you didn't cancel the account with the phone company?'

She shakes her head, colour creeping along her cheekbones. 'I kept hoping it would eventually turn up – that's why I got this cheap prepaid one in the meantime. I never imagined that some-one had stolen it and was using it to rack up an enormous bill in my name!'

'Kim,' I say suddenly, my memory sparking. 'Kim is the per-son who stole it.'

'What?'

'I rang it the other night by mistake and someone called Kim answered. At the time I just assumed the phone company had allocated the number to someone else – but obviously not if the account is still in your name.'

'Kim,' Jeanie repeats slowly in an ominous tone.

'Do you know her?'

'It's *Kimmie*.' Rage glazes her eyes. 'My *sister*.'

Kimmie is the third – or fourth, I can never remember which – sister in the family.

'Are you sure?'

'Yes. *Yes*. Jesus, my own sister stole my phone!'

'No, it can't be true. It must be a different Kim,' I reason. It seems too outrageous.

'It *is* true. I *know* it is. I was with Kimmie the day I lost the phone.' Jeanie folds her arms abruptly and I notice her hands are curled into fists. 'I must have left it behind at her place and she just helped herself.'

I'm still not convinced. 'I don't know, Jeanie. I think you're jumping ahead of yourself.'

'This is just like something she would do. She's cracked in the head, that one. She's always been trouble – Mum should have kept her on a tighter rope.'

As she speaks, Jeanie picks up the house phone, presumably to confront Kim, or Kimmie as she's known to her family.

'I'm going to kill her, absolutely kill her . . .'

Luckily for Kim, she doesn't pick up.

The next day at work I'm absorbed with refining my presentation to Net Banc when Nicola appears out of nowhere. Due to the firefighting nature of her job, it's rare to see her away from the training floor, and I usually I go to visit her rather than the other way around.

'Hey.' I smile. 'What brings you to this neck of the woods?'

'Do you have time to grab a quick coffee?'

'Sure.' I save my spreadsheet. 'An internal or external variety?'

'External.'

It's even more rare for Nicola to leave the premises outside the lunch hour. Something is up.

We go downstairs and cross the road to one of the thriving cafés. Perching on stools inside the window, we wait for our coffees to be made.

'David's lost his job,' Nicola divulges.

'Oh, no.'

'He went into work as normal yesterday morning, got called to his boss's office and was promptly informed that he was redundant, effective immediately. He had ten minutes to clear out his desk and was home within the hour.'

'That's awful. Is he upset?'

'He's shocked. He still can't believe it.'

'Was he the only one?'

'No. The bank made thirty staff redundant yesterday and there's a chance that there'll be more next month.' Our coffees arrive and Nicola cups hers with both hands. 'Do you know the worst part?'

'What?'

'As of yesterday, there are thirty excellently qualified investment bankers looking for work in Melbourne's CBD.'

'Oh.'

'David's panicking already. He spent all last night making contingency plans – if he's out of work for one month, two months, three months, six months . . .' Nicola leans closer, her voice becoming even more urgent. 'And as part of his contingency plans, he thinks it's a good time to move in with me – one rent to pay, one set of household expenses and all that.' From the appalled look on Nicola's face, she isn't all that taken with the idea of David moving in.

'Have you talked about it before now? Moving in together?' I enquire diplomatically.

'Yes, but that was when he had a *job*.'

'So you only want to live with him if he's working?'

'Of course! I don't want him hanging around my flat all day and living off me.'

'That's really harsh.' I'm feeling less diplomatic now.

'Well, it's how I feel.'

'You're being unfair, Nic. It's not like he can help being unemployed. He needs your support.'

'Maybe, but *I'm* your friend, not him, and so you should be on *my* side.'

'It's not about taking sides! Do you have any idea how bad David must be feeling right now?'

'Obviously not as good an idea as *you* seem to think you have!' she sniffs.

'My brother was unemployed . . .' I say without thinking.

'I didn't know you had a brother.' Nicola's phone beeps. She casts her eyes down to check the message. 'I'm wanted back on the floor. No rest for the wicked!'

I can hardly disguise my relief. Getting into a discussion about Liam was the last thing I intended. I usually go to great lengths to avoid talking about him, for fear I'll break down. Now, after this last-minute reprieve, I feel a sense of vertigo as I stand up from my stool, as though I've stood too close to the edge of a cliff, images from my past swirling in a fog below, waiting for me to lose my balance.

Sorry, Liam. I'm so, so sorry.

'Don't forget that Harry Dixon is coming in on Friday,' I say on our way out, using work as a means of stabilising my feelings.

Nic doesn't seem to mind, or even notice, the change in subject. 'I haven't forgotten.'

I take her arm and propel her across the street before the crossing light has changed to green.

'We'll be of no use to Harry if we've both been run over,' she says when we reach the other side. 'Do you always cross the road like that?'

I ignore the question. 'Harry will have a few other people with him, maybe three or four in total.' We enter the building and walk into a waiting lift. 'I want you to show him how easily the Telelink employees have been accommodated. Take him to the server room and introduce some of the technicians – he loves anything to do with IT. Afterwards sit him down in the break-out area for a coffee so he can get a real feel for the place.'

'Anything else?' Nic asks sardonically. The lift stops at the fourth floor and the doors open.

'Yes, there is something else.' I can feel the vertigo again, enhanced by the realisation I'm in a lift that's presently suspended a long way off the ground. But I can't let Nic go just yet, not without reiterating what I said earlier. 'Don't be mean to David, Nic. Don't make him feel as though he's diminished in any way just because he doesn't have a job. Remember, he needs your support.'

I see David for myself in the Mitre on Friday after work. He's dressed in his usual corporate gear, designer suit, an expensive-looking pale blue shirt and a set of cufflinks I haven't seen before: for some strange reason, I keep a tally of David's cufflinks.

'Have you got another job already?' I enquire, looking him up and down.

'I wish.' He pulls a face as he glances down at his clothes. 'I'm dressed like this because I went to see a recruitment agent today.'

'And what did they say?'

'That the market is virtually dead and I should expect to be out of work for a few months.'

'Oh, I'm sorry, David.'

'The worst thing is that I bumped into one of my ex-colleagues in the foyer and it brought home to me that there are thirty of us looking for work in this "virtually dead" market.'

Before I can think of another sympathetic response, Nicola has joined in on the conversation. 'Whose turn is it to go to the bar?'

I shake my head at her. 'That's all you ever think about.'

'That's all that's important.' She has an edge to her voice.

'I don't want anything,' I declare. 'I'm going soon.'

'Where are you going?'

'Up town.' I've arranged to meet Matthew for dinner.

'I'll go.' David puts down his drink on a nearby table and has soon melded into the crowd.

'Oh, come on, stay a while longer,' Nicola pleads. 'Let's drink to Harry Dixon and a very successful tour this morning.'

To her credit, Nicola did a superb job of impressing Harry: when I met him later on he was somewhat in awe of our facilities and technical capabilities. I don't want to be overly optimistic but I can't help feeling excited at how promising it looks.

'I can't stay. Sorry.'

She eyes me suspiciously. 'Why? Who are you meeting?'

She still doesn't know about Matthew. Neither does Jeanie. At the start I didn't say anything because I assumed it wouldn't last. If I told them now, almost three months later, they'd both be incredulous that I've kept him secret so long, and quite hurt too, I imagine. It's hard to find the right time for what feels like such a momentous discussion.

'No one you know.' I gulp back my drink. Now is definitely not the right time to tell her. 'I'll see you at work on Monday.'

On the main street outside there's a blustery wind that wasn't evident in the sheltered garden of the pub. Burrowing my chin into my jacket, I stride against the wind, my thoughts jumping around, a new one with each gust. Poor David; Nicola really should be nicer to him. I must tell Nicola about Matthew. And Jeanie too. *Especially* Jeanie. I'll tell her as soon as the rift with Kimmie is sorted out. She'll be in better form then.

My phone rings. It's Matthew.

'Hey.' I smile, a reflex whenever I hear his voice. 'Are you there already?'

'No. Sorry, Caitlin, I have to cancel on you.'

'Why? What's up?'

'I have the names.' He sounds elated.

'The names?'

'The names of the kids who beat up that boy. I want to keep going until we've brought them in. I'm really sorry. I hope you understand.'

I understand more than he could ever realise. 'It's okay,' I assure him in a voice that reveals nothing of what I'm feeling. 'I'm really glad for you. You've been waiting a long time for this.'

At home in bed, I stare wide-eyed into the shadows of my room, transported back to another time, another list of names, Mum jubilant as she announced the news over the phone.

'He has the names, Caitlin. Your father has the names and he's given them to the police. Those murderers will be brought to justice.'

I remember holding the phone in my hand for a long time

afterwards. I imagined the names scrawled on the back of an envelope in blue ink. I wondered what those men were doing at that very moment. Were they filing out of Sunday morning mass, the choir still singing in their wake? Or setting the table for lunch, laying knives and forks neatly aside large white plates. Or reading the broadsheet Sunday papers, or maybe taking a moment to play with their young children. Did they have any inkling at all that the police, and my father, had their names? I pictured them as tall men with dark hair and pale skin. They wore jumpers and jeans and were good with their hands. But I had a problem conjuring up an image of their faces. What did the features of a murderer look like? Steely eyes? Ruthless mouth? Cheekbones sharp enough to cut?

Finally, I used the phone to call around my small circle of friends and rally them to go out that night. I desperately needed to take my mind off my mother and father and the names of those men. I stood in the pub, drinking rapidly and talking just as fast, trying to stay ahead of the thoughts in my head.

'I think you've had enough.' The barman turned me down many drinks later. 'Here's a glass of water instead.'

'My father has their names,' I informed him importantly, picking up the glass of water with a flourish and spilling half of it on my hand.

Despite my cynicism and bitterness about my father and his cause, I felt hopeful that night, hopeful that justice would be done and that we could all move on. But nothing tangible eventuated from the list of names, certainly nothing that could remotely pass as closure. Ten years on my father is still seeking justice.

I hope Matthew has more success.

Chapter 24

The weekend is quiet and relatively uneventful. Nicola's lying low in a bid to 'be there' for David. Jeanie's away on a last-minute family visit, which threatens to be more confrontational than usual. And Matthew's absorbed with the names on his list, the face-to-face interviews, the charges being laid, the early-stage evidence, so critical for the prosecution cases that need to be built sufficiently watertight to withstand the system.

Over the weekend they all send me text messages, like progress reports.

From Nicola:

David totally down in the dumps. Doing my head in.

Trying to be nice to him but patience wearing very, very thin.

Want to meet for a quick drink? Need space from you-know-who!

Sighing at her short-lived attempt at being supportive, I respond to say that I don't want to go for a drink and tactfully suggest that she ask David instead as it might be just the thing to cheer him up.

Jeanie, meanwhile, is embroiled in a major family fracas.

Mum doesn't believe that Kimmie has my phone. She says I'm being juvenile and ridiculous!

I've raided Kimmie's handbag and retrieved the stolen goods. Just presented Mum with the evidence (phone AND gigantic bill).

Big family fallout. Mary and Cathy are taking Kimmie's side, Kellie and Lizzy on mine, Sally and Wendy on fence. Mum furious with us all.

I smile indulgently as I read the messages. Despite all the drama, I know things will eventually settle down and the allegiances won't last past the next family argument. Jeanie is so lucky with her family.

Matthew's messages are sporadic, sent in snatched moments, punctuation missing in his haste.

these kids seem so normal cant believe they did something so vicious and unprovoked

feel sorry for parents theyre still in denial

sorry its been such a lousy weekend for you. promise to make it up next weekend. miss you.

Though I'm in bed and on the verge of sleep, I fumble in the dark for my phone and smile sleepily as I read his last message. I picture him at home, falling into bed at the end of a long, hard, emotional yet fulfilling couple of days.

Miss you too, I text back and then succumb to sleep.

My working week starts on a bad note, with Tanya McManus announcing another drop in business levels and the need for a renegotiated contract. This news worries me, as does the fact that Jarrod reacts much less stoically than the first time. But then something happens to compensate – Harry Dixon phones to announce that he's accepting the proposal. Though his tone is clipped and professional and decidedly unexcited, I'm so thrilled that I practically squeal down the phone.

'Thanks, Harry. That's wonderful. I'm really delighted. I'll ask our lawyers to start working on the contracts straightaway.'

As soon as I hang up, I perform an impromptu victory dance around the office. Zoe takes off her headphones and joins in, dancing in her own peculiar indie style. And Jarrod, wearing a rare smile as he comes out of his office to witness the scene, pops open a bottle of champagne. The week, which started out so badly, ends on a high.

The phone rings close to my ear, jolting me awake on Saturday morning. I groan and reach a heavy arm to pick it up. 'Mum?'

'Hello, love. Did I wake you?'

'Yes.' I blink at the clock: 6 am. No wonder I feel so tired. To be honest, I'm a little hungover too. Quite a few bottles of champagne were consumed at the office before the celebrations moved on to the Mitre. 'It's very early here, Mum!'

'Sorry.' She sounds barely apologetic. 'How was your week, love?'

'Good and bad.' I yawn loudly. 'And yours?'

'It was good, excellent in fact. The reason I rang so early is that I have news. I couldn't wait any longer to tell you.'

'What news?' I feel a tinge of wariness though I'm still half-asleep. All too often Mum's 'news' is somehow related to Dad.

'They won the case, love,' she exclaims, proving me right. 'They won the civil case. The high court judge found four men responsible for the bombing and the families have been awarded damages.'

The last shreds of sleepiness fall away and I'm awake, horribly awake. '*What?*'

'They won damages of 2.5 million pounds. Your father was on the television – Maeve recorded him. She'll send a copy over to you.'

I check that I've understood correctly. 'You mean Dad's got *money* from them?'

'The money's not for your father, it's for all the families. We don't know how it will be divided up yet.'

I shake my head in bewilderment. 'Money does nothing, Mum.'

'Money is the only thing those people understand, it's the only way to reach them.'

'But money won't bring them back, Mum. Money won't bring any of the people who died back to life. Money does *nothing*.'

She's gentle but determined. 'It's a landmark case, love – you'll understand when you see the footage for yourself.'

'I'll never understand this.' I'm just as obstinate as she is.

'Maeve will send you the disc. You'll be proud when you see it.'

'You're wrong. I have nothing to be proud of. *Nothing at all.*'

Neither of us has anything else to say. I hang up the phone and realise that I'm crying, tears that feel strangely disassociated from my eyes, silently and stealthily creeping down my face.

*

All day I feel off kilter. I try to centre myself by doing my usual Saturday chores and determinedly set about cleaning the apartment. But as I vacuum and mop the floors, flashbacks persistently blot my thoughts. I see my mother's face in an array of different expressions: laughing, creased with a small worry, softened with love, shocked and distraught. I see my father's face with just the one expression, sombre, preoccupied, slightly frowning. I can't begin to comprehend how either of them can be pleased with this result. Money isn't justice, it's an insult. No price can be put on the lives lost that day in Clonmegan, or on the destroyed happiness and peace of mind of those of us left behind.

I scour the surfaces in the kitchen and bathroom, my fingers red and stinging from detergent; I should have worn plastic gloves. I see Maeve's reflection in the shower screen, looking young and lost in her baggy school uniform, with reddened eyes and a wan face. I see Liam holding a cue in one hand and a pint of Guinness in the other, standing in the shadows but yet his relief at being out of the house clearly discernible. I see Josh, racing down the line of the soccer pitch, recognisable only by the fluidity of his movements, his face a blur but real, so very real that I feel as though I can reach out and touch him right here in the bathroom. This feeling, this conviction that he's close is nothing new. It happens mostly when I'm vulnerable or when my guard is down. I sense that he's alongside me, a whisper away. Sometimes I find myself compulsively searching for his face, once even imagining him in the TV audience of *Top Gear*, his hands clapping madly, his face grinning and distinct though the show was recorded well after his death. More than once I've been convinced that he's working on one of the building sites I pass on my way to work and I've stopped to scan the plasterers in their splattered clothes smoothing crevices and other imperfections from the bricks. Obviously I don't find him but I know that he's close, still with me. We always communicated on a different level. Being dead doesn't change that.

Matthew rings in the afternoon and I arrange, without much enthusiasm, to meet him later on.

'What would you like to do?' he asks.

'I don't know.'

'Will we go for a drink?'

'Okay.'

When we meet that evening I'm still distracted, my thoughts held hostage to a different time and place. The pub is Saturday-night busy, bodies crammed together and deafening music that renders prolonged conversation impossible. The enforced silence suits my mood; Matthew asks if I would like to go somewhere quieter but I shake my head. He asks if I want to play pool and I say no to that too. More than once he asks if something is wrong. I summon a smile to indicate I'm okay and merely surrendering to the noisy atmosphere. But Matthew isn't easily fooled and, despite my preoccupation, I can't help noticing that he's becoming more and more frustrated as the night goes on.

'I think I'll have another drink,' I declare. We've been in the pub more than two hours now, hardly a few sentences uttered between us.

'Don't you think you've had enough?'

'No, as a matter of fact, I *don't* think I've had enough.' I get to my feet, my intention to flounce to the bar, but he catches my arm.

'I'll go.'

He's quickly swallowed by the crowd and I welcome the solitude while he's gone. I shouldn't have come out tonight. It isn't fair on Matthew as there's nothing he can do to improve my mood. Left alone I would succumb to the memories, and eventually sleep them out of my system.

A while later he returns with drinks for us both along with a large glass of water. He pointedly offers me the water first.

'Thanks – but I don't remember asking for this.'

'Just drink it.'

I do, and then I follow it with the vodka and Diet Coke. God, I'm so sick of vodka and Diet Coke. It even tastes stale, and my stomach clenches in protest.

Matthew hardly gives me enough time to drain my glass before demanding, 'Let's go.'

I *did* want to go home, but now, rather perversely, I don't. Still, I follow him through the sweaty, densely packed crowd to the crisp winter's night outside. He turns left in the direction of my apartment, and slows enough for me to draw alongside him, but doesn't hold my hand. I would have to be blind not to notice that he's annoyed, but I feel too listless to apologise, to make amends, to explain the black mood that's shrouded me since my mother's phone call. My hand, the one he should be holding, is cold and aimless by my side.

We reach Grey Street and Matthew stops at the crossing. I plough past him onto the street, an oncoming car that was never a real threat blaring its horn at me.

Matthew is even more furious when he catches up with me on the other side. 'Jesus, Caitlin. Are you trying to get yourself killed?' He stops me in my tracks, puts an angry, authoritative hand on my shoulder. 'What's *wrong* with you tonight?'

Before I can decide whether or not to respond, there's an almighty explosion, the sound so loud and sudden that it cracks the night apart. I scream in terror, digging my fingers into his arm, desperately trying to pull him to safety.

'Run! *Run!*' He's too large and heavy for me to move, and he seems totally oblivious to the fact that we could die at any moment. '*Matthew, move, damn it!*'

'Caitlin.' He has me by both shoulders now, shaking me. 'Caitlin, it's only a ladder come off that van.'

Another scream – or is it the same one? – drowns him out. It's thin and piercing, chilling, and it's coming from deep inside me. 'For God's sake, move,' I wail, hysterical by now. '*Get out of the way!*'

He has no idea how easy it is to die, how a short distance and an even shorter amount of time can mean the difference between life and death.

He shakes me again, and though it's only a gentle shake, my head rocks back and forth like a rag doll. 'Calm down, Caitlin. It's just a ladder. That's all.'

His words finally penetrate and the scream stops abruptly in my throat. I try to focus on what's beyond his face, a van stopped in the middle of the road, a metal ladder strewn a few metres behind, a young man, the driver, walking back towards it.

'He's a careless fool – he should have had it properly secured. But that's all it is.'

I hear him more clearly this time, and realise that it really wasn't an explosion, just the terrible bang of metal on concrete, as he said. But instead of feeling calmer, I feel sick. The last drink, the one that tasted so awful and vapid, rises up in my stomach. The last scream, still clogged in my throat, adds to the need to gag.

Matthew steers me to a nearby bench. 'Sit down. Put your head between your legs. Take some deep breaths.'

I do as I'm told. After a few minutes of dragging air into my lungs, I straighten slowly.

'Are you feeling better?' He's searching my face for clues, trying to understand me.

'Yes,' I whisper.

'What was that all about?'

'Nothing,' I say weakly. 'I just got a fright.'

'Jesus, Caitlin!' he exclaims, his frustration from earlier erupting in outright anger. 'Stop treating me like an idiot. For God's sake, tell me what's wrong with you tonight!'

His anger is daunting, not just because I've never seen it before, but mainly because it's justified, brought on by my own evasiveness. If there's one negative about Matthew, it's that I can't fob him off, at least not for long. He wants to understand me, to know me. He's always pressing for information, for details, and he has me cornered now. There's no way I can plausibly explain what just happened without telling him the truth. Well, some of it anyway.

'I thought it was a bomb.' I start to shiver uncontrollably.

His eyes fill with understanding. Just like that, his anger is gone, his face and voice are back to normal, or perhaps a shade softer than normal. 'You've actually experienced a bomb?'

My throat feels full, a sensation I get when I'm about to cry.

I gulp some air, but the tears come anyway, welling in my eyes, blurring Matthew's face. 'There was a bomb in Clonmegan. Fifty-three people were killed, hundreds more injured.' His fingers brush the tears dripping down my face. More rush to take their place. 'I was only a short distance away when it happened . . .' I can't go on. I'm crying too hard.

He gathers me in his arms, pressing me against him as though to keep me safe. 'It's all right,' I hear him say. 'It's all right, Caitlin.'

Over and over he assures me that everything's all right. Lulled by his voice and the security of his arms around me, I finally stop crying.

'It's all right, Caitlin . . . It's all right . . . I love you.'

Josh was the last boyfriend who loved me. Josh whose life has been callously valued at a certain sum of money: a share of 2.5 million pounds. This thought prompts another bout of tears that soak into the fleece of Matthew's sweater, and he continues to hold me and reassure me until I'm all cried out.

At home he makes tea and supervises me as I drink it.

'Do you want to talk about it some more?' he asks carefully.

'No. No, I don't.' I shake my head to make myself absolutely clear.

I never talk about it, not with anyone, not even Mum or Maeve who can at least understand some of what I feel. It's too distressing, even now, so many years later. I can see that this is hard for Matthew and that he feels helpless without more details on what happened. I feel sorry for him, but I can't tell him anything further. I'm already quite traumatised by what has occurred tonight.

When I finish my tea, he ushers me to the bedroom where he locates my pyjamas and helps me get undressed. He tucks me in, like a child, the bedcovers stretched tight and secure, and then lies on the bed beside me.

'Thanks.' My gratitude comes out sounding rather feeble, but it's totally heartfelt. He's wonderful, really wonderful.

'Sleep now,' he says, stroking my hair. 'I love you.'

As I close my eyes, I think that I might love him too, but I find it impossible to tell him this. I can't help worrying that fate is out there, lurking, and if I say those words aloud, declare my feelings in the same naive way I did with Josh, I'll be putting myself at its mercy. I don't trust fate, not one little bit.

Somehow I sleep, and when I wake with a start during the night Matthew's still lying there next to me, a fully clothed, slumbering guardian angel.

Chapter 25

Zoe squints at me, her already smallish eyes threatening to disappear as they focus on a point in the centre of my forehead. Her scrutiny is so intense it verges on comical. I smother the urge to laugh.

'Orange and yellow, that's good.'

'What do those colours mean?'

'Shush, I'm not finished,' she admonishes, closing her eyes. 'Grey too, both light and dark...' Her eyes pop open again, confronting me. 'There's more black than is considered normal.'

'Sorry?'

'Black – hatred, anger. Quite concerning when coupled with the greys, which denote deceit and fear.'

'Oh. Anything good in there?'

'The orange denotes ambition and yellow, intelligence.'

'Something positive, thank God,' I joke. 'Good to know I'm more than an angry, deceitful ball of hate.'

'And I see crimson,' Zoe's expression becomes sly, 'which means love, of course.'

'It does?'

'Yes. Is there something, or rather someone, you've forgotten to tell me about?'

Zoe's phone begins to ring in what I consider a very timely interruption. 'Err . . . time to get back to work, I think.' I scoot my chair from Zoe's workstation to my own.

The clock on my laptop states the time as 3.45 pm. Having my aura read has killed only fifteen minutes of a terminally long day. My phone rings and I allow it to shrill four times before picking up; no point in making it obvious that I have so little to do. It's Mike, the technician responsible for the Net Banc rollout, and he launches straight into a detailed account of what needs to be done before the much-revised start date. I listen a lot more attentively than I would have done if the conversation had occurred six months ago – when I was still relatively busy.

When I put down the phone, my ear is stinging from having it pressed too close. I should get headphones like Zoe. In fact, I'll log on to the stationery website and order a set right away, and in the process kill another ten minutes or so. There won't be any time to spare when the Net Banc rollout begins; I'll be run off my feet for a few months at least. And I almost can't wait.

Nic's in top form, a force of nature as she replenishes drinks long before glasses are emptied, flirts outrageously with men she deems worthy and finishes her sentences with peals of laughter that cause other groups to look, somewhat enviously, in our direction. Nic isn't just doing it for show. She's having fun, lots of it. In this kind of mood she's irresistible. Being single suits her much more than being part of a couple.

It's Thursday night, not one of our usual nights at the pub, but Nic was persuasive and I was keen for some excitement after another too-quiet day at the office.

Nic leans close. 'Man alert. Traditionally dark and handsome. Paying for his drink at the bar as I speak.'

I swing my head to take a look. The man in question is handsome, too handsome if there's such a thing. David is off the scene, callously dumped by Nic the week after he lost his job. She's already been on several dates with other men, ironically all the same prototype as David, the only difference being their employment status. I can't help hoping that David gets a job soon, paying even more than his last one, and that he'll saunter into the pub one evening smelling of money and success and snub Nic in the way she deserves. I check myself: I'm being mean. I look back at Nic and raise my shoulders in a non-committal shrug. The man at the bar, though Nic's type, is not mine. My type is currently sitting behind his desk in the St Kilda police station, wrestling with paperwork. Or maybe he's out in the car with Will. This pub, this very corporate and high-flying scene, isn't his thing, which is one of the reasons I never arrange to meet him here.

'You should get Zoe to read your aura,' I say, changing the subject.

'Why would I do that?' Nic snorts.

'It's fun.'

'What did she have to say about yours?'

'That it showed I was incredibly intelligent and ambitious.'

Rather conveniently, I omit to mention that I am, at least according to my aura, in love. Crimson, if I recall the colour correctly. Since that June night Matthew's told me many times that he loves me. He whispers it, his voice so low and breathy in my ear that I sometimes wonder if I've misheard. His eyes, though, reaffirm the message, their brilliance softened by the depth of his feelings and, when I don't respond in kind, growing hurt.

I also omit to mention that my aura reveals me to be deceitful. If I admitted this to Nic, I could immediately prove it correct by telling her that I've been secretly dating a police officer, a sergeant no less, without her knowledge. The extent of my deceit sounds worse than it is, though. For a start, Nic isn't exactly easy to confide in. She's very cynical about men at the moment; well, she's always been cynical but she's even more so since the split with David. Nic's use-and-abuse attitude towards men isn't the kind of philosophy that encourages me to open up about Matthew and the terrifying love that I feel for him.

The reason I haven't told Jeanie is harder to pin down. From a logistical point of view alone, it makes sense to tell her. She's spending more time at the apartment these days, her travelling budget slashed after recent cutbacks in her firm. If I told her about Matthew, I could at least have him around more often. Because I haven't told her, we spend most of our time at Matthew's house, which also happens to be the preferred gathering place for his flatmates' extensive network of friends and colleagues. An average night at the house is like being in Melbourne Central Station, and about as romantic!

But telling Jeanie means trusting that fate doesn't have

something terrible in store, trusting that things will work out okay. Along with everything else I lost that day in Clonmegan, I lost the ability to trust in the future. And for that reason it feels safer to keep this relationship secret, to hug it deep inside.

Nic throws back the last of her drink and presses her fingers to her lips to contain a hiccup. 'You know, Caitlin, you're a bad influence on me.'

'No, Nic, you're the bad influence.'

She shakes her head theatrically. 'I beg to differ.'

I grin. 'Beg all you like. It's *always* you that's the bad influence.'

Nic eyes the bar and its surrounds, no doubt working out the most aesthetically interesting route to get there. A few moments later she lurches off to get more drinks and, no doubt, flirt madly with the investment banker she spotted earlier. When she's out of sight, I check my phone and see that there's a message from Matthew: *Hope you're having fun.*

Matthew would disapprove if he saw how drunk I was. He would get me some water and set about persuading me that it was time to go home. He worries and fusses too much, which is sweet of him but totally unnecessary. Suddenly I can't wait for tomorrow night when we'll have the apartment to ourselves: Jeanie's going to a music gig in the outer suburbs and staying over with a friend of the band.

Miss you, I text back. It's true. Despite Nic's bubbly company and the high from all the alcohol I've managed to consume under her *bad influence*, I feel lonely for him.

*

Matthew stands in the hallway, bearing a bunch of flowers and a self-conscious smile.

I eye the flowers, gerberas in pink, orange, yellow and red. My day feels brighter just by looking at them. 'Are those for me?'

'Who else?'

I lean over the flowers to kiss him. 'What did I do to deserve this?'

'You deserve them for being you.'

Guilt swells inside me. If he knew how drunk I was last night and how hungover earlier today, he would not think me deserving at all.

He follows me to the kitchen and, at my request, takes down a glass vase from a shelf that's too high for me to reach. I free the flowers from the cellophane wrapping, noticing from the label that he purchased them at a supermarket rather than a florist. I imagine him at the checkout, sheepish as he waited in line, the flowers held low but still attracting benevolent smiles from women in the vicinity.

'I not only come bearing flowers, I have a movie too,' he announces, removing a DVD case from the inside of his denim jacket.

'Great!' I glance at the title of the DVD. 'I've heard it's good. You go and set it up while I organise the snacks.'

Matthew abandons his jacket on the back of one of the kitchen chairs and disappears into the living room. I finish arranging the flowers and centre the vase on the kitchen windowsill where the bright colours will be illuminated further by the morning sun. I twist the lid off a bottle of beer and open a Diet Coke for myself: I can't face alcohol after last night.

'Ready to go?' I enter the living room with a drink in each hand and a bag of popcorn wedged under my chin.

'Yeah. What's this about, though?'

I'm in the process of putting down the drinks when he asks the question. When I look up, I see that he's holding the disc Maeve sent me, the one with the coverage of my father. It's labelled: *Dad – BBC news.* Of course Matthew would be curious at seeing such a title. I curse inwardly. I shouldn't have left the disc hanging around.

'It's just some coverage of my father on television.'

'I can see that. Why was he on TV?'

I take a shallow breath. 'He was involved in a civil law suit . . . It was related to the bomb I told you about.'

'Can I watch it?'

'Aren't we meant to be watching the movie?'

'I mean after the movie – we can put it on when it's over.'

Quite obviously, he believes this is a reasonable request. He wants to know more about my family, my background, and what better way than to watch this disc, Professor Jonathan O'Reilly centre stage.

'I –' It's unfair of him to back me into a corner like this. What can I say to dissuade him, to convince him that it isn't a reasonable request at all? Why is he always so damned interested in every single thing about me?

Understanding dawns on his face. 'Have *you* watched it, Caitlin?'

'No.' The disc has been sitting next to the DVD player since last month.

'Why?'

I snap. 'Because I don't speak to my father and I have no desire to see him, in person or on TV. Now, for God's sake, can we watch the movie?'

He treats me to a piercing look before he takes the remote and presses play. We sit on the couch, a careful distance between us. I drink some of my Diet Coke, regretting that I didn't opt for something stronger. *Damn it, damn it, damn it!* I should have thrown the disc in the rubbish bin – or at least put it somewhere out of sight.

Lost in self-recrimination, I miss the opening scenes of the movie. The storyline evades me. Matthew isn't concentrating either. He's staring too hard at the screen, his fingers agitatedly drumming his denim-clad knee. I slide my hand over his, stilling it. 'Sorry for snapping.'

He doesn't answer. His eyes bore into the screen. A few minutes later, though, his hand turns upwards to clasp mine, his way of saying that I'm forgiven. I move closer, nestle my head on his shoulder and for the next hour and a half luxuriate in his closeness, paying only scant attention to what's happening on the screen.

Matthew raises his head to look blearily across at the trilling phone on the bedside table. 'Aren't you going to answer it?'

'They can leave a message.'

I know it's Mum with her usual Saturday-morning wake-up call. She'll be in a chatty mood, eager to share the minutiae of her day and week, and I can't reciprocate, not with Matthew lying here next to me. She'll be able to tell from my reticence that someone is here, and the questions will follow: *Who's with you? Is it a man? What's his name? Is it serious?* God forbid, she's so fond of chatting with Jeanie she might well demand that Matthew be put on the line so that she can say hello. No, it's better to let the phone ring out and to call Mum later, maybe tonight.

Matthew looks from me to the phone and back again. He says nothing but his expression shows that he understands more than he's willing to say. The ringing stops and the unanswered phone promptly joins ranks with the unwatched disc, the fact that I haven't yet committed to go to Deniliquin to meet his parents and, even more significantly, haven't yet told him I love him, forming a malignant cell, a tumour on what's otherwise a perfect relationship.

Chapter 26

I'm running late. My glucometer isn't working: the batteries are dead. A search through the bathroom and kitchen drawers follows, during which I find practically every other type of battery in the universe except the ones I need. Not being able to test my blood makes me feel ungroomed, like I haven't washed my face or brushed my teeth.

Another delay happens over breakfast.

'Where did those flowers come from?' asks Jeanie, her mouth full of toast.

The gerberas are vivid and requiring explanation as they stand in their vase on the windowsill. I curse myself for not putting them in my room. Of course Jeanie would want to know where they've come from; the only reason she hasn't asked before now is that she wasn't home for most of the weekend.

'They were on special at the supermarket so I picked them up,' I reply airily. I *am* planning to tell her about Matthew. Very soon. But not now, when I'm already late for work.

Jeanie is distracted by my mention of the supermarket. 'That reminds me, we have no washing detergent. Or butter, for that matter.' She begins a spontaneous shopping list on a scrap of paper torn off an old bill – we were both too busy to do the usual Saturday grocery shop. Now, as we jointly compile a list, I'm keenly aware of minutes ticking by but I'm unwilling to excuse myself until I'm confident that Jeanie's attention has fully moved away from the flowers on the sill.

But there's yet another delay ahead: an unexpected and very disconcerting phone call that comes while Jeanie and I have headed to our separate bedrooms to get ready for the day.

'Can you get that?' Jeanie shouts from her room.

'I'm late! Whoever it is can wait until later.'

On my way out the door, noticing the message light flashing on the phone I have second thoughts. Impulsively, I pick up the receiver and listen to the message.

'Hello, Caitlin. It's Dad here. How are you? Already gone to work, I suppose. Well, speaking of work, I was ringing to let you know that Maeve has accepted a position in the history department as an associate lecturer. I thought you'd like to know because your mother mentioned that you were worried about her. I'm sure Maeve will ring you herself to tell you all the details. Anyway, no other news from this side of the globe. Only that your mother said she didn't hear from you over the weekend, so it would be great if you could give her a buzz and let her know that you're alive and kicking. Goodbye, love. Take care now.'

I put the phone back in place and glide out of the apartment and down the stairs. Outside the blue sky and sun seem to hold the promise of spring, but the biting breeze is a harsh reminder that it's still officially winter. I walk slowly, abstractedly, in the direction of the tram. Halfway there I stop, sit down on a bench and think about my father's message.

Maeve has a job, a full-time job, *at the university*. Dad has obviously orchestrated this turn of events. He must have persuaded Maeve to send in an application, and put in a good word for her with his peers in the history department. Mum was right: Maeve listens to Dad. *They get on well.* God, I'm not feeling jealous, am I? No, I'm happy for her, regardless of what it proves about her relationship with Dad. Maeve has a job, a *real* job. She's no longer a student, she's a teacher. I'm so happy for her I feel tears stinging my eyes. Blinking down at my watch I realise I've just missed my tram. Ten minutes until the next one: I know the timetable by heart. I'm *really* late now.

Still sitting on the bench, my thoughts once more revert to Maeve. But other memories are activated by association – Liam, Josh and Mandy, whose contact details have lain untouched in the drawer of my bedside table since Easter. I try to visualise an older, more mature Mandy in the supermarket aisle, two kids in tow. Then I try to visualise Maeve, also looking older and more mature, lecturing a roomful of cocky first-year students.

I come back to the present with a start, check my watch again and realise I will have to hurry or risk missing yet another tram.

*

I walk with my hand enclosed in Matthew's. This stroll along the beachfront is impromptu: Matthew planned to cook me dinner at his house but some friends of friends are planted in the kitchen there. He then suggested cooking at my place but I discouraged the idea; as far as I know, Jeanie doesn't have plans to go out. So we ate in one of St Kilda's many restaurants, not as nice as having him cook for me but nice enough all the same, and now we're walking off the food.

The salty wind whips against my face and I breathe it deep into my lungs. The beachfront is relatively quiet, just a few joggers and power walkers, their silhouettes svelte against the dusk. I don't know if it's the taste of the sea, something familiar about the blue-grey-orange splotches in the sky, something set in train by my father's phone call this morning, but suddenly I feel as though it's Josh by my side, his hand cradling mine, and that we're walking near the docks in Belfast, the huge ship-building cranes, Samson and Goliath, about to come into view.

I shiver and Matthew moves his hand to my waist to pull me closer to him. 'Are you cold?'

'Not really.'

'Someone walk over your grave?'

I half smile and walk on without answering. My thoughts flicker back and forth between the present, with Matthew, and the past, a walk I must have had with Josh at one time; the sky or the wind or the feel of Matthew's hand in mine must bear enough similarities to that earlier occasion to trick me into thinking it's then instead of now.

Gradually, my thoughts return fully to the present. Matthew's silent by my side, his head bent. He's taken his hand away from my waist without my noticing and both hands are shoved in his pockets as he strides forward against the wind. He looks out of sorts; come to think of it, he looked that way at various points in the meal earlier on. Without talking or checking that I want to walk in that direction, he turns to lead the way out to the pier where we pass a few fishermen fishing off the side and a teenager weaving along on his skateboard.

'You're quiet tonight,' I comment lightly.

'Yes, I guess I am.'

'Bad day at work?'

'No. Work's okay.'

I take a breath, a breath that doesn't seem to have enough air in it. 'Something to do with me, then?'

'Yes, you could say it is.'

'What is it?'

I notice him take a shallow breath of his own. 'I'm not sure where this is going, Caitlin, where *we're* going . . .'

'What do you mean?'

'I feel our relationship is one-sided.'

I stop and put one hand on the railing. I feel weak, as though my knees could buckle at any moment. 'That's not true.'

'You're holding me at arm's length, you tell me as little as possible, you won't let me in . . .'

'I tell you plenty!' My voice lacks strength. 'More than I've told anyone else.'

'No, you don't.' He shakes his head, his expression resolute, immoveable. 'You tell me as little as you feel you can get away with.'

'Don't be ridiculous.'

'I'm not being ridiculous. You know it's true. I know practically nothing about your family and your upbringing, and you go out of your way to keep me from meeting your flatmate and your friends. God, you don't even answer the phone when I'm with you!'

'Matthew —' I pause, stuck for words. I was aware that he was watching and, to some degree, forming conclusions, but I'm still stunned by the evidence of my own transparency and the extent of what he's assimilated. There are things I can say in my own defence, explanations, but they involve digging deep into the past and bringing up matters that have no place on this pier where the world appears calm and beautiful and – other than the two of us arguing like this – completely free of conflict.

'I can't get close to you, and if we aren't close then you have to ask if there's any point to this . . . to us.'

I move away from the support of the railing. 'Well, if that's how you feel . . .'

'No, that's not all.' He puts a hand on my shoulder, anticipating that I was planning to walk away. 'I'm not finished with you. You drink more than you should —'

'I drink way less than most people on a night out!'

'You're a diabetic, Caitlin. You can't use what other people drink as a yardstick. You won't wear your bracelet – you wear *nothing* that identifies you as a diabetic. If I found you on the side of the road, I wouldn't know how to help you. Such a simple thing – wearing the bracelet, keeping yourself safe – but still you resist.'

'God, I didn't realise you had such a litany of complaints about me!' I cry.

'They're not complaints – but there are things, *big things*, between us. This recklessness, this disregard you have for your health and safety really bothers me. The crazy way you ride your bike, how you cross roads without looking . . . sometimes it feels like you're hell-bent on breaking the rules and putting yourself at unnecessary risk.'

'Now you sound like my father,' I say accusingly.

Matthew jumps at this mention. 'Why do you hate him so much, Caitlin? Is it because of the affair? Do you *still* hold that against him?'

There's a bitter taste in my mouth; I wet my lips and swallow, but the bitterness does not go away. 'The affair – the divorce – they were the last straw . . .'

'So something happened before that? Was it to do with the bomb? But he's not part of the IRA, is he?'

'No, of course he isn't!'

'From what I can tell from the internet, he's been pivotal in bringing to justice the people who planned the bomb. He seems like an essentially good man . . .'

I stare at him incredulously. 'You checked on the internet?'

'What else could I do?' He shrugs without looking at all apologetic. 'You certainly won't tell me anything.'

A little belatedly, I realise that I googled Matthew too. But that was different. I hardly knew him then, so I wasn't exactly snooping behind his back. 'Well, if you search for long enough, the internet should be able to tell you everything you need to know!' I shriek, sounding petulant and childish even to my own ears.

Matthew looks deep into my eyes, past my sarcasm and anger to where I'm at my most vulnerable. 'What I don't know is who died that day,' he says in a voice so gentle it could undo me if I'm not careful. 'All I know is that it was obviously someone important for you to be like this so many years later, still too devastated to talk about it.'

My breath catches in my throat. Does he have any idea that the answer to that question will reveal everything he wants to know about me and more: the core of why I am the way I am, a truth I will never come to terms with.

'Some things are private, Matthew,' I say brokenly after taking a few moments to gather myself. 'If you can't respect that, then maybe there is no point to us.'

'I respect your right to privacy, of course I do,' he insists, his voice still unnervingly soft. 'But being secretive, as you are, is completely different to being private.'

Quite clearly, he's not going to let it drop. He intends to stay here and badger me until he gets answers, as though I were a criminal.

I push his hands away from my shoulders and step back, almost losing my balance as I do so. 'Just because you're a police officer doesn't give you the right to know everything. Nor does it give you the right to preach to me! I should have known you'd be like this. I knew at the start that I shouldn't get involved with someone like you, but I stupidly did all the same!'

I walk away, my walk becoming a jog, the wind flapping my jacket and stinging my eyes that are humiliatingly full of tears. I don't need to turn around to know that he's watching, forming more conclusions and probably deciding that this is the end for us. Damn him. Damn him and his need to know every single thing about me. Damn his non-stop observing and his 'genius' deductions about my personality and my life. Damn him for googling my father on the internet. Damn him.

He's right about one thing, though. I'm too devastated to talk about any of it: the bomb, my father, or the terrible, terrible fact that I didn't just lose my boyfriend that day, but my brother too.

Josh and Liam lost together. It still defies belief.

Chapter 27

Later that night, unable to read or sleep, I lie on my bed, staring at the ceiling. There's a cobweb on the cornice by the window and I think, without any real commitment, that I should brush it away when I'm cleaning on the weekend. There are a few small insects trapped inside the light fitting – another thing, I decide vaguely, that should be cleaned. Wouldn't it be nice to be able to clean your life the same way you can clean a room? To mop up the hurtful words that spilled from your mouth. To scrub away the messy arguments. To scour and clean until your stained past is restored to something fresh and more appealing.

The phone rings. I hear Jeanie pick it up, her voice a distant murmur. A few moments later there's a knock on my bedroom door and she sticks her head in. 'Your mother's on the phone for you.'

'Okay, I'll pick it up here.' Woodenly, I reach my hand across to the handset on the bedside unit. 'Hi, Mum. What's up?'

'Nothing's "up",' she replies brusquely. 'Only that I haven't heard from you all week! You weren't there when I called at the weekend . . .' She pauses, making it apparent that she's waiting for some sort of explanation.

I close my eyes and see myself in bed with Matthew, the tan of his skin against the white bed linen, the dark rash of stubble across his face, the quizzical look in his eyes when I chose not to answer the shrilling phone. Though I felt bad at the time, I'm glad now that I didn't pick up. If I had, Mum would be enquiring about Matthew right now. And I would have to tell her that we had a big argument and that it's probably all off.

'I went away for the weekend,' I lie.

She must know that I'm not being truthful because she doesn't ask her usual questions: where I went, who with. In fact, she doesn't say anything at all for a few long moments.

'Are you going to stop taking my calls now as well as your father's?'

'Mum, don't be ridiculous!'

'I'm not being ridiculous. I'm just asking. Because you have this black side to you, Caitlin, this unforgiving streak that seems to make it relatively easy for you to cut yourself off from people.'

'Mum!' I lever myself up in the bed and swing my legs over the side so I'm sitting hunched over. 'What's wrong with you? Where's all this coming from?'

'Did you watch the disc Maeve sent?'

'No, not yet.'

'Do you have any intention of watching it?'

'I don't know,' I reply, honest now.

Her sigh is ragged and weary. 'You know, it's one thing not wanting to talk to him on the phone, it's another altogether not to be able to bring yourself to watch him on the television. That's bitterness in the extreme.'

'I'm not bitter!'

'Then what are you? It's a disc, Caitlin, it's only a disc. He can't talk directly to you, he can't touch you or even see you. It's an image of him, a recording, that's all, yet you can't bring yourself to watch it. If that's not bitterness, then what is it?'

I don't answer. I don't know what it is, what the correct label might be, and I'd rather not be having this conversation at all.

'You know, you're too like him, that's the problem. You're both perfectionists, and that's why it's so hard for you both to deal with what happened. But at least *he* found an outlet, a way to come to terms with it. *You* haven't dealt with it at all.'

'I'm not like him, Mum!'

'Yes, you are. That's why you can't forgive him. You're self-righteous, just like him –'

'I don't want to talk about this. I'm tired.'

'I can forgive him, but you can't. Why, Caitlin? It's been eleven years. Don't you think it's high time to move on?'

'Mum, I'm *tired*. I haven't had a good day. I –'

'*I've* moved on,' she persists. 'Why can't you? Why, Caitlin?'

And this is when I crack. In a matter of moments I go from being relatively disengaged to being infused with a dark, dangerous rage. '*I lost my brother.*' God, it hurts to say it. A sharp stabbing hurt that's as fresh as though it happened yesterday. 'I lost my boyfriend *and* my brother,' I scream at her.

'I lost my only son,' she shoots back, tit for tat.

'Dad sent Liam into town that day feeling useless and worthless . . .'

'Maybe he did,' she doesn't miss a beat, 'but that was only one day out of twenty-two years. There were many other days, days when your father cheered him on at his matches, when he taught him how to swim, how to ride a bike, how to drive, when he gave him money to go out . . .'

'I don't care.' I can't seem to control the volume of my voice, even though I know Jeanie must be able to hear in the room next door. 'All I care about is *that day*. How Liam felt. It's bad enough that he died, but to die feeling that he had no value, no worth, because he was unemployed! *Dad* made him feel that way and *that's* what I can't get over. And, while we're at it, I can't brush aside the fact he wasn't there for us afterwards, or that he thought it was a good time to *screw his secretary*!'

'I know, Caitlin. I know all that happened.' Mum's tone has softened. 'Instead of pulling together, our family pulled apart. It can happen either way with grief –'

'You're *always*, *always*, *always* making excuses for him!' I scream over her, tears streaming down my face, fury and hurt swirling inside me.

'Love, I know how –'

'Are you happy now? Are you happy that you started this?'

'Of course I'm not happy.'

'Our family is broken. Nothing can put it back together, least of all me forgiving Dad. Liam is dead, you and Dad are divorced, Maeve has been in her own little world –'

'It is not broken. I'm the first to admit it's not perfect –'

'Jesus, Mum, it's so far from perfect it's laughable.'

'Caitlin, you can't just –'

'I'm going to bed, Mum. I'm tired – I told you at the start that I was tired.'

Pressing the 'end' button on the phone, I cut her off. I sit on the bed, shaking, taking deep breaths to try to expel the anger, the bitterness from my system. It's a long time before I roll beneath the bedcovers, my body feeling weak and tender, the tear-dried skin on my face taut against the softness of the pillow. I leave the light on, needing the warmth and comfort it bestows upon the room.

The morning sun blazes through the kitchen window, intensifying the colours of the gerberas, a reminder of Matthew that I don't want or need. Though I slept surprisingly well, I feel chronically tired as I sit in the over-bright kitchen. My cup of coffee is not reviving in any way; it tastes bitter in my mouth and leaves me feeling thirsty and slightly sick. I pour myself a glass of iced water from the jug in the fridge and I'm sitting down again when Jeanie comes in.

'Is it just boiled?' She nods at the kettle.

'Ten minutes ago.'

She flicks the switch and the humming of the kettle fills the kitchen. Barefoot and with tousled hair, she gets herself two slices of bread and pops them in the toaster. Then, while she waits for the kettle to boil and the bread to toast, she leans back against the counter, her arms folded as she looks down on me in my seat. 'That was quite a spectacular argument you had with your mother last night.'

'Sorry.' I make a face. 'I didn't mean to be so loud.'

'Loud and quite cruel, I'd say.'

'I wasn't being cruel.' I shrug defensively. 'I was making a point, that's all.'

'Mission accomplished. Pity, though, that what you were saying didn't make any sense!'

'Hey, whose side are you on?' I feel a flare of annoyance.

'Yours, of course, which is why I tell you when you're being stupid and unreasonable. Last night you were both, by the way.'

I glare at her. 'Don't you start on me too! I'm *really* not in the mood.'

Jeanie's toast pops and I jump at the sound. God, I'm feeling fraught this morning.

For a while nothing is said. Jeanie butters her toast and makes herself a cup of tea while I finish my glass of water and return to my cup of coffee, which is now cold and even more bitter.

Jeanie can't contain herself for long, though. 'You think every family is perfect but your own,' she declares as she chews on a mouthful of toast.

'I never said that.'

'Not in so many words. But it's apparent in your lack of regard for your own upbringing and in how you glorify everything about mine.'

'*What?* Don't be so ridiculous!'

Jeanie swallows and her voice becomes clearer, harsh even. 'You have no real concept of what it's like to grow up in a big family, Caitlin. It was chaos in our house. Every Saturday morning I went to netball and when I got back my mother would look at me puzzled and ask, "Where have you been all this time?"

Every week we had the same exchange – and she still didn't remember that I had netball on Saturday mornings! She didn't know where we were half the time.'

'Interesting anecdote, but what's that got to do with anything?' I ask, replying to her harshness with sarcasm of my own.

'I bet your mother and father knew where *you* were all the time.' Under the soft bed-tousled hair, Jeanie's expression is uncharacteristically hard. 'I bet they came to watch your netball matches –'

'Netball? I don't think so!'

'You know what I mean – the netball equivalent in Ireland, whatever sport teenage girls play over there. I bet your parents were there, cheering you on. I bet they came to watch and clap every time you got an award at your school assembly. I bet they bought you a brand-new bike every other year, a nice shiny scratch-free model, and well before you had outgrown the last one too. You might think that your mum and dad were too strict, too controlling, but at least you weren't *invisible* to them as I was to mine.'

I get up and throw the rest of my coffee down the sink. 'You know, I think I'm ready to go to work now.'

'There's no need to be sarcastic – or to run off to work. I'm just telling you some truths. I'm fed up with this hard-done-by attitude you have –'

'Oh, shut up, Jeanie,' I burst out as I turn around from the sink.

'My own grown-up sister stole my phone. How's that for a fucked-up family?'

'*Leave me alone.*'

'There's no such thing as a perfect family, a perfect mother or father or sister,' she rants, as though she hasn't heard me. 'You're childish to even think there is . . .'

'I said *leave me alone*, Jeanie. I've had enough!' My shrill voice reverberates in my ears.

I stomp from the kitchen to the bathroom where I brush my teeth so vigorously my gums begin to bleed. A few minutes later, shoes jammed on my feet and handbag strap pulled tight on my shoulder, I leave without saying goodbye, the slam of the apartment door the only contribution I have to make. Despite my bravado, my hands are shaking and my stomach feels really queasy now. What a horrible beginning to the day! I rarely have arguments with Jeanie, I can't even remember the last time we exchanged a cross word. What's wrong with her, picking a fight like this? Just like Matthew and Mum last night. What's wrong with all of them?

Chapter 28

'Harry! Hello, Caitlin here. Just letting you know that every-thing is on track. The technicians have the networking solution fully worked out . . . Yes, they say that the system will be a direct image of your own . . . Yes, amazing technology, isn't it?'

Twirling my pen in my fingers, I gaze out the window as I listen to Harry speak. I'm calm and businesslike on the phone, but the argument with Jeanie keeps replaying in my mind, mud-dling together with the fights I had with Mum and Matthew to form one screaming voice, and the queasiness in my stomach has not settled down.

'The training manuals are at the printers, Harry – I'll send you some when they come in. They look good. Lots of pictures, nice-sized text, easy on the eye. I should have them to you by Friday.'

I run through more details, practical matters like the

synchronisation of the three rooms, contingency plans for sickness and no shows, and how we'll translate feedback into improvements. After this call with Harry, I must make two other lengthy and detailed phone calls, also related to Net Banc. Then I have a facilities meeting to attend, lunch with a prospective client, and another internal meeting in the afternoon. It promises to be a busy day. Right now I need to be busy, to be distracted with work and things to do. Thank God it isn't like some days of late where I've had too much time to think.

'Yes, the rooms will be ready the day before, Harry, and you can come for a walk through. Put your mind at ease. No problem . . . Anything else, just give me a call.'

I put down the phone and take a moment to draw breath. During that tiny fragment of time, my eyes veer to my mobile phone where it lies impassive on my desk. I pick it up, press a button and the screen accommodatingly lights up. No missed messages or calls. Not yet, anyway.

Without stopping to acknowledge the empty lifeless feeling that seems to have transferred from my phone to my insides, I make my next call, to Mike, who releases an exaggerated groan at the mere sound of my voice. Despite his feigned despair, Mike clearly thrives on the size, complexity and technological challenges of the Net Banc job. As he talks, I find myself carried along by his enthusiasm and, once again, offer a quick prayer of thanks that it's a busy day.

'That was a very nice lunch.' Brent Newson wipes the corners of his mouth with his napkin and regards me convivially from across the table. 'And this is a very nice restaurant. Overall a pleasant change from the ham sandwich I usually have at my desk!'

Brent is in his late fifties, his hair grey and concentrated on the lower half of his head, his face round and amiable. He wears large glasses, presumably for reading the fine print and small details that underpin his job. I called him and arranged this lunch after reading a quote he made to a journalist about burdensome new regulations in the insurance industry and the ongoing challenge of keeping staff up to date and properly trained.

'You're welcome, Brent. Actually, this place is one of my favourites, so it's a treat for me too.'

The restaurant, on the banks of the Yarra River, has a panoramic view of the historical shipping wharves and the city beyond, and the food, Japanese with an Australian twist, is always exquisite, though I haven't eaten much of it today. I can't seem to overcome the nausea that's churning in my stomach.

Brent folds his napkin and puts it on the table. 'You make a really strong case for outsourcing, Caitlin,' his eyes blink behind his glasses, 'but I know from experience that our management team, and board, believe that such a move would involve more cost and less control.'

I look across at him, hold his gaze. 'I have an excellent financial model that can work out the real cost of internal training. You'll find that it's not only easier to outsource, it's invariably cheaper too. And there's a very valid argument that you would regain control rather than lose it.'

His lips move into a smile. 'Well, you're welcome to come onsite next week and show me how your model works. If the results turn out as you say they will, maybe we'll be in a position to put forward a convincing argument to the board.'

Pleased with the progress we've made, I decide this is a good note on which to end the lunch. 'Sounds like a plan, Brent. Would you like a coffee?'

He glances to the dessert menu that the waitress put on the table while we were deep in discussion. 'For some reason, I'm in the mood for a liqueur. Or maybe a port.'

I beckon the waitress. 'Do you have any ports or liqueurs you'd recommend?'

'We have a very nice twelve-year-old tawny port,' she replies in a perfunctory tone.

I glance at Brent who nods. 'We'll have one port, please.'

He looks crestfallen. 'You're not joining me?'

I hesitate. Liqueurs and ports are generally off limits: too much sugar. 'I really shouldn't, but make that two!' I say to the waitress.

Her smile seems to hold a hint of disapproval, as though she's aware I'm breaking the rules, taking a risk. She collects the laminated menus and returns a short while later with two glasses of port and the bill.

Raising my glass, I clink it with Brent's. The port is heavy and sweet in my mouth, laden with sugar and guilt, but still it's nice to connect with a client at this level and to round off a successful lunch with something a little decadent for us both. Strictly speaking, Brent isn't a client, he's a prospect. But I feel good about him, about Insurassist. I haven't started to work out all the different components yet, but the basics are there: a profitable cashed-up company, a strong need for change, a decision maker who's easy to deal with, and an agreed follow-up meeting next week. After a barren few weeks, it's nice to have something substantial to work with again, something I can pour myself into and get lost in.

Already a few minutes late for my afternoon meeting, I hurry through the office and pass by my desk to pick up a notepad and pen. Zoe, talking on the phone, waves me down before I can rush off again.

'Jarrod has been looking for you,' she says, her hand covering the mouthpiece.

'He'll have to wait – I'm running late for my meeting.'

'He's come around twice.'

'Did he say it was urgent?'

'Not in so many words,' she admits. 'But he had that cat-on-hot-bricks look about him.'

I laugh. 'He always looks like that! I'll be back in an hour.'

I set off for the meeting, the notepad clutched to my chest, the pen jutting between my fingers like a cigarette. Light-headed from the port, it takes some effort to refocus my thoughts from the early-day buzz of Insurassist to the more mature, expectation-ridden relationship that Net Banc now is.

'You're late,' Nicola announces as I slip into the meeting room on the fourth floor.

'Sorry, I was delayed wooing a prospective client.'

'Well, lucky for us that you're out there selling hard while we're busy trying to figure out how to deliver on your promises!' Nic's smile softens her sarcasm.

'What did I miss?'

She glances at the other faces around the table. 'We're talking about feedback, how we can gather it quickly and effectively on day one, and translate it into tangible improvements by day two. Of course we have our questionnaires, but we also need an earlier gauge of how things are going.'

The meeting goes on for another fifty-five minutes and we discuss a few ways to get a quick view of how the trainees rate the course, but nothing is decided. We finish on the most popular agenda item, food and catering, and as I catch the lift upstairs my thoughts are still preoccupied with avocado chicken tortilla wraps and orange almond mini-tarts. All the talk about food reminds me that I forgot my lunchtime shot of insulin and I pass by my desk again, to get my bag.

'Jarrod –' Zoe begins.

'I know. I just have to go to the ladies. Then I'm heading straight for his office.'

In one of the cubicles, I lift up my top and stab the needle randomly in my stomach. I can almost feel the insulin begin to work its way through my system, spreading under my skin, supplying what's lacking, what cannot be produced naturally. Suddenly remembering the batteries for my glucometer, I make a mental note to drop into a pharmacy on the way home.

Opening the door of the cubicle, I pause in front of the mirror, running a hand through my hair. My face looks slightly flushed, my eyes bleary. I'm tired, but in a weird way I'm wired too. Hopefully my work days are starting to regain their momentum. Today I'm busy, legitimately busy: I have lots to tell Jarrod when I stop by his office.

Feeling thirsty, I lower my head and drink water from the tap at the basin. I dab the excess water from the corner of my mouth with a tissue and then coat my lips with thick, shiny gloss. Before leaving the restrooms, I can't help taking a quick peek at my phone. Still nothing from Matthew.

'Hey, Jarrod.' I breeze into his office. 'You were looking for me?'

'Yes, I was. For the last few hours, in fact.'

'Sorry. Had one of those days.' I help myself to a seat. 'I don't want to count my chickens, but my lunch with Brent was *very* promising. I'm meeting him again next week.'

'Good.'

I pause, waiting for Jarrod's usual rapid-fire questions and needless advice on how to further secure the prospect, but nothing's forthcoming. Jarrod seems strangely uninterested.

'And things are progressing fabulously with Net Banc,' I continue while Jarrod gets up from his desk and walks behind me to close the door. 'The technicians have some really innovative ideas. I think we'll end up with a great blueprint for other jobs of this scale.'

Jarrod walks back behind his desk but doesn't sit down. 'Good,' he says again.

I can't ignore his apparent lack of interest. 'Is something wrong?' I ask a little puzzledly.

Jarrod opens his mouth and closes it with a sigh.

'What is it?' I press. Is he working his way up to telling me that he has resigned? Is that why he seems so disengaged? I'm surprised to realise that I'll be sorry to see him go. On the whole he's been a decent boss and I've learned something from his fastidious approach, though I hate to admit it. On the positive side, his departure is an opportunity for me, a chance to put myself forward for his job, a long-awaited step into management.

'I'm sorry,' he begins, his voice sounding deeper than usual. 'Because of the global financial crisis, we've had to cut headcount . . .'

So he isn't resigning, he's being made redundant. I didn't expect that!

'Unfortunately, your job is one of the ones we've decided to let go.'

I'm not hearing him correctly. This cannot be true. '*My* job?'

'Yes – I'm sorry, Caitlin.'

'*I'm* leaving? But I –' My voice breaks. Disbelief and shock combine to form a hard, impassable lump in my throat and it hurts to swallow. 'Are you really saying that I have to leave?'

'I'm sorry.'

'But I have deals happening: Net Banc; Insurassist will come through too, I'm certain of it. And I was the one who did all the hard work for Telelink . . .'

'I'm sorry.'

It's irrelevant how many times he says he's sorry, or how evidently sincere his apologies are. 'This isn't fair, Jarrod,' I howl at him.

'Things like this are never fair,' he agrees morosely, 'and there's never a good way to deliver bad news like this.'

'Please, Jarrod, don't do this to me.' I'm horrified to hear myself begging. 'I can bring in more business, and more than pay my way –'

'I'm sorry. I know how hard you work, how much you put in,

and this has honestly been one of the most difficult decisions of my career.'

Staggering to my feet I feel stunned, like I've been hit by something heavy.

'I have your payout cheque here.' Jarrod has this sad, sympathetic expression that doesn't suit his face. I much prefer when he's being a pompous know-it-all.

'I've never been unemployed, Jarrod. Not since I left Ireland.' Is that pleading voice really mine? 'Are you sure you can't delay this a few months?'

'Sorry, Caitlin. It's company policy. You have to clear out your desk and go.'

It comes to me then: the gauge that Nicola was looking for in the meeting. We can use balls, small red and green balls. If people like the training they throw a green ball into a basket, if they don't like it they throw red. Simple. I don't know how or why the solution has materialised right at this moment; there's nothing in Jarrod's office that's red or green, and the topic of conversation is as far from feedback mechanisms as one can get. It's a strange, strange time for the idea to come into my head.

I take the cheque and paperwork from Jarrod's outstretched hand and walk unsteadily towards the door.

'Are you all right, Caitlin?'

'Sure,' I reply, utterly defeated.

If there was a basket at the door, I'd hurl a red ball into it. This day has not been a good day. The busy feel, the momentum with Net Banc, the promise of Insurassist, all put a deceiving veneer on what was bad underneath. It started out bad and now it has ended that way too.

Chapter 29

The laneway at the back of the Mitre buzzes with a healthy mid-week crowd, the patrons attired mostly in dark suits and white shirts. Black and white never fails to look good together. The contrast makes the white look whiter, and the black even more severe, something to be taken seriously. The combination lends the illusion of things being clear-cut, straightforward once you keep to the rules. In this setting, with office blocks hovering in the skyscape, the monochrome clothing conveys purpose, power and status. These are the people who bark orders down the phone, stride into meetings, sign, with an arrogant flourish, their names to letters and other documents that need their authority. In my knee-length pinstriped skirt and white top, I blend in perfectly. But for one difference: as of two hours ago, I'm unemployed. Any purpose, power or status I possessed is now gone, left behind in Jarrod's office like an unwanted file.

'Here,' Nic, back from her third visit to the bar in the relatively short time we've been here, thrusts a glass into my hand. 'Get this down you.'

I take the glass and swallow half its contents, desperate for the alcohol to take effect and to soften the hard lump that's rotating inside my chest. *I'm unemployed, I'm unemployed, I'm unemployed.* No amount of alcohol will take the menace from these words. I feel insecure and half-terrified, all of the knowledge, confidence and experience of the last ten years wiped out in one stroke.

I look around, searching for familiar faces, or for other people with shell-shocked expressions like mine, and supportive friends like Nicola making frequent, bolstering trips to the bar. There's nobody else I can see, nobody I know from work, nobody who looks like they've just lost their job.

'I think I was the only one.' I take another tasteless but fortifying gulp of my drink.

Uncannily, as though it heard me, Nic's phone beeps with a message. 'Nathan's gone too,' she reads slowly, 'and three girls from accounts. So, it's not just you.'

From the expression on her face, she's hoping this news will make me feel better, less singled out, but I feel the same: shocked, frightened, sick. 'You'll find something else, Caitlin.' She pats my arm reassuringly. 'You're smart and presentable and qualified. There are always jobs out there for people like you. Companies make vacancies for people like you!'

Smart and presentable, maybe. Qualified, no. Who will hire me without a degree? What did Dad say? You need that piece of paper.

'I'm not qualified, Nic,' I say slowly, wearily. 'I don't have a degree. I left Ireland without finishing it.'

I have nothing to back me up, to prove what I'm worth.

'Oh. I thought . . . I assumed . . .' Nic's voice trails off. She's beginning to look uncomfortable, as though she'd rather the conversation would move on.

'You know, Nic, I thought of something we could use to get instant feedback from the Net Banc attendees, a quick gauge of how they feel about the training . . .'

'That's hardly your concern now!'

'I know, but humour me. I thought that we could have a basket set up at the door and a tub of balls, red and green balls. If the trainees like the training, they throw a green ball in the basket. If they don't like the training, they throw a red. It'll be easy to count the balls, get an initial sense of how we're going. It's fun and quick. Obviously, we would follow up with detailed questionnaires later.'

'You're still hung up on that juggling, aren't you?'

'No, I'm not.'

'You are!'

'I'm not. I'm just using the concept. You have to admit it's a good idea. You should use it. Harry would like it. I know he would.'

'Caitlin, Harry isn't your concern now.'

'He was until a few hours ago. I can't switch off so easily.'

Nicola rolls her eyes and looks around again, brightening suddenly. 'Derek's here.'

I swing around. 'Where?'

'At the bar.' She raises her hand in a casual wave.

I spot Derek in time to see him return Nic's wave. With a weird sense of déjà vu, I register the details of him: the confident half-smile directed at the bar girl as he tosses his change into the tip jar on the counter; his shirt, open at the collar, and his tie, loose and soon to be discarded; his swagger as he moves away from the bar, raising the rim of his beer glass to sip as he walks. Does he have the bike parked outside? No, he wouldn't be so stupid. I stare at him, watch every step of his progress until he's virtually out of sight in a far-off corner, and all the while he steadfastly refuses to acknowledge my presence.

'Nice that you two are so friendly!' I turn back to Nic. 'He won't as much as look in my direction.'

She shrugs. 'You're a reminder that he lost his licence for six months and broke up with his girlfriend, that's all.'

I'm taken aback that she knows these details. 'Did he tell you this?'

'Yes.'

Obviously Nic is friendlier with Derek than I've given her credit for. They must have got to know each other during the implementation, finding common ground over late nights, early starts and shared objectives. Now that I think about it, Nic is as much of a flirt as Derek is. They would have been close within a couple of days of working with each other.

I feel quite piqued by this, and then piqued at myself for even caring. 'Oh well, I suppose Derek's not my concern anymore either.'

'No, as a matter of fact, he's not.'

My mood plummets even further. What am I going to do? How will I find the strength to start from scratch, to carve a niche and a future in another company, to find and foster new clients like Telelink and Net Banc?

'Here's something to help your mood.' Nic's voice plays over my thoughts. 'Look over your shoulder. Discreetly!'

'Why?'

'The scenery has improved rather dramatically.'

I know without looking that it's a group of men – designer suits, dark good looks, arrogant smiles: Nic's usual type. 'Not interested.'

Nicola rolls her eyes again. 'You're missing out . . .'

'Really,' I muster a smile, 'I don't care if I am.'

While Nic assesses the new arrivals from under her lashes, I consider checking my phone, which is tucked away in my bag. I know with painful certainty that there are no missed calls or text messages: I would have heard it ring or beep if there were. It has remained eerily silent all day. Nevertheless, I've continued to check it intermittently, a reflex I can't seem to help. No point in doing so again. No point at all. *He's not going to call. He's done with you. He thinks you're reckless and immature.*

'Time for another drink, methinks,' declares Nic, and puts down her empty wineglass on a nearby table before walking slowly, catwalk style, towards the bar. She passes a group of men, I assume the same ones she was eyeing up earlier, and flicks her hair ever so slightly. All three of them openly check her out. She doesn't let on that she's noticed, which of course she has; she's quite professional in how she flirts.

As I stand waiting for her to return, I think about going home. I could follow Nic to the bar, tap her on the shoulder, and inform her that I don't want another drink because I don't feel like I belong here. I'm not one of these people: I don't have a job.

I am not what I seem, I could declare to Nic and anyone else who cared to listen. *I'm wearing a suit but I'm really unemployed.*

But I feel sluggish, my arms and legs too leaden to make even the slightest movement, not to talk about the mammoth effort of following Nicola to the bar. In what seems like no time at all and yet an eternity, she's back, three sets of eyes again closely following her progress.

'Did they notice me?' she asks, her lips hardly moving.

'You can talk properly. I'm sure they can't lip-read.'

'You never know. Well, did they?'

'Notice you? You know they did!'

'I wonder how long before one of them comes over.'

I throw back a good portion of the fresh drink she's just handed me. It tingles through my body, dissipating some of the heaviness in my limbs. 'Ten minutes,' I respond, suddenly more in the mood for her games. 'No, five – five minutes before one or all of them swarms over to you.'

'And you too,' Nic adds generously.

'Me too,' I agree without a shred of enthusiasm.

I can't help myself then: I take out my phone. Check its blank screen. No missed calls, no unread messages.

I knew this! Why do I keep checking and double-checking the obvious? He hasn't called, and it's pretty clear now that he's not going to.

I'm angry with myself for being so pathetic. What's wrong with me? Big deal that he hasn't called. Big deal that he's no different to all the other men over the last eleven years. Big fat deal.

'You know, Nic, men are bastards. All of them. Especially the nice ones.'

Nicola laughs. Her eyes are focused over my shoulder. 'Don't turn around, but there are three bastards coming in our direction.'

'Really, Nic, I'm not in the mood.'

'Well, *get* in the mood.'

'It's not that easy.'

I'm as angry with Matthew as I am with myself. *He held himself out as different.* Someone I could trust. Someone steady and reliable and safe. He had no right. No right at all. He didn't even make it through our first real fight. *Pathetic.* So much for him being in love with me!

Flashes of other fights, with Josh, replay in my head. Sudden arguments that spiralled out of nowhere, shouting, furious gesturing, slamming doors. But we always made up, and after each argument our relationship seemed deeper, tighter, with a new level of understanding. Is that what love is, being able to fight and make up and be closer as a result? But love is other things too: having someone you want to be with *every single day*, someone who's stimulating without being annoying, who makes you feel content without feeling bored, whose imperfections complement your own so as to make a more complete whole.

'Tell them to go away,' I blurt as I sense the men approaching from behind.

Nicola laughs.

'I'm not joking. Tell them to go away.'

'Caitlin, what's wrong with you?'

'Nothing.'

What's wrong is that I'm waiting for Matthew to call. *All day* I've been waiting. I can't believe that he hasn't, that he would let things end like they did last night; it goes against everything

I know about him. He obviously doesn't love me – if he did he would have called by now. Josh is the only one who ever loved me, *really* loved me. He loved me without needing to hear my voice, my laughter. But he's dead. Eleven years now. Dead and buried. Like Liam. In different cemeteries, though they died side by side.

How can I tell Nicola all that?

Nicola's smiling, on a completely different wavelength to me. 'Are you *drunk*? Four drinks and you're *drunk*?'

I consider the question. The music and pressed bodies and noise have receded into the background. Nic's face is all that I can see. It's close, really close. Her head is tilted to one side, her eyes crinkled, her mouth open in a grin.

'I might be,' I slur.

Nicola's eyes are lovely. They have tiny green flecks. And her lipstick, that red, is so bright and lovely too. It suits her, really suits her.

Nicola's hand clutches my arm. 'You're swaying. I've never seen you so pissed.' She's still grinning, though.

'Lovely smile, Nic. You're lovely.'

The men come, Nicola's men, holding beer bottles in their hands and introducing themselves with predatory smiles. I feel myself retreat until my physical body is left standing in place, nodding and smiling as appropriate, and the rest of me hovers in the air, looking down. It feels nice, very nice indeed, to be above all the people and noise, to be so high. I'm floating, totally at one with the stratosphere, only mildly concerned by matters of employment and love and all the other minutiae that those on earth have to deal with.

Is this what it's like for Josh and Liam? Floating above the world? Watching me and everyone else?

Down below Nic tosses her hair, flirting and trying to decide which of the men, if any, is worth playing for. Over in some far-off corner is Derek, friends with Nic now, still stubbornly blaming me for the accident. Somewhere out there is Matthew, shy, sweet, perceptive, demanding answers, not loving me enough to call today; and how ironic that I wouldn't have met him in the first place if it wasn't for the accident.

Thanks for that, Derek. Thanks for facilitating that first meeting with Matthew. Or do I mean no thanks? What does it matter! I like it up here. Nothing seems to matter that much at all.

No sooner have I had this thought than I start to fall, the floor rushing up to meet me. Hands grab my arms on the way down.

'Caitlin? Caitlin?' Nicola's voice.

'She's blacked out.' A voice I don't recognise.

'Clear back, everyone. *Clear back!*'

I don't hear the rest of what's said.

This was a bad day. A bad twenty-four hours, in fact. I'm more than happy to be out of it.

Part Three

Chapter 30

When I first open my eyes, I feel relaxed and quite pleasantly vague. My eyes drift from left to right; it's taking some effort to focus. I conclude that the bed I'm lying on must be quite high off the ground because I feel as though I'm floating in midair. The realisation that I'm not in my own room causes momentary but mild confusion. There's a thin white blanket tucked neatly around my lower body and a metal industrial-looking bed end. The room is compact, the walls a bland inoffensive colour, and the light spilling from the window suggests that it's sometime in the afternoon. This prompts me to check my watch and it's only then I realise that there is something attached to me: a drip.

Awareness pricks my bubble. Immediately, I begin to recall snatches of the events that have led me to this bed, this hospital. Matthew, standing on the pier, his face uncharacteristically severe, his eyes knowing more than I can deal with. My mother, the accusations, the blame, the terrible truths released down the phone. Jeanie, provocative and hurtful words spewing from her mouth. Jarrod's expression strangely sympathetic. Nicola steadying my arm, grinning. *'I've never seen you so pissed.'*

The door opens and a nurse comes in. She sees that I'm awake and gives me a warm smile. 'You're back in the land of the living, I see,' she proclaims and unhooks the chart from the end of my bed.

'How long was I out?' My voice sounds weak from disuse.

'A couple of days.'

A couple of days. Not hours. *Days.*

'Does anyone know I'm here?' I manage, despite my shock.

The nurse gives me an odd look before she writes on the chart. 'Of course. Your boyfriend has been here . . .'

My boyfriend. Does she mean Matthew?

The nurse takes my pulse and listens to my heartbeat and checks my feet. 'And I've seen a girl here too.'

Probably Nicola.

'Blonde hair.'

Jeanie. I fight the sudden onslaught of tears.

The nurse's voice is kind. 'It can be a little overwhelming waking after something like this. Don't be too hard on yourself, now.'

It's only then that I hear her accent. The edges have been softened and polished but its origins are undeniable. I falter, a question stuck in my throat. *What part of Belfast are you from?*

She's bent over the chart again. If only I could get a closer look at her name tag . . . The irony doesn't fail to strike me: here I am, more than a decade later on the other side of the world, tubes feeding insulin and other fluids into my body, and it's still about names. That reflex, to pinpoint religion and political affiliation, has endured through everything and is as strong as ever.

The nurse hooks the chart back onto the bed, slips a pen into her pocket and turns towards the door, all without giving me a clear view of the tag pinned neatly to the front of her white short-sleeved shirt. 'I'll be back later. Press the button if there's anything you need in the meantime.'

I'm on my own, wondering if there is anything I need. There are, in fact, a few things that I need right now. I need to know how Matthew – if it was indeed him the nurse saw sitting by my bed – found out I was here. I need to know if Jeanie is still upset with me. For that matter, I also need to know if Matthew is upset with me. And, of course, my mother. It's quite a list of people I've managed to put offside.

I lie still for a long time, thinking about how I can make amends, worrying that I can never put things right, seesawing between the present and the past. At some point, feeling heavy and weighed down by it all, I close my eyes and sleep.

I dream that I'm in Belfast City Hospital. The nurse has a much stronger accent, so pronounced that I'm finding her hard to follow. Her name is Margaret Donaldson.

'My first boyfriend was Protestant too...' I tell her conversationally.

'Good for him,' she replies tartly.

'He died in the Clonmegan bombing.'

She softens immediately. 'I'm sorry, love.'

I nod and we share a moment of silence.

'Your mother came in while you were sleeping,' she says, taking her turn at being the conversational one.

'She did?'

'Aye. She was crying a lot.'

'Oh, no.'

'She kept saying that she'd thought you were taking proper care of yourself . . .'

'My glucometer was dead, it needed new batteries,' I confess shamefacedly. 'I know I should have made the batteries a priority, but there was so much else going on.'

'So you were a bit careless . . .'

'Yes, I was.' My voice is laden with guilt. 'I wasn't taking proper care of myself.'

'Well, that much is clear to your poor mother now!'

I wake with a jolt, the nurse's admonition ringing in my ears, a taste of guilt in my mouth. I'm inordinately relieved to find that I'm not in Belfast City Hospital and that my mother's recriminations and very justifiable disappointment don't have to be dealt with. Well, at least not right at this moment.

I press the buzzer to call the nurse. The light flashes red in my hand, indicating urgency, and I feel a little embarrassed that I'm calling her only to ask her name and what part of Belfast she's from. The urgency is not of a medical nature, but it is otherwise genuine, and I cannot begin to explain how badly I need to know.

Later in the day, after the dinner trolleys have been wheeled away and the smells of food have dissipated into the usual hospital smell of disinfectant, there is a rap on my door. It's Matthew. He fills the room even from the doorway, vibrant and purposeful against the bland clinical backdrop. He's in uniform. On his way to work, I guess from the pristine condition of his blue shirt.

'Hello.' My lips tremble into an uncertain smile.

'Hello.' His response is formal, distant. Still, he's here, and given the circumstances I'm grateful. He pulls up a seat and sits next to the bed, his arms resting on his knees.

I plunge in at the deep end. 'I'm sorry, Matthew. Everything you said was justified.'

'That doesn't matter now.' He looks down at his hands, shaking his head slightly.

'But it does matter,' I insist anxiously. 'And I'm *really* sorry.'

'Okay. Apology accepted.'

The silence that follows is filled only with hospital sounds: the rise and fall of nurses' voices as they pass outside, the squeak of wheels down the corridor, faint beeps from machines in other rooms.

'How did you find out I was here?'

'I rang your mobile phone and Nicola answered.' He *had* called in the end. I should have known he would. I should have trusted him. 'Of course, Nicola had no idea who I was,' he adds in a flat voice.

'I'm sorry,' I reiterate. I'm gripping the blanket, the cotton scrunched under my tense, furled fingers.

This time he acknowledges my apology with a slight nod that gives nothing away.

'Do you know if anyone has told my mother?'

'Jeanie called your mother.'

'You've met Jeanie?'

'Yes. Someone else who was totally unaware of my exist-
ence,' he says in that same detached tone, but his jaw is rigid
and it's suddenly obvious to me that that he's holding his feelings in check, that this formality is a front. *He* doesn't trust *me*.
And given my secretiveness and erratic behaviour, who could
blame him?

'I'm sorry,' I say yet again. There are so many things that
I am sorry for, I'm in danger of losing track of them all. 'I
found it difficult to talk about you, to tell them how serious we
were . . .'

He looks at his hands again and then at me. 'Look, Caitlin,
I don't need to be validated by your friends. That's not what
I'm about.' His voice trails off but I know that he's not finished.
I wait, my heart drumming, creating a peculiar sensation in
my chest. Finally he continues, 'All relationships reach a point
where you are either honest about who and what you are, or you
walk away.'

I'm distraught. I can't walk away from him. Not again. Not
ever. '*No, I don't want to walk away*,' I say urgently. 'Do you? Do
you want to walk away?'

'No, I don't.' He sounds resigned. 'But I'm not prepared to
go on as we were either. I need to know who you are – I need to
understand why you do the things you do.'

I nod. I understand what he's saying. And so I summon everything I have, every ounce of strength and courage and endurance,
and try to explain. 'It's not easy for me to be honest, about either
my feelings or my past. What's here and now is fine, but what
happened before is not, and I thought I could put it behind me,
that I could leave it for dead. It's taken me this long to realise that

I can't. It's alive, it's part of me, it's everywhere. Even the nurse here is from Belfast: her name is Mona and she's Catholic, not Protestant like I first thought . . .'

I realise that I'm all over the place, that I'm not making much sense, not to myself, definitely not to Matthew. 'I don't know where to start!' I cry in desperation.

'Start anywhere.' Emotion flickers in his eyes. His shield is slipping. This gives me hope and an injection of strength.

I take a breath and try again, taking a step back in time and making a big effort to talk more slowly. 'My father brought us up believing that if we kept to the rules, everything would be fine, nothing bad could happen. But something bad did happen, something *very* bad, and maybe that's why I can't see the point of rules . . .'

No, that's still not the right starting point; Matthew looks more bemused than enlightened.

Another breath. Another attempt. 'The bomb I told you about was a car bomb. It went off in the middle of town. Josh, my boy-friend, was killed . . .'

I hear him suck in his breath and his hand reaches to take mine. Tears pour down my face. *Now* we are underway. 'Josh was deaf, he didn't even hear the blast, but he knew that some-thing was wrong so he went back to clear people away from the car. He was standing in the worst possible place . . . there was nothing left of him.'

'I'm sorry,' Matthew says quietly. His hand tightens on mine and I feel his strength.

'That's not all,' I sob. 'My brother . . . my brother was killed too . . .'

Matthew has stood up from the visitors' seat and is now sitting on the bed next to me. His arm curls around my shoulders and he gathers me as close as he can.

'Liam was three years older than me.' My voice is hoarse and uneven. 'He was annoying and exasperating, like all brothers, but we were very close. He was brilliant at sport, but he couldn't get a job, not coaching or doing anything remotely related.'

My head is buried in the crook of Matthew's neck. Though feeling wrung out and emotional, I feel a sense of safety too which, ironically, reminds me of my father and the piece of the story I've not yet told. 'Neither Josh nor Liam would have been in town that day if it wasn't for my father. We had no reason to go into town, we were all perfectly happy to spend the afternoon at home, until Dad started picking on Liam . . .'

I start to cry in earnest, my tears blotting Matthew's shirt. A few minutes pass before I can utter the last of what I need to say.

'You asked me why I hate my father. There are a few reasons. Dad was there for everybody else, providing support for the whole town, with the exception of his own family. We should have had first call – we needed him the most. The affair, doing that to my mother while she was still reeling from the loss of her son, was like a slap in the face for us all. But at the root of everything is the fact that Dad's intolerance and lack of understanding drove us into town that day . . . We had no reason to be there, *no reason at all*, only that Dad couldn't bear to look at Liam a moment longer. In effect, it's like he sent Liam and Josh to their death . . . How could I not hate him for that?'

Chapter 31

Josh was my first love, and I loved him so instinctively and with such devotion I thought it would last forever. Maybe it could have, I don't know, but considering how young we were, there was every possibility that we would have eventually split up, perhaps one of us breaking the other's heart.

But Liam should have been a given, he should have been there always, forever. He should be married now, to some nice local girl, with one or two kids – boys, little rascals with red hair, thick legs and an obsession with kicking balls of all shapes and sizes. Instead, he's dead. I have no brother now and never will again. Even though it's been eleven years, I can't seem to come to terms with this stark, irreversible fact, and now I realise that's why I shut out what happened to him. Difficult and heart-breaking and unfathomable as it was, I did manage to process Josh's death – but Liam's I simply couldn't accept. In my mind, he's frozen at the stage he was at before he died: afternoons spent booting a ball against the side of the house, low, powerful shots, honed through frustration and boredom; coming in on Saturday nights, eyes glazed, a smirk on his mouth, spirits raised by the combination of pool and beer. On one such occasion, Mum smacked him when she saw how intoxicated he was, forgetting in her anger that he was a man, not a boy. There was a moment of stunned silence before he laughed, and then she laughed, and so did I, until tears ran down our faces.

I remember Liam on the day of the bombing, slouched in the armchair, one leg hooked over the armrest, joystick in his hand. My father was parked in the other armchair, occasionally looking up from the papers he was marking to frown at Liam. Josh and I were on the couch, my head resting against his shoulder as we both read our books, content to be together despite the tension building around us.

'For the love of God, Liam, would you put that thing away and find something constructive to do with yourself!'

My father's low, contemptuous voice permeated the room. If he had shouted in anger, I imagine Liam would have instantly retaliated. But contempt is harder than outright anger to answer, and Liam was mute in its wake.

My father's aggravation increased even further at this lack of response. 'Did you hear me? You've been playing that thing all week. I can't bear to see you doing something so utterly useless. *There must be something else you can do, Liam.*'

Liam still persevered with the game, glaring at the screen, jerking the joystick back and forth, a tic working at the side of his mouth.

'What's wrong with you?' Dad was relentless. 'Are you too lazy to even answer me now?'

Liam quite obviously didn't have the energy or imagination to craft an answer that would satisfy my father. There was a dangerous pause.

'Answer me, damn it. Show some *bloody* respect.'

Liam's answer, when it came, was not what any of us expected. He hurled the joystick across the room, the wire dislodging from the PlayStation and trailing behind it like a ribbon. It whizzed past my father's ear before crashing into the wall behind him. Liam leapt up from his seat. 'There! You can fucking well keep it for all I care.'

Josh and I exchanged alarmed glances and stood up too.

My father, apoplectic with rage, was the last to get to his feet. 'Get out of this house,' he roared. 'Get out *now*!'

'Don't fucking worry,' Liam spat, his fists clenched. 'I'm going.'

Josh, worried about Liam's fists and what he might do with them, took his arm and forcefully assisted his departure.

'Why are you always picking on him?' I screamed at Dad. 'Why can't you leave him alone?' Not waiting for an answer, I ran after Josh and Liam. I found them outside, standing by the front gate. Liam looked pale and depleted, as though his anger had bled out of him.

'I'm going into town,' he muttered.

'We'll go with you,' I offered as a show of solidarity.

That was how we all ended up going into town that day. Josh and I walked the first leg with Liam, before he detoured to pick up a friend. Later on, when the town centre was evacuated, Liam was standing on the opposite side of the road from us, close to the dark-green car. I exchanged a shrug with him and pointed in the direction of home. He shook his head; I knew he had no desire to return to the house and sit in the same room as my father, being made to feel so inadequate and worthless.

Josh was uneasy, though. He kept looking back over his shoulder, at the car, at Liam. He felt compelled to go back. Josh and Liam were side by side when the bomb exploded, Josh's hand on Liam's arm as he tried to convince him to come home with us. The blast took them both. Nothing was left of them. Nothing but the ash that hailed from the sky and landed on my arms as I screamed their names.

I harbour some guilt about that day, guilt that's been eating away at me. I should have said more, I should have stood up for Liam properly, shown unflinching support, attempted to defuse my father's contempt. I never got to say sorry to him for privately thinking he should have been trying harder to get a job, for not fully empathising with his situation. As I raked through the rubble with my bare fingers, the apology was burning in my throat, and it has been ever since.

I'm remembering other things too, details I had pushed to the back of my mind and mislaid with the passing of time. My father driving me to dancing, to swimming and friends' houses, never complaining though it must have been inconvenient and annoying. The little gifts he occasionally brought home from work, pens, pencils, brightly coloured stationery he knew I liked. And the day, a few lifetimes ago, when Mandy and I fell off our bikes . . .

After I said goodbye to Mandy at the corner of the street and walked the rest of the way home, I took my dented bike around the back where Liam was taunting Maeve with a basketball, bouncing it around her and laughing at her attempts to gain possession. They glanced my way but didn't notice the state of me or the bike. I knew I wouldn't be as lucky when I got inside.

As I sneaked in the back door, as inconspicuously as possible, my parents were in the kitchen, Mum at the sink, Dad setting the table for lunch. Mum looked over her shoulder with a smile. 'Hi, love.' Her smile fell away when she saw my torn and bloody knees. 'Jesus, Mary and Joseph! What happened to you?'

'I came off my bike.'

'How?'

'I hit a pothole.'

'Were you going too fast?' This was from my father and I turned to look at him.

'Maybe a little.'

Mum left the sink, drying her hands on her skirt, and came over to assess my injuries. 'Where does it hurt the most?' she asked sympathetically, her hands on my shoulders, her eyes looking me up and down.

'My knees and my hands.' I turned up my palms to reveal the stinging grazes.

She tutted at the shorn skin and steered me to a seat. 'Come here and sit down. Let me see those knees . . .' Blood had glued the fabric to my skin and I winced as she lifted it away. 'Sorry, love, I'm trying to be gentle. I'll clean it and put some cream on and it'll feel a lot better.' She went to the bathroom to get the first aid box and I was left to face my father's wrath.

'You were lucky to get off so lightly.'

I said nothing.

'Where did it happen?'

'Just outside town.'

'Did you cycle home afterwards?'

I gulped. I didn't want to tell the truth, but my bike was outside and clearly not roadworthy. 'I got a lift . . .'

His eyes narrowed dangerously. 'You got a lift!' he repeated. 'And from whom did you get a *lift*?'

'A farmer. He had a trailer, he put the bikes in . . .' I trailed off, knowing there was nothing I could say to remedy the situation.

Mum returned from the bathroom and, sensing the friction, paused in the doorway.

My father's expression was forbidding. 'You got into a car with a stranger?'

'Mandy was with me,' I said feebly.

'So you're as stupid as each other!'

Mum turned on him, her eyes blazing and her voice harsh. 'Jesus, Jonathan, the girl is battered and bruised. Can you get off your high horse for once and show some sympathy?'

Through welling tears, I saw the anger drain from my father's face and in a matter of seconds he softened into a different man. He came over, sat down next to me and lifted me onto his knee. I buried my head in the curve of his neck, where I could smell the familiar musk of his aftershave.

'Sorry, love. I worry about you – about road accidents, about men in cars who don't have good intentions . . . about everything, really.'

Sitting there, in the warm crook of his arm, I understood his worries, and I knew for once where he was coming from. And I felt safe and loved in the way that only he could make me feel.

Now I find myself remembering that sense of being protected, of being kept safe. I had all but forgotten that side of my father. His generosity too: the brand-new bike he bought me a few days after the accident, metallic blue with drop handlebars, multiple gears and narrow high-pressure tyres; the allowance he paid into my bank account when I was at Queen's; the money he gave to Liam to supplement his dole. His weakness was Liam's unemployment. It grated at him, frustrated him no end; it was his Achilles heel. In almost every other respect, Dad was dependable, decent and fairly level-tempered.

My feelings about him seem to be in a state of flux, taking new perspective from the memories and nuances I'd all but forgotten about, changing hour by hour, softening. I'm aware that this shift in how I feel about him has in fact been building, against my will, over the last few months. Matthew's balanced opinion of Steve, Sophie's cheating ex-husband, along with Jeanie's assertions about her own imperfect family have played a part. The realisation that Maeve and Dad have a relationship, a working father–daughter relationship salvaged from the wreckage of our family, has played another part. By the time I finished listening to his voice message, the one about Maeve's new job, the one where he sounded like a normal, caring father instead of a distant, opinionated professor, there was a chink in my feelings, a significant shift that I could no longer ignore. Maybe that's why I fought so hard with Matthew and Mum. I was hanging on to the hatred, fighting for it, because it's all I've known for the last eleven years and in its own way it's helped me survive, kept me going.

These thoughts about my father are confronting and they leave me feeling so drained that I usually fall asleep before I reach any definitive conclusion or decision on what to do about him.

Chapter 32

Mona is back. She was off yesterday and I missed her. She's the only nurse who stops to chat. We talk about how I'm feeling today, the weather outside, the news and, with the preliminaries over, we talk about home. Mona has been here twenty years, ten more than me. She has two teenagers, born and raised Australians.

'They talk and act like Aussies,' she smirks, 'but their skin is bluey white and the two of them couldn't look more Irish if they tried!'

I laugh, trying to imagine two Irish-looking, Australian-sounding angsty teenagers. Mona's husband is also from Belfast. They emigrated straight after they got married.

'Australia was our honeymoon, in effect. And we're still here, still on honeymoon.'

'Why did you choose Australia?'

She grimaces. 'I couldn't wait to get out of Belfast. I wanted to get as far away as possible. If I could have practically gone further away than Australia, I would have!'

That sounds familiar. I briefly wonder how many of us there are, Northern Irish who have run as far away as they practically can.

'Do you miss home at all?' I ask.

'It took me a long time to miss it. To want to go home again. But now, aye, I do.'

'Have you been back?'

'Three times in all. The last visit was two years ago.'

'Did you find it different?' I'm surprised by how curious I am.

'Aye, I did. There's construction and new buildings and a bit more sophistication to the place. There's still division, though, two sides with very different views and opinions. But I've real-ised that's not entirely a bad thing. There's no denying that Belfast has heart, that the people are passionate and prepared to stand up for what they believe in. When my kids mope or say they don't care about things, I feel like shaking them. They have no idea how good they have it. Give me passion rather than complacency any day!'

Mona doesn't look remotely like my mother but her turn of phrase and kindliness remind me of her. I haven't spoken to Mum. She phoned twice, once when Mona was changing my drip and another time when the doctor was here and it was equally inconvenient to answer. The nurses at reception updated her on my progress and scribbled a message onto a pink slip that they brought in later with my meds. *Your mum called. Very wor-ried about you but glad to hear you're doing better.*

I tried to call her back last night. The phone rang out and I left a message of my own: 'Hi, Mum. Just letting you know I'm okay and that I'm going home the day after tomorrow. I'll talk to you soon.' I hung up feeling extremely relieved that she wasn't there to receive the call, and extremely guilty for being so relieved. It's not really making the apology that I'm dreading: it's facing up to how much I've let her down. Mum has got through the last eleven years on the reassurance that I was safe, and that Maeve was safe, and that nothing bad would happen to her remaining children. But I didn't keep myself safe. I exposed myself, and her, to another potentially disastrous situation, and I can only imagine just how rattled and insecure she is feeling right now.

I haven't spoken to Jeanie either. According to Matthew she's in Brisbane on business but she'll be home tomorrow to greet me when I come out of hospital. I'll apologise to her then, straight up, no fuss. No fancy words, just a plain 'I'm sorry'.

So many apologies. So much making up to do.

At least Matthew and I have moved past apologies.

'Everyone in this ward must think I'm in trouble with the law,' I joke when he turns up later in the afternoon, in uniform again. He was here twice yesterday, before and after his shift, a figure of authority just like now. But only until he smiles, whips off his hat and squeezes me in a hug.

'Well, you *were* in trouble with the law, Miss O'Reilly.' He grins. 'I've received a number of complaints against you, but given the extenuating circumstances I've wiped your record clean.'

Suddenly I don't feel like joking around. There's something I need to say, and this feels as good a time as any. The words have been bubbling inside me for days now. I reach to take his hand in mine. I'm shaking, petrified. 'I love you,' I croak.

I wait, almost expecting the world to stop on its axis and everything in the room to come crashing down now that I've tempted fate by making such a bold declaration aloud. Nothing happens.

Matthew gathers me closer to him. 'I know you do,' he says.

What a lovely, reassuring thing to say! Maybe he guessed all along that I loved him, or maybe he just figured it out over the past few days. Either way, Matthew officially now knows *everything* about me, my past, my present, plus a sketch of my future and his part in it. This makes me feel quite shy and exposed, but I know that's more to do with my emotional immaturity than anything else. I also know that in time this shyness will pass and what I've revealed – about the bomb, my father, Josh and Liam – won't seem so monumental. It will recede from the forefront of our lives and take its rightful place in the background.

Matthew is the ideal person to tell everything to. He has perspective, something which, quite frankly, I've lacked. He doesn't just see my story as one of wasted lives, simmering hatred, never-ending grief and a broken family. He sees survival, resilience, hope, and a better future that has, against the odds, been forged from all the loss.

Matthew sees the big picture, the higher cause. In that way he reminds me of my father.

'I love you,' I tell him again, my voice muffled against his shoulder but definitely more confident.

*

I'm home, in my own bedroom, and I can see from my bed that it's a beautiful day outside. The sky is blue and cloudless, and the sun has genuine warmth. Jeanie is going to the races today, one of the first meetings of the season. I can picture the scene: girls in strappy dresses and high heels, men perspiring in shirts and trousers, flutes of champagne sparkling under the sun, commentary booming from the speakers as horses thunder around the course, the jockeys on their backs a moving blur of colour. I went with Jeanie to last year's meeting. It was a perfect day, too.

The phone rings. I don't want to talk to anyone but I answer, reluctantly. 'Hello.' My voice is flat and verging on inaudible.

'Caitlin! You're home. How are you? Are you okay?'

Tears spring to my eyes. 'Yes, Mum. I'm okay.'

'How are you feeling?'

Good question. I feel weak. Embarrassed. Stupid. 'I'm okay.'

She knows that I'm not okay. 'Jeanie told me that your sugar levels went too high?'

'Yes.' I squirm and a wave of heat travels up through my body that has nothing to do with the blazing sun outside. 'So high that I got ketoacidosis.'

'Jesus, Caitlin. Jeanie didn't say anything about that.'

'Jeanie wouldn't know the medical term, Mum.'

'You could have died. Good God, Caitlin, you could have died . . .'

I don't know how to respond to this. Of course I've had this thought myself over the last few days, but it's different when you hear it aloud.

I could have died. Without seeing her. Or Maeve. Or even Dad.

'You told me you were taking care of yourself, Caitlin.' She sounds angry and close to tears. 'But you clearly weren't telling me the truth.'

I didn't tell her the truth. Not about my health. Not about my job. Not about Matthew. I was drinking too much and playing Russian roulette with my sugar levels. I was worried about my job for months before I lost it. I had feelings for a man that were so deep they scared me. She knows none of this.

'Telling the truth is not always the right thing to do,' my father used to say at his lectern. 'Not when it has catastrophic effects.' Of course I couldn't respond with this. She'd know I was quoting him.

'I'm sorry, Mum. I didn't want to worry you, that's all.'

'You didn't want to worry me . . .' She repeats in a high-pitched voice. 'Do you have any idea what it's like for me? Can you imagine how it feels to be thousands and thousands of miles away, and getting only a glossed-up version of my daughter's life? Do you know how powerless that makes me feel, how useless? Don't I deserve more? Whether it's pretty or not, don't you think I deserve the truth?'

'I'm sorry, Mum,' I say again, and I mean it. I see now that she's always done her best to tell me the truth: about herself, Maeve, my father, and all the ups and downs of the last ten years. As a result, our conversations have sometimes been uncomfortable and painful, but she's ultimately done the right thing in letting me know what I ought to know. When Liam died, our family came apart at the seams: I ran away, Dad had the affair, Maeve became disengaged. As Mum put it, instead of pulling together, we pulled apart. But Maeve and Dad have since returned to the fold, Maeve with a new level of maturity, Dad as a friend and co-parent. I'm the only one who hasn't come back. I *want* to be back in their midst, at least emotionally if not physically. I'm ready to be pulled back in. I've been lonely a long, long time.

'I was in a relationship again . . . I met someone – Matthew – and we'd had a fight that day.' I belatedly try to explain. 'And I lost my job, Mum. You of all people would know the impact that had on me . . .'

Later, when I've hung up the phone and tears are streaming down my face, Jeanie comes in. She's wearing a sexy black and white print dress, precariously high shoes, her outfit topped off with an oversized hat of silky black feathers that stick out at all angles. The hat would have me doubled up in laughter if it weren't for the fact I'm crying.

'I'll stay with you,' she offers when she sees the state of me. 'I can watch the races on the TV.'

I should tell her not to worry about me, to go and have some fun, but I don't. She kicks off her heels; for some reason, though, she doesn't think to take off the hat. The bed sinks with her weight, her arm around my shoulders is firm and reassuring and I know how lucky I am to have her as my friend.

Chapter 33

I'm holding the paper sleeve with Maeve's handwriting on it: *Dad – BBC news*. I slide the disc into the DVD player and sit back on my heels as I wait for it to load. The picture is fuzzy at the beginning but the colours eventually become clearer. Standing outside a courthouse the reporter, holding a black umbrella to shield himself from heavy sheets of rain, speaks in a strong Northern accent.

'In a landmark civil case, a high court judge in Northern Ireland has found four leaders of a paramilitary organisation responsible for the 1998 Clonmegan bombing that killed fifty-three people and injured hundreds more. The attackers phoned in the bomb threat but gave police the wrong location, which led to the evacuation of people from the centre of town to the top of Chapel Street, right next to where the bomb went off. The bomb happened just months after the signing of the Good Friday Peace Agreement that promised a new era of peace between Catholics and Protestants in Northern Ireland. The paramilitary organisation claimed responsibility for the bombing but no one was found guilty in a criminal court. In 2001, the families of some of the victims decided to go down another route to seek justice and brought a civil case to the high court.'

The camera moves from the reporter to the man standing next to him. I feel a lump in my throat when I see my father. He's older, his hair more grey than brown, his skin pale and finely lined, his dark trench coat doing nothing for its tone. It seems like he has aged by more than the ten years it's been since I last saw him.

Professor Jonathan O'Reilly lost his 22-year-old son, Liam, in the attack, I read at the bottom of the screen.

'The families of the victims are very pleased with today's result,' my father begins, his eyes staring out of the TV and into my soul. 'Finally, we've got justice. Finally, we have recognition of the terrible crime these men committed. I stand before you wearing the cost of that crime, a son that's lost to me, a family that's broken. I, and everyone else involved in this lawsuit, would have preferred a criminal conviction, but today's verdict at least shows that terrorism is a costly business, and the people who fund it and carry it out are liable for *all* the costs involved.'

He's tired; I can tell by the droop of his shoulders that this trial and the years leading up to it have taken their toll. I can also tell how proud he is from the angle at which he's holding his chin.

The camera moves to another member of the committee and I feel bereft without my father. Tears trickle down my face and I'm vaguely aware that I must make a strange sight, kneeling in front of the telly in the middle of the day, crying like a baby.

The reporter is speaking again. 'In his judgment, Mr Justice Devlin found there was overwhelming evidence that the four men bear responsibility for the Clonmegan bomb . . . And he concluded that he was "satisfied to a very high degree" that the paramilitary organisation itself was also liable for the deaths. The families were awarded more than 2.5 million pounds in damages.'

Finally, the camera comes back to Dad and this time I'm ready to take in every detail. His features, especially his eyes, are as striking as ever. His voice is rich and articulate. He may be older and somewhat tired, but my father still presents as a very attractive and intelligent man.

'Yes, we will be pursuing compensation,' he confirms, 'though this case has never been about the money. It's about what's right and wrong. What happened in Clonmegan was wrong, and the only way to right the wrong was to seek justice, some form of punishment for those involved.'

There is more news coverage on the disc and I watch and cry my way through every minute of it. I can see now that this civil case wasn't about money; it was about finding a realistic way of hurting and punishing those responsible for killing Liam and Josh and all the other victims. I feel guilt and sadness that I've only just realised this important fact, only now when I can see the end result for myself. No one but my father

could have got this far. No one else would have had the req-
uisite strength, commitment, intelligence, political expertise
or that driving sense of right and wrong. I, for one, thought
he'd never get anywhere, that he was banging his head against
a brick wall and that he'd cast his family aside for nothing.
But he achieved what he set out to do: the impossible, justice.
I thought he wasn't there for me, that he'd done nothing to
help me and cared about me in only a cursory way, when all
the time he was seeking justice, putting everything he had on
the line, including his family. I realise now, from the deep,
deep relief and the sensation of lightness that's pervading both
my body and my mind, that I needed justice every bit as much
as he did. The truth, stunning enough to momentarily quell
my tears, is that my father could not have done more for me
than this.

The next day I'm up from bed and clearly on the mend. I make
myself breakfast and then do some small chores: unload the
dishwasher, sweep the kitchen floor, wipe the bathroom basin. I
read a little and fall asleep with the book in my hand.

At four o'clock the phone rings. It's Nicola, sounding a little
sheepish. 'Hey, how are you feeling?'

'Good, thanks. Much better.'

'I'm thinking of finishing early today and coming around to
see you, if that's okay.'

'That would be great.'

I haven't seen Nicola since the night I blacked out. She phoned
me while I was at hospital and arranged a time to call in and

visit, but something came up with work at the last minute and she had to cancel.

I do another mini tidy-up as I wait for her to come, wiping down the kitchen table and setting out two cups and some nuts and grapes left over from a basket that Jeanie sent to me at the hospital while she was away in Brisbane.

Nicola arrives at five thirty, her expression rueful. 'Sorry, it was harder to get out the door than I thought.' She kisses my cheek awkwardly. 'But you'd know that better than anyone!'

Well, I used to know, but not anymore. Nicola walks towards the kitchen in her black shirt, pencil skirt and stiletto shoes. I'm wearing jeans and a plain white T-shirt, and right at this moment I feel very unemployed.

She fishes in her large shoulder bag and puts a box of chocolates on the table. 'I brought you these . . .'

'Thanks,' I say indifferently.

She's even more ill at ease now. 'You *can* eat chocolate, can't you?'

'Yes, in very limited amounts.' I fill the kettle and switch it on. 'How's work?'

'Oh, you know, same as ever.'

I wait for her to expand. I wait for details on Zoe and Jarrod and all the others but she doesn't provide them. It feels as though a line has been drawn, and she's on the inside of the line and I'm on the outside.

'Tea or coffee?'

'Coffee, thanks.'

I busy myself making two coffees. We sit across from each other at the table. I open the chocolates but neither of us takes one.

'What are you going to do with yourself now that you're a lady of leisure?' she asks in a more conversational tone.

'Get another job as quickly as possible.'

'You can afford to take a holiday for a few weeks, though, can't you?'

'Yes, but I don't want a holiday, I want another job.'

'The market is tight at the moment – it might be better to wait a few weeks.'

'I'd go crazy if I was out of work that long.'

We sip our drinks and the atmosphere becomes slightly less strained.

'It was scary, seeing you black out like that,' she says. 'I don't think I've ever been so freaked out.'

I smile wryly. 'Sorry, I didn't mean to give you such a fright.'

'I thought you were just very drunk – lucky that the paramedic didn't write you off the same way! He made me look in your wallet and that's where we found the card. He said you should've been wearing a bracelet.'

'Yes, I should have been,' I admit. 'And I will in future.'

Nicola's coffee cup is empty. So I ask if she'd like another.

'No, thanks, I'm right.' She's getting ready to leave. I can sense it.

'How did the Net Banc training go today?'

'Sorry?'

'Net Banc. Today was their first day of training, wasn't it?'

'Yes, yes, it was. It went fine. All A-okay.'

'And Harry Dixon, was he happy?'

Nicola raises an eyebrow. 'He's not exactly what I would call the happy type.'

I smile. 'Did he ask for me?'

'Yes, he did.'

It's like getting blood from a stone. 'And?'

'And I *obviously* had to tell him that you were gone from the company. And he was *obviously* even less happy then.' She picks up her oversized handbag from the floor and sets it on her lap, heralding her imminent departure.

'Did you use my green and red ball idea to gauge how the trainees felt?'

'No, no, I didn't.'

At that the awkwardness becomes unbearable.

'Well, thanks for calling around,' I say, the first to stand.

'No worries. Sorry again that I didn't get to the hospital to see you.'

As we walk towards the door, it occurs to me that she hasn't once referred to Matthew. Considering that she spoke to him when he called my mobile that night, I expected our conversation today to include more than a few very curious questions about him and how long he has been in my life.

At the door she gives me another clumsy kiss on the cheek. 'See you soon, okay?'

I nod. 'Okay. Bye, Nicola. Say hello to everyone at the office for me.'

I close the door, feeling strangely certain that I will see Nicola once or twice again, but that will be all. My mother would describe Nic as a friend for a season. Now that we no longer work together, the season seems to be over.

*

Dear Mandy,

I know this letter is out of the blue and many years too late. All I can say is that it's taken me this long to properly come to terms with what happened. Losing Liam and Josh like that, one moment seeing them side by side and then the next knowing they had become part of the black cloud of smoke, was something I thought I'd never get over. When I got on that flight to Heathrow and then to Sydney, I never wanted to set foot on Irish soil again. I didn't just cut off the country, I cut off my family and friends too, everyone but my mother. To be brutally honest, if Mum had been strong enough, I would have cut her off as well. I was desperate to get away, crazy with grief.

Life is good here. I have nice friends and I've done well in my career. I've played hard and worked hard and done my best to distract myself. Now I can see that if I'd stayed at home I wouldn't have had so many distractions to hide behind, and perhaps I would have done a lot better at working through my grief. I would have come home hundreds more times to a house that was missing Liam and I expect that over time I would have learned to live with that loss without my heart freefalling every single time. I would have provided comfort to my mother and Maeve, and would be on speaking terms with my father – at least, I'd like to think so.

I'm sorry that I cut you off, Mandy. That I wasn't there when you needed someone to talk to, to console you through your own loss, and to give you the courtesy of consoling me through mine. I'm sorry that I didn't answer the letters you sent when I first came here.

If it means anything, I think of you often. Mum tells me that you have two kids, boys. Have they got freckles and heads of wild curls? I see you as being a great mother, no nonsense but lots of fun. I don't know what your husband looks like and that feels weird.

I'm going to send this letter via my mother in the hope that she'll bump into you again soon. I know you gave her new contact details the last time you met but I put them aside and now I can't find them. It feels quite old-fashioned, writing a letter. These days everyone writes emails or texts or communicates through Facebook. Writing a letter is kind of like going back in time and, given the circumstances, it feels right.

I hope that I will hear from you and that you'll send me some photos of your life now. I can see myself going home for a visit sometime next year and I'd dearly like to make contact and amends before then.

Lots of love always,
Your friend,
Caitlin

Chapter 34

There are, in fact, *two* days that will be forever etched in my mind: the day I met Josh McKinstry, which I have already told you about, and the day I found out that my own body was less than perfect, incapable of performing one of its most fundamental functions, producing its own insulin. I was twelve years old and for months before my diagnosis I had been steadily losing weight even though I was always hungry and thirsty and was eating and drinking more than ever before. I was moody, lethargic and not very nice to live with. Mum and Dad initially put my symptoms down to pre-teen hormones, and it was only when I started to get recurring infections that they took me to the doctor. The GP ran some tests and when he got the results he immediately referred me to a specialist.

Dr Flynn, a gentle grandfatherly man, took one look at my skinny, wasted body and told me we were lucky to catch the diabetes when we did. 'Many of my patients end up with keto-acidosis before they're diagnosed.'

'What's that?' I asked.

'Nausea, vomiting, extreme thirst and, in severe cases, loss of consciousness. It's a life-threatening condition and sometimes the first symptom of previously undiagnosed diabetes – so count yourself lucky, young lady,' he added with a smile.

I followed the doctor's gaze as he turned to my parents, and it was only then I saw just how shocked they were. Mum looked as though she was trying not to cry, and Dad looked sad and vulnerable and not at all like his usual upstanding self.

'I can see that you're both finding this hard to take in,' Dr Flynn said kindly. 'Sometimes this disease is as hard on the parents as it is on the children. Shock is a normal first reaction, as is fear and resentment, and even grief. You all have a relatively short time-frame to learn complex new information and to make considerable lifestyle changes. You will initially fear and resent those changes, and you will feel sad that your lives have been altered forever. It's rather overwhelming for children and parents alike.'

That night I couldn't sleep. I lay listening to Maeve's gentle snoring, the whistle of the wind outside and the murmur of my parents' voices downstairs. I knew that they were talking about me. I strained to hear what they were saying, the rise and fall of their voices, the words they chose as they discussed my imper-fections. Finally I got out of bed and stealthily opened the door of the bedroom. The carpet on the landing felt plush under my feet. I carefully stepped over the creaky top step and sat halfway down the stairs, shielded by the banister and the shadows. My mother was crying in the kitchen.

'How did we not know, Jonathan? I feel so guilty that I waited this long to take her to a doctor. I should have known it wasn't normal to be that skinny.'

'I know. When I think about what could have happened . . .'

Feeling ill at ease, I tucked my nightdress around my legs. I knew that I would be in big trouble if they caught me eavesdropping like this, but I wanted to know what they thought, what they *really* thought and felt, what was behind the brave face they'd both donned since leaving the doctor's.

'I feel like I've failed in my role as her parent. My job was to make her feel safe and secure as her life unfolded. Now she will have this burden, this fear, every day of her life.'

'I know, Paula, I know. It's so hard to accept that it's there for the long haul, that there's no way to correct it, to cure it. But at least now we know what's *wrong* with her.'

His choice of phrase struck a chord. So there *was* something wrong with me.

'I guess we'll all have to learn to live with it.' Mum's sobs intensified.

I heard the rustle of Dad's clothes as he moved closer to comfort her. 'Yes, we'll have to get used to it, make the adjustments that need to be made. She won't ever have perfect health. It's disappointing, devastating, for her and for us . . .'

To my ears, they both sounded a long, long way from 'living with it'. I got up and tiptoed back to my room.

In my bed, I was just as alert as before. 'You're a freak, Caitlin O'Reilly,' I whispered into the dark. 'Your body can't even do one of the most basic things it's meant to do. Freak! Freak! Freak!'

Meeting Josh when I was eighteen defused much of the bad feeling, the self-loathing that still lingered from finding out that I was different to everyone else. Josh was different too; his body didn't work as it should either. But he had so many other things going for him that his deafness, his imperfection, ceased to matter. Josh helped me put the diabetes into perspective and to understand that it was only a part of me, not everything.

Those two days, when I met Josh and when I found out I was a Type 1 diabetic, were turning points. My life was taken over, commandeered in a new direction, and the repercussions have cascaded down through every day since. Now, the day I lost my job, fought with my mother, my friend and my boyfriend, and ended up in hospital, looks like it will be another one of those turning points. It's left me fragile and wary of my body and what could happen if I don't take proper care of it. It's made me realise how much I love my family, my friends and Matthew. I have been granted perspective, again. My childhood was not unhappy, I was loved and valued by my parents. My father is a perfection-ist, but so am I, and the truth is that the current rift in our family is more because of me than him.

I'm half-awake when the doorbell rings. Matthew's arm is slung around my waist and I'm sure that I have a smile on my face. It's early Saturday, the street outside is peaceful, no bustle, no cars, no weekday madness. Even the birds are unusually quiet. I open one eye and check the clock: 7.15 am.

Late yesterday I got a call from Harry Dixon asking me to come and see him next week. As soon as I recognised his voice, I wondered what he wanted, why he was calling me. I didn't have to wait long to find out: niceties are not part of Harry's repertoire, and he was as cranky and abrupt as ever. He said he had a 'proposition' for me. Harry's not the type to waste his time or mine and I suspect his 'proposition' is in fact a job offer. Net Banc is an excellent company, rated highly by analysts and employees alike, and Harry, beneath all the fire and brimstone, would be a loyal and decent boss. I won't find out until next week but having this meeting on the horizon already makes me feel much more secure about my employment status.

The doorbell rings again.

Matthew's arm moves against me, his fingers splaying on the curve of my hip. 'Is that coming from your door?' he asks without opening his eyes.

'I was pretending it wasn't,' I reply and reluctantly roll away from the promise of those fingers.

I throw on some clothes, wondering who could be at the door. Jeanie is away again, her travel budget reinstated. Nicola is not a morning person – unless she's decided to pop in on her way home from an all-night party – and anyway, she hasn't been in contact since we spoke last week. More likely, though, it's a neighbour, locked out of their apartment or in the throes of some other domestic emergency. On tiptoe, I peer through the peephole. The man standing on the other side is familiar to me, but he's older and not as upright as he used to be. It's been ten years and three months since I last saw him. I lower my heels. My chest feels tight and I can literally feel the blood draining from my face.

I'm aware that I have a choice, that I don't *need* to open the door, yet I do so with surprising ease.

'You wouldn't come home, so I came here,' my father says in greeting.

I open the door wide enough to let him in. His eyes sweep across my apartment, gauging in an instant how I live. Then he turns and looks me in the eye.

'I was a hypocrite. You were right in that regard, and it's been a harsh realisation for me.' His accent is so strong and pure that I feel like I've come home. 'I should never have put anyone or anything before my family. I never will again.'

I nod. I know that he's here with Mum's blessing, that they've conferred as parents and friends, and decided he should come here to see that I'm all right. The knowledge that this conversation has happened between my parents makes me realise that my family is not as fragmented as I had feared.

Matthew comes to stand in the bedroom doorway. He's directly behind my father and bears witness to what is said next.

'I'm sorry, Caitlin.'

Funny how those two words can melt away years and distance, how they can right any wrong.

I step towards him and his arms await me. 'I'm sorry too, Dad.'

I feel genuinely proud of him and what he has achieved. Since watching the disc, I'm more at peace. You see, I was hanging out for justice every bit as much as he was and now that it's been achieved I can finally trust, not only in the legal system but in everything: my family, my friends, and in fate and what it may or may not have in store. Despite his remarkable feat in driving that landmark civil case, I'm aware that my father has made many mistakes over the past eleven years. He should have been more supportive to my mother, and they would still be married if he'd saved even a small part of himself for her. He should have given Maeve more support and guidance too, been quicker to help her past the schoolgirl stage she was frozen at for years. And when distance softened the edges of my hatred, he should have reached out to me, insistently, until I understood that my hatred was born from the deepest love, that I was the most like him of all his children and that I could never be fully happy without his approval and without him in my life.

I see each mistake with a new level of understanding. Before me is a softer, multi-dimensional, flawed but essentially altruistic man.

My father is less than perfect.

Like me.

Like Josh and Liam. And even Matthew, who will come forward at any moment to shake my father's hand.

Acknowledgements

While *Less Than Perfect* is a work of fiction, those who are familiar with recent Irish history and politics will be able to recognise that I drew on the Omagh bombing and the remarkable achievements of the Omagh Support & Self Help Group for inspiration. Professor Jonathan O'Reilly, Caitlin, Josh, Liam and all the other characters in the book are completely fictional, but their loss, grief, bravery, tenacity and ultimate triumph reflect the extraordinary strength of the Omagh people.

Thanks to Jacqueline Gabb, Sam Bartlett, Matthew Longmore, Stephen Cohen and Aleisha Davis for your technical assistance. Without your knowledge and experience certain parts of this book would not have been possible. I'm hugely grateful (and quick to add that any mistakes are totally my own!).

Thanks to my usual gang of readers, Rob Carroll, Amanda Longmore, Ann Riordan and Brian Cook (my fabulous, multi-talented agent). As always, your recommendations have made this book much better than I could ever achieve on my own.

Thanks to Cate Paterson, publishing director at Pan Macmillan, for your wonderful ongoing support, and a big, enormous thanks to my publisher Alex Nahlous for your excellent suggestions and editing. I feel *extremely* lucky to have had you working on my book (and I promise I don't hold that massive you-know-what change against you!). Thanks, too, to Clara Finlay for caring enough to go through the manuscript word by word and doing such a scrupulous copy edit.

Thanks also to Dianne Blacklock and Liane Moriarty, fellow authors and great sounding boards on all things book-related. Dianne and Liane and I like each other so much that we produce a periodical newsletter called *Book Chat*. If you would like to subscribe, just go to my website: www.bercarroll.com. And check out Dianne and Liane's books – you will love them.

Being one of six, I have lots of my own 'big family' experiences to draw from. But being one of eight and thirteen has a lot more street cred – so thanks to Jeanie Edwards and Stephen Cox for allowing me to steal some of your hilarious anecdotes.

Finally, thanks to Conal McKeever (sorry for cornering you with questions at all those parties), and to Erin Downey, Donna Heagney, Matt O'Mahony, Orla Quilligan and Gillian Henery. And thanks to all my readers. I hope you like this book. I've wanted to write about the North of Ireland for a long, long time.

ALSO BY BER CARROLL IN PAN MACMILLAN

Executive Affair

Claire Quinlan is unlucky in love and fed up with her life in Dublin.
So when an opportunity arises to transfer to the Sydney office of
her company, she grabs it. She sets up house in Bondi with her old
friend Fiona, finds a new boyfriend Paul, and is sure that her life has
changed for the better.

But her new job and boyfriend are more challenging than she
imagined. She finds herself falling for the handsome American vice-
president, Robert Pozos. Robert is sophisticated and charming and
very complicated. He spells another broken heart, but she just can't
seem to stop herself . . .

Then Claire uncovers a corporate fraud and she suddenly doesn't
know who she can trust. Everyone has something to lose: Robert,
Fiona, Paul. But Claire, who always played it safe, is risking the
most . . .

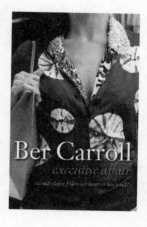

Just Business

Niamh Lynch appears to have it all: a high-flying career, a handsome, successful husband and a loving family. But looks can be deceiving.

From the moment she has to deliver the terrible news that there will be heavy redundancies at her workplace, her marriage crumbles and her life falls apart.

Certain cracks have been there for a long time, since her family left Ireland. Others are new. Who will catch her as she falls? Her mother whom she can't forgive? Her father from his grave? Or Scott, a man who has just lost his job, but who seems to understand her like nobody else does.

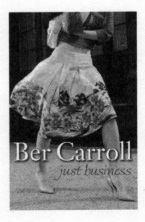

High Potential

Katie Horgan should soon be made partner at her law firm, but her love life is going nowhere – until she meets Jim Donnelly. Jim is smart, handsome and, like her parents, Irish. But he already has a girlfriend.

When Katie is sent to Ireland, she happily settles into her work at a clinic that provides free legal advice to the homeless. She befriends Mags who makes it her business to initiate Katie to Dublin's social scene. Then Jim Donnelly comes home on a visit, and everything begins to unravel . . .

The truth comes out, about Jim, Mags, and the reason that Katie's parents left Ireland – and Katie learns that life is not as black and white as she always thought.

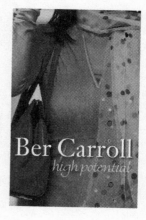

The Better Woman

Sarah Ryan grows up in her grandmother's house in a small Irish village. Sarah is clever and ambitious and eager to move away from the sleepy village. She fully believes that John Delaney, the boy-next-door and her first love, will be right by her side . . . until he breaks her heart.

Jodi Tyler is raised on Sydney's northern beaches amidst a close and loving family. But Jodi has a secret, a tragic secret which leaves her determined to make a success of her life. Like Sarah, Jodi's grandmother ends up providing her with a home. And when Jodi falls head over heels in love, she too ends up with a broken heart . . .

This is a story of two remarkable women who face all life's challenges head on – and those they love and lose on their journey. Set in Ireland, Australia, London and New York, Sarah and Jodi make their way in the world unaware that their lives are running in parallel and it is only when they both want the same thing that their paths will finally cross . . .